Blorfindel Brighteyes
Part One
Child Of Bondage

Jonathan Gerkin

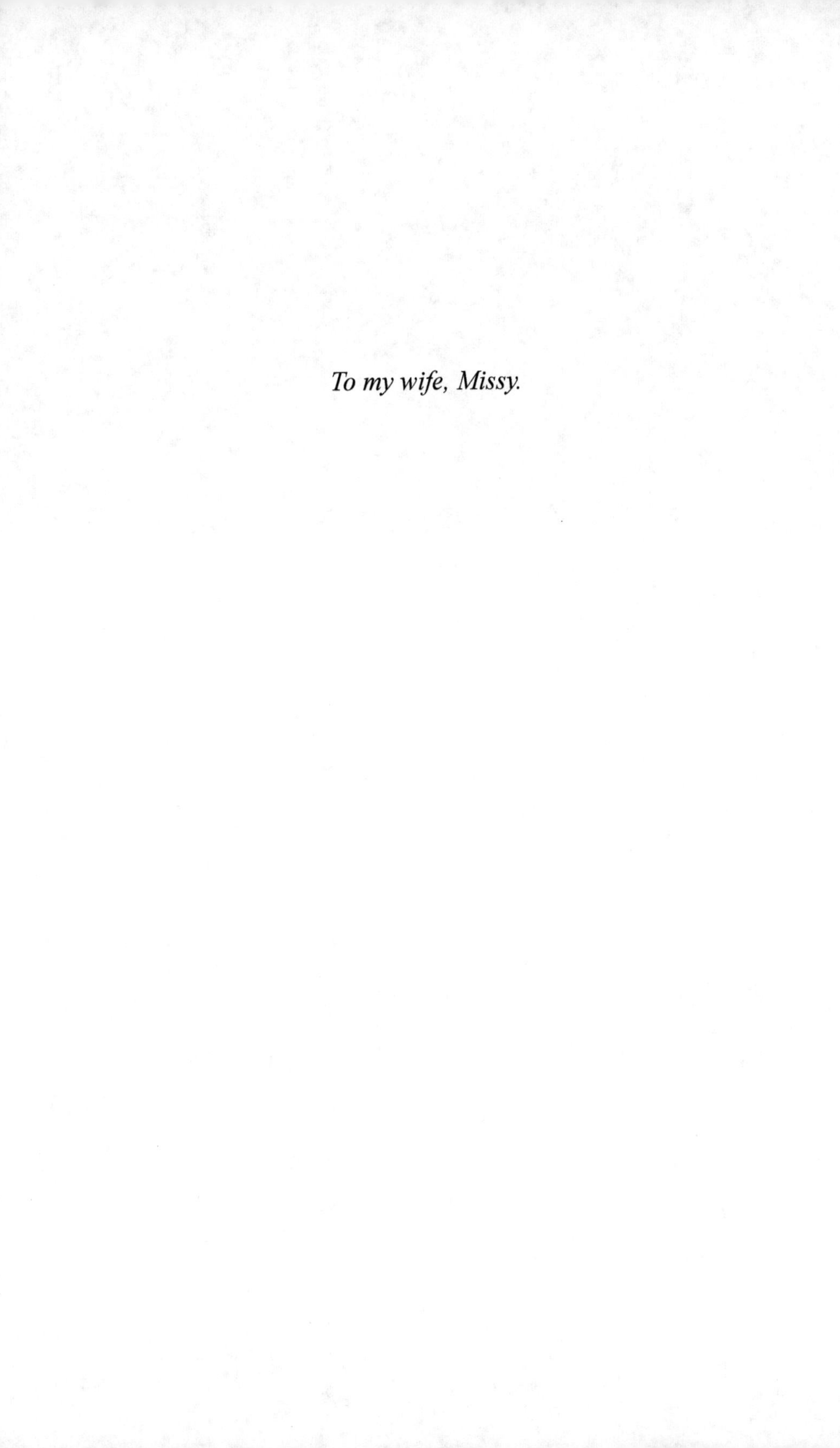

To my wife, Missy.

Acknowledgments

Tom P for providing the forum where the first character sketch of Blorfindel Brighteyes was introduced.

Roberta G, Colleen C, Mark M, and Nathan S for providing the forum and feedback on the design of the world and cultures presented in this work.

In addition, feedback from Sylvia D was of great assistance in developing the final text.

And, in everything, Missy for being my sounding board, critic, inspiration, and motivation.

Table of Contents

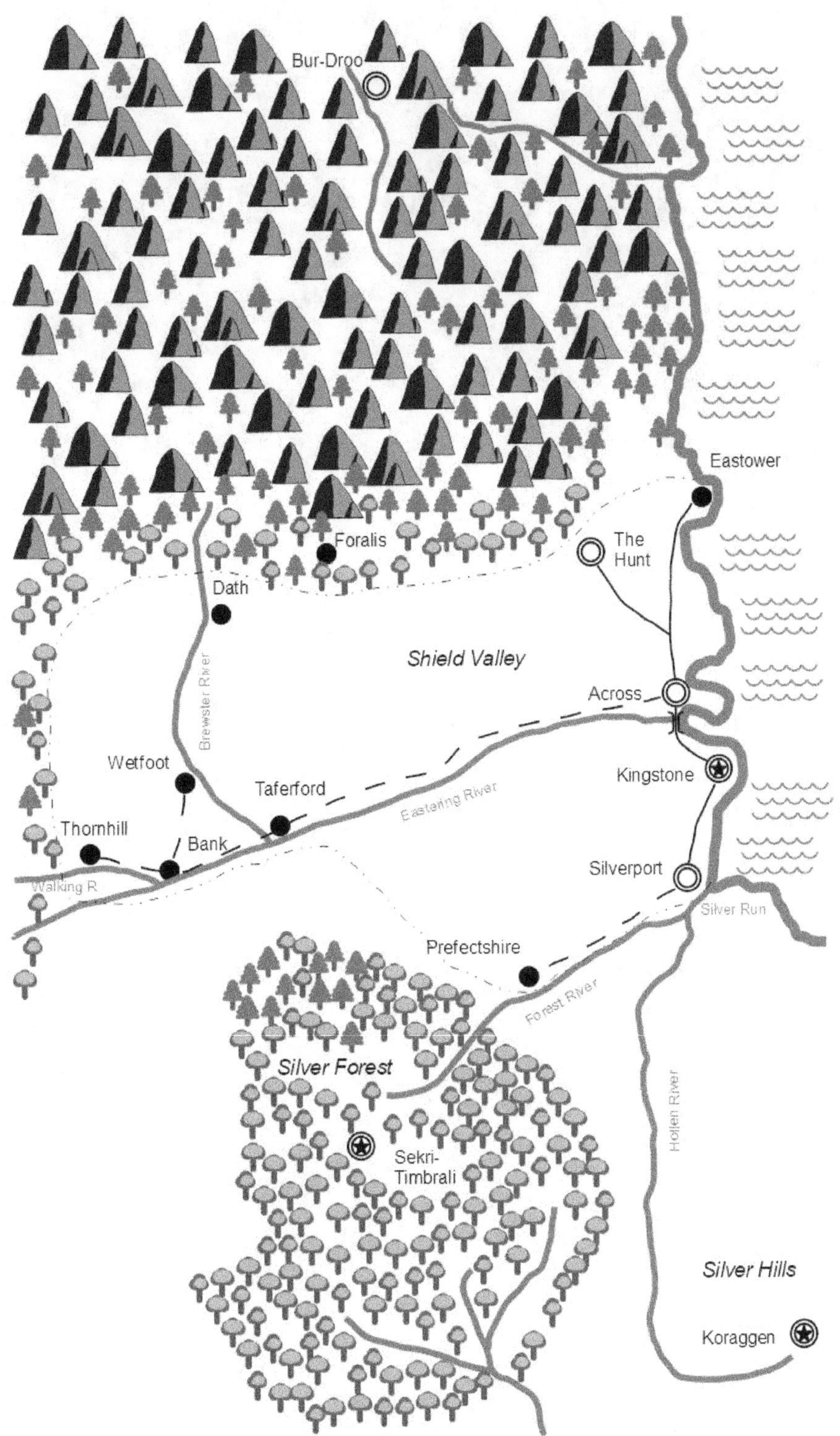

Bur-Droo
Eastower
Foralis
The Hunt
Dath
Shield Valley
Brewster River
Across
Wetfoot
Kingstone
Taferford
Eastering River
Thornhill
Bank
Silverport
Walking R
Silver Run
Prefectshire
Forest River
Silver Forest
Hollen River
Sekri-Timbrali
Silver Hills
Koraggen

Chapter 1

The Fall Of Foralis

Ghinlihil was a Fitheran child. His eyes were blue and his hair was blonde, just like his father. At four feet and 45 pounds, he was considered large for his age. This was hardly surprising since both of his parents – Laliam and Jilwanis – were taller than average. Laliam was considered a giant among the Fitherani at five feet six inches and 111 pounds.

The Fitherani existed to appreciate the details of the forest and they were given many years to do so. Fitherani did not call themselves old until they has seen twelve centuries. Ghinlihil was eighty-one years old. He still had fifty-four years of training ahead of him before he could attempt the archery test that would make him an adult.

Ghinlihil and his parents lived in Foralis. Foralis had been founded as a frontier village nearly a thousand years earlier. Many of the founders were still residents. It was a beautiful place, with carefully tended trees surrounded by the wild forest, and mountains to the north that lit up when the sun got low. At any season of the year, it seemed the perfect place for a Fitheran to be.

The world had changed since the village was founded. The Tafers had built a nation – The Shield Valley – south of Foralis. Tafers tended to be a foot taller and twice the weight of a Fitheran, but it was very rare for one to survive one hundred years. While the large and quick-lived Tafers had few dealings with the Fitherani, they were at least peaceful neighbors. To the north were Kutel lands. They were another matter entirely. The Kutel existed to destroy and they considered Fitherani a special delicacy. In size, they fell between the Fitherani and the Tafers. They were slower in mind and body, but their lives were short and brutal. Few survived to forty years, though there were Tafer scholars who speculated that they might live to sixty if they could be protected from each other. Kutel raids on Foralis became bolder and more frequent as the years passed.

Laliam Steelhand and Jilwanis Sharpeye had come to Foralis, separately, to help defend it. They first met on the edge of Foralis. They married in Foralis. They built a home and started a family in Foralis. She was the second best archer of the village.

Lalliam Steelhand was the tallest and strongest of the Fitheran archers of their village. He was the only one who was as deadly in close combat as he was with his bow. The two light swords that hung from his belt were beautifully made, but they were not ornaments.

Ghinlihil played with an arrow as he watched his father read the signals from the returning woodsmen. Somehow the gray fletchings felt right on his fingertips, still he was impatient to shoot the arrow, not just hold it. Lalliam bent to whisper in his son's ear, "There are Kutel nearby. Go straight home and wait there." The whisper was far softer than the rustling leaves in the wind, and even Ghinlihil's sharp ears had to strain to hear. Ghinlihil hesitated for an instant: he wanted to stay. He had never seen a Kutel before, though he knew a good deal about them and could even speak their language. He knew that Kutel were as ugly as the Fitherani were fair. Their skin was dark purple or gray and frequently marked with scars and sores. They had large mouths usually with protruding fangs, tusks or sometimes both. In spite of their legendary ugliness, Ghinlihil longed to see one with his own eyes. In his youthful enthusiasm he wanted to be part of the ambush and stand with the adult Fitherani as they defended the village. Ghinlihil knew that he was too young. His archery training had just begun six years ago.

Ghinlihil could think of no argument against his father's command, so he turned for home. The familiar woods slid past with just the slightest breath of a summer breeze. Soft shoes crinkled dry edges of dead leaves. By Fithern standards Ghinlihil was stomping through the forest. It was all the protest that he dared to raise – his father would not approve, but he would not say anything.

Lalliam waited. His bow was ready. He stood in the bowing branches of a fir tree and swayed with them when the breeze blew. He frowned at the sound of Ghinlihil's footsteps. Even so, he felt that his son was in no particular danger. The Kutel would not hear or see him before Lalliam was ready to shoot. As the other Fitherani archers settled into their hiding places, they disappeared even from Lalliam's view. *I can fall back to Ermingo when the Kutel see me,* he thought. He looked back to mark the tree that Ermingo had taken – a sturdy oak eighty yards behind him and hardly visibly through the forest. Emingo was the best archer of Foralis and he would anchor the second line. Lalliam waited, listening for a disturbance in the night-buzz of the summer forest. An hour passed, but Lalliam did not stir. Even as he waited for battle, the air scented by the fir was pleasant to him.

Solsung, the Kutel shaman, was the leader of this war band. His orders from the Wizard-King were very clear: "Keep the war band moving toward the town. Do not stop for anything except killing. Move as quickly as you can without losing control. Kill all of the Fitherani in the village. No prisoners. No torture. Burn the houses. All of the young die, too. Do not stop for anything until they are all dead. Only cut trees if you have to to get at the Fitherani." The Wizard-King did not give such detailed orders often – Solsung had only heard them once before, fifteen years ago. The plan worked then, and it would work now.

The Wizard-King said that it was important that his war band did not take prisoners. It was the only part of the mission that Solsung did not like – he could have made a lot of money on slaves. Clearly, there was a Fitheran here that the Wizard-King wanted dead, and he was taking no chances. Because Solsung did not know which one, he had to kill them all.

He had a strong war band – more warriors than he could count. Sixty-four of them, including both of his shield bearers and his best tracker, were his grandsons. He also had a barren female in front. She was useless, except to flush out an ambush. He was given a young one because she could move as fast as the rest of the war band. She actually could move faster than the armored warriors, but she had to be threatened by the archers or she would not move toward the Fitherani. Of course, everyone expected the Fitherani to kill her first.

The first Kutel stepped into Laliam's view. She was a beater. The Kutel often put an old or barren female in front of their raids to flush out defenders. Lalliam trusted the fir tree to hide him and let her go by. She jogged past Lalliam and though she was not twenty feet away she did not see him. Her eyes darted around in stark panic, but did not penetrate the low fir boughs that separated her from the Fitheran. He stood still and waited for the first combatants. Soon the Kutel that he could see outnumbered the Fitherani by five to one. These were becoming normal odds.

Lalliam was looking for their leader. A well placed arrow could often cause the Kutel to rout. A Kutel without a commander would not face mortal combat. If Lalliam could shoot the leader none of the others would step forward and become the next to stop an arrow.

He saw the leader. *The raid stops here,* Lalliam thought. Smaller than most of their leaders, he looked like quite an average Kutel. He was a hand or so less than six feet, and well under two hundred pounds. His fangs were somewhat dull with age and his long, flattened nose showed signs of being broken repeatedly. His leathery skin was bleached nearly gray and only his scars showed the more normal Kutel coloration of dark purple-gray. His yellow eyes betrayed no more wit than the average Kutel, which was not much, indeed. The hides that made up his armor were scorched, and he had the ceremonial lightning-trident. Even with the totem of the Kutel lightning-god, Karakak, had it not been for the shield-bearers Lalliam might not have singled him out. Each of the Kutel in front of the leader had an over-sized round wooden shield, much too large to be helpful in combat. Their only purpose was to shield the Kutel leader. This commander was well protected by his shield bearers. Lalliam took careful aim.

Another Fitheran shot first. Lalliam loosed his arrow as soon as he heard the bowstring. The other archer's arrow hit the beater behind him and she shrunk to the ground shrieking. The Kutel broke into a jog while Lalliam's arrow was in the air. Lalliam had not expected the Kutel to increase their pace and his timing was off. The arrow hit the edge of a heavy wooden shield in front of the Kutel leader.

Solsung heard an arrow hit one of the shields. His shield bearer did not cry out. The Kutel shaman did not care whether the younger Kutel suffered a wound, only that his shield wall would not falter. Solsung looked around for the Fitheran who shot at him and he saw Lalliam drawing another arrow under the fir tree. *He is the biggest Fitheran I have ever seen. He must be the leader. I wonder if he is the one that the Wizard-King is afraid of? If I keep him alive, can I barter him to the Wizard-King? No, he would just send a bigger war band after me.*

Karakak had granted Solsung a fear spell to use on the leader of the Fitherani. *If the Fitheran leader runs away, they will all follow him. We still have to run them down after they run away, though.* The Kutel leader cast his spell from relative safety behind his shield-bearers.

Lalliam's heart froze. Suddenly he knew, absolutely knew that the Kutel were here for his only son, Ghinlihil. *They will keep coming, throwing their lives away, until they get him.* The other Fitherani expected Lalliam to withdraw and reform the line either with or behind Emingo. He did not stop to reform his line. He ran for the village. They all knew something was horribly wrong, but Fitherani were trained to battle without speaking, and they could only follow his example.

Lalliam was puffing when he reached his home. It was a modest wooden structure between two oak trees. He planted those trees himself: one for his marriage to Jilwanis and the other when Ghinlihil was born. While some homes had more trees planted around them, it was an entirely typical home in the village of Foralis.

He threw open the door so fiercely that he nearly hit his wife with it. He was surprised to find Jilwanis just behind the door, slinging a quiver full of arrows over her shoulder. Her platinum hair and silver eyes seemed to glow to him. Her smile could still take his breath away, but now her face was an archer's mask of deadly calm.

"Take Ghinlihil to the Tafer village!" He nearly shouted. In his own mind he thought, *I will rejoin the battle when I can, but my first duty is to family.* He did not question where the thought came from. The fear spell turned the Fitheran's imagination against him.

"You take him, you're faster." Jilwanis knew even as she spoke that he would not flee the village. She looked up to meet his blue eyes. "They'll want my arrows in the battle."

She would leave him to the Kutel! Lalliam's fear-addled mind screamed. *If we can only get him to the Tafer village, the Kutel will not get him.*

Ghinlihil stood around the corner and listened to his parents argue over who would have to take care of him. Nothing could have made him feel more like a baby.

"Take him now!" Lalliam ordered. *That was a mistake,* he knew. The Kutel's magic couldn't make him forget two hundred years of marriage. He tried logic, "The Kutel draw closer all the time."

Jilwanis did not like orders, *He thinks he can command me like one of his soldiers!* "Then you'd better get moving." She pulled her bow from behind the door and strode out to battle – or would have. Lalliam's hand clamped down on her shoulder and stopped her in her tracks.

Lalliam had never laid a rough hand on his wife before, not even in play. He was called Lalliam Steelhand after the Fithern fashion: his second name was not a family name, but a description. His grip and his fist made him a byword in Foralis, and he used far too much of that strength on Jilwanis just then. *No good will come of it,* he knew. *Raise the trees! Ghinlihil is more important than your pride, Fitheresse.*

"Let go of me," Jilwanis hissed. She had never been angry with Lalliam before – not like now. She could tell something was very wrong, but her anger took over. *Am I supposed to carry Ghinlihil the twenty miles to the Tafer village?*

Ghinlihil could sense his father's fear and his mother's anger. Tears began to well in his eyes. *They think I'm a baby and a bother. They don't want me here. I can go to the Tafer village by myself.* Ghinlihil backed away from the doorway. *They are fighting because of me. I can take care of myself. I am in the way here.* He had been told to move silently when the Kutel were around, so he slipped out the back window and ran down the path toward the Tafer village. He left a trail of tears behind.

Ermingo mouthed a curse as he ducked behind another tree. It was not the advancing Kutel that bothered him. He had killed thirteen of them so far and he still had two thirds of his arrows left. He was undisputed as the best archer of Foralis, and one of its first settlers. His oath was for Lalliam. *Fool! The young warriors look to you for strength and you run away!* Then, calming himself to shoot yet another Kutel, he softened momentarily. *Lalliam has a family now.* That made Ermingo jealous and just as angry.

Ermingo fought a personal vendetta. A Kutel's poisoned arrow took Callia, his fiancée, seven centuries ago but not a hundred yards from where he now stood. On that day he took the name Ermingo Coldheart and he never married. He looked forward to the Kutel raids with a red-hot rage that belied his cold-hearted name.

Another Kutel stepped out in front of him. Ermingo's arrow was one of two that pierced its heart. The other archer retreated after shooting.

I would be a grandfather by now, if she did not… if the Kutel had not… Ermingo forced the thought out of his mind. The Kutel continued to pay for the murder, though none of them knew of it. If the Kutel had historians even they would have forgotten the ancient skirmish. It was of no great consequence to the Kutel, and fifty of their generations had passed since it took place.

More and more of the Fitherani fell back to warn or check on their loved ones. Lalliam was a respected warrior, renowned for bravery and skill as well as his incredible strength. If Lalliam could run away to check on his family, so could they. Except for Ermingo, the unmarried Fitherani were young and none had two hundred years' experience. As a group they had far less motivation to risk their own lives to defend the village. They loosed arrows at the Kutel from the safety of the trees and gave ground whenever they were discovered.

Ermingo was forced to withdraw to the edge of the village.

Solsung the Kutel shaman clapped his hands in a prayer of thanksgiving and joy. The Fitherani were running. As always their arrows were depleting his war band, but his shield bearers were unharmed and he was the safest Kutel in the forest. Half of the Fitherani had fled the battle at a run. Solsung could afford to trade soldiers for yards now. His war band, however, started counting their fallen comrades and hiding from arrows. *That will never do.* "We'll chew the bones of the Fitheressi tonight! Leave the Fitherani to the crows!"

The thought of eating Fitheressi flesh put heart back into the Kutel. They pressed on at a jog, leaping over the bodies of the Kutel who had gone before. "Slow enough to keep together, fast enough that the Fitherani can not stand and shoot," that was the plan, and it was working. He could see the first of the Fithern houses. Solsung screamed, "Karakak light the fires!" He sneered when the houses remained. He was not important enough to the Kutel god of lightning for all of his prayers to be answered. For now it did not matter. The Kutel had brought torches, and soon they were lit.

The young Fitherani archers began to focus their arrows on the Kutel with torches. Ermingo was not distracted. In the back of his mind he saw Callia, her face distorted in pain and fear, and her once red lips turned as blue as her eyes and quivering from the Kutel poison. Tears did not bother Ermingo's aim; he had seven hundred years' practice shooting and crying.

He tried to whisper and shout at once, "The archers first!" It cost him his advantage. The Kutel archers shot their arrows at the sound. Two ichor smeared arrows stuck in the elm tree that hid Ermingo. They had him now. He could not break cover to shoot back, not when the slightest grazing meant slow death. He could only hope that the Fitherani took his advice and killed the Kutel archers before the skirmishers surrounded him. He looked back at the youths falling back and shook his head. He heard the pounding of hobnailed boots as the Kutel approached. *Come on, shoot! They are in the open!* No arrows came from the retreating Fitherani.

Ermingo drew his sword and dagger. Fear mixed with frustration and bitter anger. Ermingo was not a young Fitheran, but he was not quite ready to die yet, and he knew his chances in close combat with Kutel. His sword and dagger felt awkward, unnatural. He was much better with a bow. He leaned his bow against the tree and cut it in two with his sword. *The Kutel will not have my bow to send their foul shafts.* In a strange moment of clarity he saw that his angry swing also cut away some tree bark. For an instant he pressed his forehead against the course bark and apologized to the elm, but then his thoughts were on the Kutel: *I may not be Lalliam Steelhand, but I will not be the first to bleed on these leaves.*

Then the Kutel came.

It's a trap, Solsung's reason screamed, *When have the Fitherani given up so easily?* Reason, however, has very little sway over Kutel, even Kutel as old as Solsung. *Forty-five years old is an unnatural age. If I live no longer, the Fitherani will remember me forever!* Solsung virtually led the charge into the Fithern village.

More than half of the Kutel band survived the charge into the village. They smiled and laughed and drooled on themselves as they threw torches into the Fithern homes. Solsung laughed along with them. He laughed and clapped for Karakak. *The Fitherani expect their homes and their trees to last forever. They have nothing that I cannot destroy.*

Chapter 2

Rescue

Ammoss walked quietly down the forest path. *Quietly, not quite silently*, he thought. Ammoss could hear a slight rattle as the black iron bands that made up his armor ran against one another. It was a good compromise that allowed him free movement and distributed the weight of his armor well. He still frowned at it so hard that his black whiskers bristled. It made him second guess whether he should have given up stealth and ridden to Foralis, instead. He tried to be silent whenever he walked alone.

Ammoss usually preferred to be alone when he walked in the forest, but not this time. Tonight he was racing to catch a band of Kutel before they got to Foralis. He had come across their trail three days earlier and went at once to Dath, his adopted home. There he tried to raise some aid for the Fithern village. No one came. They each had their excuse: "The Kutel have never made a successful attack on Foralis in hundreds of tries." "The warriors might be needed at home if the Kutel turn to raid here." "Besides," they said, "who wants to march all day to what is probably a false alarm?" Ammoss had seen many alarms. *The false ones are the best kind.* He was ready to respond to either kind. All of this added up to him walking the Northeast Path alone.

Ammoss carried his bow on his back. *It's too dark for bow work,* Ammoss thought. *Too dark for me, anyway. The dark will not bother the Fithern archers.* To the Fitherani, night was like a cloud. "The horizon passing over the sun," was the expression. The Kutel could also see well in the dark. That put Ammoss at a disadvantage. He drew his sword.

Ammoss was a Tafer, a big one. That was his advantage. He was three inches over six feet and his armor rebelled against his two hundred fifty pounds. Ammoss smiled at a pleasant memory, *My extra girth is Shandi's fault.* In two years of marriage he had put on seventeen pounds. A fool might think that he had gone soft, but only a great fool. Ammoss was a veteran of many battles and a formidable fighter in any environment. In the quiet forest that he loved he was terrifying even to his allies.

Few could manage a 52 inch blade in one hand. To Ammoss the sword's weight and balance were reassuring, and the magical runes on the blade spoke of anger, blood and death. Ammoss had taken the sword from a Kutel hoard years ago, but the runes were of Fithern origin. Ammoss could not make sense of that, since the sword was far too big for the Fithern fighting style. One thing was clear: this was a weapon made to kill Kutel.

Ammoss cursed himself for letting his mind wander. He needed to be alert if there were Kutel about. He fiercely hoped there would be, then was assaulted by guilt. He did not want to like killing Kutel, it made him feel barbaric. He asked himself the same questions whenever he was hunting Kutel: *Is it not wrong, after all, to hate the Kutel just for being Kutel? The wolves that attack sheep are not evil and it is totally natural for a fox to eat a hare. Why shouldn't the Kutel attack the Fitherani?* He responded to his own questions with a snarl: *The Kutel are not animals. They speak a language and use tools. They are close enough to Tafers to interbreed.* That thought always raised his hackles. Such unions were almost exclusively involuntary. *They kill their own young and eat them if they are weak. They use their old and barren women as fodder to flush out ambushes. They seek only to dominate or destroy.* Ammoss almost worked himself into a rage. *I will kill them wherever I find them.*

He almost ran over a little Fitheran on the path before his mind snapped back to the present. As children the fine-limbed and light Fitherani could be mistaken for Tafer children. Most people would have to check their ears to tell the difference. Ammoss knew that no Tafer child would be anywhere near here. He became instantly alert. Everything about the chance meeting seemed wrong. *The young Fitheran should not be alone in the forest with Kutel about. He should have heard me coming and hidden himself. He should have been watching unseen as I passed by.* Like their ears, Fithern hearing was halfway between that of a Tafer and a cat.

Ghinlihil stopped in front of the Tafer warrior with his mouth hanging open as if to say something. He could think of nothing to say. His first instinct was to run away, but he was running to the Tafers for help, and here was one almost at his doorstep.

Ammoss could hear the heavy footfalls of Kutel on the path ahead. He lifted the Fitheran with his left hand and set him on a low maple branch. "Climb quietly," he whispered. Ammoss could speak Timbrali – the Fithern language – fluently. Now was not a good time for conversation. The Fitheran began to climb.

Solsung whined to himself, *I had been doing so well!* His band had burnt the village and killed the Fitherani by ones and twos. He had orders from the Wizard-King of the Kutel: there must be no survivors. Solsung hated the Wizard-King, but he feared him even more. Everyone was afraid of the Wizard-King, so everyone chased the last Fitheran.

Only ten of his Kutel had survived the raid. *That is good, I do not have to share the booty with many.* The problem was that the Kutel found the trail of one fleeing Fitheran. Now Solsung had to run headlong down the forest path to try to catch the little Fitheran. The remainder of his war band kept ahead of their shaman. They knew that he would use his trident on any of them if they slowed enough for him to reach them.

Ammoss moved one tree further down the path before stepping behind an eight-foot-tall maple stump. There he waited for the Kutel. *Less than twenty, by the sound.* He unstrapped his war hammer and held it ready in his left hand. It looked like nothing more than a wooden handle driven through a large iron spike, but it was light and quick and balanced for throwing. The weight helped balance Ammoss' long sword.

Solsung's favorite grandson was leading the way. He was following a trial of tears in the dust when he passed an old tree. A yard and a half of blue steel flashed white runes of power in the faint moonlight. His bearskin armor could not stop it.

The reek of an open bowel told Ammoss that he need not be concerned with that one anymore. He did not so much as glance back, but kept his eyes on the Kutel before him. The Tafer's war hammer caught the next Kutel in the forehead and sent him to the ground. Ammoss felt a slight satisfaction that its head hit the trail before its back. He stripped a quadriceps from another Kutel with his sword before they reacted at all.

Solsung had not planned for a Tafer. *No matter. Tafers are not much bigger than Kutel, after all. The odds are still seven to one.* He did not count himself.

No matter what his rationalization, the real reason why Ammoss hunted the Kutel was because he was good at it. He was sorry that they could not present him with more of a challenge. *One on eight is too easy.* He cut down two more with a left and right sword stroke, then shattered the rib cage of another with his hammer. The Kutel all flailed at Ammoss with whatever weapons they had, but by the time their blows landed he had moved on. The best that they could do was scratch his armor before two more fell in four pieces. They were on the edge of panic.

Solsung suddenly realized that the odds were very badly against him. The shaman prayed again to Karakak. He prayed that the Tafer would hold still long enough for his remaining warriors to mutilate him. Solsung could only use this prayer once per night, but he had never been denied the magic since he gained the courage to ask for it.

Ammoss felt a dull wave course through his body. He could hear one of the Kutel speaking in a language that was not his own. *Magic! A priest of Karakak!* Ammoss recognized the singed armor and crooked trident that marked the shaman of the Kutel lightning-god. Ammoss fought through the spell's force by willpower borne of confidence. In his mind he counted off his gods and weighed them mightier than Karakak.

A Kutel used the distraction to make an attack. Ammoss turned the Kutel axe with a backhand of his sword. He guided the weapon away from his chest, but the axe beak scratched his arm as it went by. Ammoss' return stroke caught the Kutel under the chin. As he drew the blade across its jaw he parried a spear thrust with his hammer. He then stepped down hard on the spear shaft. Off balance from the clumsy thrust, the Kutel was carried to the ground by his spear. When Ammoss' sword came free from the other Kutel's palate the Tafer let it swing over in a broad arc and strike the one that was now bent over in front of him. Its spine snapped.

The Kutel shaman had never seen a warrior like this. The blood of his war-band fell like rain in the trees. *I am dead.* Solsung fought down his rising panic. *At least the Tafer will kill me quickly – better than I will get from the Wizard-King if a Fitheran escapes.* He held his trident in both hands and warily advanced on the Tafer. Solsung did not wait for the Tafer to attack. He stabbed quickly out and back. It was meant to make the Tafer stand off. He came away unharmed. Solsung had been in personal combat many times in his rise to leader status and his confidence was returning. *My trident has the longer reach. I just might kill him.*

Ammoss saw the Kutel pause to think. He threw his hammer at it so that he could get a double grip on the sword. When the Kutel ducked right to avoid the hammer, Ammoss knocked its trident aside with his sword. He stepped quickly past the points and struck the Kutel full in the face with the heavily weighted pommel. The trident fell from nerveless fingers as the Kutel fell to the ground. Ammoss stepped past, then rocked down and backwards to drive the sword point into its throat.

Ammoss looked around for more Kutel as he collected his war hammer. He smelled smoke. *It is probably from the Kutel. That's a bad sign.* He quickly cleaned the blood from his weapons and armor before returning to the tree where he left the Fitheran. He spoke quietly up the tree trunk, "Come on down, it's safe for now."

Ghinlihil was sixty feet up the young maple when the Tafer spoke to him. The tree swayed when he dipped his head, "No."

Ammoss could not think of which language to curse in. He regained control. "Come down and I'll take you to Dath, my village. We can go back to Foralis when it's safe."

Ghinlihil had to admit that he was going to Dath in the first place. However, he was too high in the tree and it was having trouble with his weight. He hardly dared to breathe for fear the trunk would snap. He held on so tightly that the bark dug into his face.

"It's well enough if you're scared. I'm scared too." *Scared that you will fall out of the damned tree.* "We'll go back to my house and have cold tea." *Fitherani have a weakness for tea.* Ammoss liked it himself on a hot night. Shandi usually kept a pot in the cellar for him.

That got Ghinlihil to begin a careful descent. "I'm too little for tea."

"Not after tonight, Fitherandel," Ammoss looked at the faint orange glow farther up the path. Fires still burned in Foralis. "Not after tonight."

When Ghinlihil got to the ground Ammoss moved him quickly away from the battle scene. *That is not for young eyes.* He chuckled to himself, *How old are those 'young eyes' I wonder?* "I'm called Ammoss." He waited for the Fitheran to reply before asking, "How are you called?"

"Ghinlihil."

Ammoss translated the name, "'The wind that makes the leaves dance.' A little wind would be nice tonight."

Ghinlihil was dressed very sensibly for a warm night, in silks and soft moccasins. Ammoss' armor was oppressive. It was hot and it did not fit properly anymore. There was no sign of a breeze now.

Ammoss and Ghinlihil walked for miles in silence. Occasionally the little Fitheran would have to break into a trot to keep up. Ammoss would slow his pace when he noticed. Ghinlihil was doing well to take two steps for every one of the Tafer's.

Ammoss was willing enough to slow down. He had been walking all night at a quick pace to catch the Kutel, only to stop within a half a mile of Foralis. *Even so,* he thought, *one Fitheran is worth a night's march.* He laughed aloud. Some slavers would mount entire expeditions in hope of capturing a Fitheran. They ate less than a Tafer and could be willed to the owner's heirs. *Slavers are no better than Kutel, and harder to spot.* Ammoss spat on the path to clear the idea from his tongue.

Ghinlihil stared wide-eyed at the Tafer's strange behavior. Even when he was walking quietly, Ghinlihil was fascinated with Ammoss. *He is so HUGE.* Ghinlihil had never imagined anyone bigger than his father. Even when others had explained how big the Kutel and the Tafers were, he could never make his mind imagine anyone bigger than Lalliam Steelhand. *What will father say when he finds out? He is probably glad to be rid of me.* Ghinlihil's eyes teared up again.

I guess I cannot blame him for crying, Ammoss thought. *What can I do to cheer him up?* He thought about a song, but he did not know any in Timbrali. "Do you speak Shield?" Ghinlihil dipped his head 'no' again. *Just as well.* Ammoss was no musician.

Ghinlihil broke the silence, "Is it far to Dath?"

Is it? To a little Fitheran, maybe. It is a long way to walk twice without a proper rest. "We'll get there tomorrow. It's a long walk for me, but I'm heavy, you're light." That, at least, was true, though Ammoss could not tell how light. *Certainly less than seventy pounds, probably much less.*

"How do you get to be so big?" Ghinlihil only came to the Tafer's hip.

"I eat a lot." – *Too much* – "Tafers are bigger than Fitherani, a little bigger than the Kutel on average. No, not really. 'Round about we are, but other places Tafers are no bigger than Kutel. We're a tall people in the Valley of the Shield."

They come in different sizes? Ghinlihil was overwhelmed.

Most of the journey to Dath was made in silence. The forest almost demanded silence from them. It was so still that their own footfalls rang in their ears.

Ammoss was surprised that Ghinlihil walked the whole way. He had expected to carry the youth for the greater part of the morning. *I'd have made a camp,* he thought as he turned off the path toward his home. *I could not have managed the armor and the Fitheran together.* In spite of his fatigue, or perhaps because of it, he smiled at himself. *I would have carried him and my armor and walked until I dropped, for pride.*

Soon his house appeared around a bend in the narrow path. "This is it." His house was actually unfinished – at least Shandi said so. He planned to finish another room this year. It was a large house. In Dath it was second only to the home of Sheildmaster Roun.

Ammoss had originally thought to live only in the four downstairs rooms and leave the upper story empty. The second floor overhung the lower by three feet all the way around. The idea was to make the structure easy to defend. Ammoss lived too far from the center of Dath to expect very much help during a Kutel attack. His intention was to make his home the most defensible place in town. Then the townsfolk would be tempted to abandon their homes to fight from his. This theory had never been tested.

The house was built over a well that he used only when the weather outside was very bad. A stream ran nearby that provided water for regular use. The cellar had room to provision three or four families for a winter. Four years earlier he had hosted two families from town for the winter after a fire had left them homeless. Ammoss had moved his own smokehouse the following spring to make sure that it did not happen to him.

Shandi had turned the dark brown fortress of a house into a home. She was the daughter of Talor, the Shieldmaster of The Hunt, *A man worthy of the title,* Ammoss thought. Ammoss had gone to him three years ago to help him fight the Kutel there. Ammoss would admit (though only to himself) that Shandi was not the most beautiful girl he had ever met. In fact, prettier girls lived in Dath whose fathers would have married any of them to Ammoss for the dower. Shandi was a practical girl, and coming from the aristocracy, she was wealthy enough in her father's house that his money was not the lure that landed her. That meant a great deal to Ammoss. There was more between Ammoss and Shandi than the sharing of work or wealth. Almost every day Ammoss thought of one or two things about Shandi that he thought were special. *She can ride a horse cheerfully. She will clean a fish, or a deer, and cook it – and cook it well.* That was the way she had captured Ammoss in the first place. Even now, though she paid a local widow to help clean, Shandi did all of the cooking. She even brewed ale for him. (She drank it too, but he considered it his ale.) They had been married for two years, but he still asked her permission before taking anything from the kitchen.

A great shaggy black and white splotched dog bounded around the corner of the house and down the path toward Ammoss and Ghinlihil. The little Fitheran was terrified. He stood wide-eyed and still. With each bound the beast came eight feet closer. Chunks of earth and the sparse grass flew into the air behind it.

Ammoss wanted to shout, to tell the dog to stop, but he knew that the dog would not obey. He counted bounds until the sixth. The rope around her neck ran out and her hindquarters past her head gracelessly. She composed herself quickly. Straining against the rope she began to bark his welcome home. Ammoss realized that Ghinlihil was holding his breath. "Truck's just happy to see me." His voice sounded more weary than reassuring. "There must have been dogs in Foralis."

Ghinlihil had known that dogs came in different sizes, but he never imagined one to match the size of Ammoss. Before he could frame his reply, a big sweaty Taforam opened the front door. The white powder on her apron indicated that she had been baking. The hope of food overcame both fatigue and fear. Ghinlihil began walking up the path again.

"When I asked you to bring me something nice from Foralis, I didn't mean a Fitheran." Shandi gestured at Ghinlihil. She spoke in Shield. "You look worse than I do, and I've been baking in this heat." She paused long enough to see that Ammoss had nothing to say. "Oh, be quiet Truck!" The dog kept barking. Shandi ignored her, "I'll bring out sausage and cheese. The bread isn't quite ready yet." She left the door open when she re-entered the house.

Ammoss walked up and sat down beside the path in the green grass. He was just far enough from the house that Truck could reach him, but not jump on him. He was too tired to be playful, and not especially hungry.

Ghinlihil could not understand a word that the Taferam had said. *She left the door open, and that must be a welcome.* When he got within reach of the dog he got a thorough sniffing from a wet nose. After a few words from Ammoss the dog went back to try to get her master to play.

Shandi reappeared with a big wooden platter. She held it too high for Ghinlihil to see anything on it except the top of a pewter pitcher. She put it down on a tall stump that had been flattened to make a sort of table. She had wanted Ammoss to hollow it out for a bird bath, but he had said that it would breed mosquitoes. She stood by the stump guarding the food from Truck until Ammoss and the Fitheran arrived.

"How is Foralis?" She tried to sound casual. Shandi understood that the Kutel were dangerous. *So many reasons to appreciate her,* Ammoss thought. He surprised her with a kiss.

Ammoss cut a sausage in half and handed a piece to Ghinlihil. "Eat," he said in Timbrali. He poured tea into three wooden cups, then he spoke to Shandi in Shield. "I didn't get to Foralis." The smell of spicy sausage was waking him up. "I found his one on the road being followed by Kutel. I think I saw fires." He took a bite of sausage.

She saw the fresh mark on his arm and understood that battle had taken place. *At least this time he cleaned the blood off his boots before tracking it all over my floors.* She resisted the urge to fuss over the wound. He had more knowledge of healing than she did. It was something that bothered her. She felt that it was her job to take care of him, as she had taken care of her father and brothers when they were wounded.

Fires in Foralis, that is bad news. Her kitchen not withstanding, it was too hot to light fires. *Fires could only mean that the Kutel did some real damage to the Fithern village. Even signal fires would mean that they needed help, and Shieldmaster Roun did not send any help.* Kutel had set fire to The Hunt when Shandi was a child. Most of the town was saved, but the burns and the destruction and the stench that lasted all winter composed one of her strongest memories. *The poor Fitherani.* "We should send men to see what help can be made."

"Roun should have sent men yesterday, then there would have been no fires." Ammoss began unbuckling his armor with welcome relief. He looked to see Truck stealing the end of a sausage from Ghinlihil's hand. The Fitheran was asleep sitting up. "I'll go back to Foralis tomorrow and see what condition the Fitherani are in." He then threw his armor aside, lay back in the grass, and immediately fell asleep.

Shandi picked up the platter and hesitated, looking at the Fitheran. *I should put him to bed. Maybe they sleep like that? Besides, why wake him just to put him to bed?* She carried the leftovers inside and let Ammoss and Ghinlihil sleep in the sun. *Oh, I will have burnt the bread!*

Ghinlihil awoke with a start. *Where am I?* He leaped to his feet. Pain shot through his legs and he wavered for just a moment. Pain won out over panic and he sat back down.

He saw Ammoss lying in the grass an arm's length away (the Tafer's arm's length; he was well out of Ghinlihil's reach). Instantly memories of the following night washed over him, backwards. He remembered spicy sausage, the dog, the long walk. The memory of the battle did not affect him very much, it was too foreign – unreal. He remembered his parents arguing. He began to cry again. *Do they even want me back?*

Suddenly a Taforam – *What is her name?* – was babbling and fussing over him. He could not understand what she said, but she gave him some dried banana chips. *Father says they're too expensive.* Then she began painting his legs with a strong smelling dark potion. It made them feel different, but not particularly better. She picked him up, carried him inside, and set him on a fresh bed with clean linen sheets. She was still talking.

"I don't understand," he said.

Shandi sighed. "Just rest," she said, knowing that he would not understand. *What does he want? His mother, probably.* Pity washed over Shandi. *I do not have her to give you.* "Ammoss will find her in the morning." The Fitheran just stared. *That was pointless. What if Ammoss does not find her? Well, the Fitherani take care of their orphans. They are decent folk.*

Ammoss did not want to open his eyes yet. The afternoon sun shone red through his eyelids. *Dog breath! That is what woke me up, dog breath.* It was not getting any better. He opened his eyes a slit. Truck was sleeping with her muzzle pointed at his nose. Ammoss slowly got up. He noticed that Shandi had collected his sword and armor. *Good girl, it might have got cold enough for a dew tonight.* The thought struck Ammoss as odd. *I have been sleeping with the dog and calling my wife a "good girl". That should be the other way around.*

He picked up his war hammer and walked slowly into the house. *If I were Shieldmaster, I would have a page to look after my armor.* The thought stuck in his mind when his eyes adjusted to the light inside. There was a boy sleeping on a cot next to the empty fireplace. His mind struggled with the memory: *Fitheran. Ghinlihil. I have got to have a look at Foralis in the morning.* He staggered up the stairs to bed.

Ammoss woke early with a heavy head. *Sleep hangover: too much sleep.* Shandi was still asleep. *She probably had things to do yesterday.* He went downstairs to get something to eat. When he walked through the front room, he found Ghinlihil lying awake in bed. "Come, we'll have fresh bread and butter," he said in Timbrali.

Ghinlihil followed Ammoss to the cellar where he cut a slab of butter. He then followed the Tafer to the kitchen where he picked up two loaves of dark crusty bread. Ammoss made a poor show of giving thanks for the bread, to no one in particular, and broke it in half. He gave half to Ghinlihil and began buttering the other half.

"I'll be riding back to Foralis today," he said between mouthfuls. "You should stay here, our guest, for now. I'll be back tonight and if all's well you can go home tomorrow."

If they want me back, Ghinlihil thought. His eyes teared up again.

Ammoss had expected the Fitheran to brighten more at the idea of going home. "Don't worry, the Kutel look fierce, but they're not really good fighters. Battles always look worse than they really are." Ghinlihil was not responding. Ammoss gave up trying to be cheery and changed the subject. "Don't be too hard on Shandi today. She doesn't speak Timbrali, but she'll do her best to be a good hostess."

Ghinlihil ate quietly. Then he went with Ammoss and watched him saddle the big horse. He stood next to Truck and they both watched the big Tafer ride away on his sturdy chestnut warhorse.

All was not well in Foralis. Nothing at all was well. The only good thing was that the rains of the previous week had prevented a forest fire.

The village was burnt to the ground. Charred beams stood mournfully in the noonday sun. In many places the fires had not been hot enough to burn the corpses. Crows gathered there. The scene that met Ammoss was both grizzly and desolate. The town was a confusion of charred black and blood red. The smell made his horse skittish. Even a veteran like Ammoss could not block it out of his mind.

Any Fitherani who survived will not return here, except perhaps to meet one another and move on. The Fitherani had no tradition or custom for honoring the bodies of the dead, and generally buried or burned them only to get them out of the way. They would not feel compelled to return just to tend to the dead.

Ammoss dismounted and walked around the village looking for fresh tracks. He found none, outside of a lone wolf who came for carrion. *If Ghinlihil's parents survived this, they will come looking for him at Dath.* He also checked the Kutel footprints to see if any of them where about. He found signs of a few deserters, and the trail of eleven that he fought on the path. He saw no threat written in the ground outside Foralis. He saw no hope in the ground inside Foralis, either. Ammoss collected his horse and rode home that afternoon.

Ammoss, like Solsung, had been mistaken; there were a few Fitherani who escaped Foralis. Three days after the battle, the survivors of Foralis gathered and prepared for the journey south to Sekri Timbrali, their homeland. Many years passed before they discovered, to their lasting shame, that they had abandoned Ghinlihil.

For most of his ride home Ammoss was occupied with regret at the loss of Foralis and its Fitherani. Eventually, this gave way to his loathing of the Kutel. *It was a great victory for them. Their captains will be bolder now, forgetting past defeats. How long before they attack Dath?* His thoughts also wandered on to Ghinlihil. *We will have to keep him, of course, until someone comes to claim him.* By the time the sun got low enough to make Ammoss squint, he could no longer think of the razing of Foralis as wholly evil. That surprised him. *Shandi wants children.* He did also, but he had not yet admitted that even to himself. *We have had no success of our own so far.* By the time he returned home, he had talked himself into adopting Ghinlihil if no one came for him.

Shandi's day with Ghinlihil had been an unexpected pleasure. She had been living on the outskirts of Dath since marrying Ammoss and she had almost no contact with children there. She missed them dearly; all of her little cousins and their friends, and the servants' children who were always underfoot. She had expected the language barrier to be more difficult with Ghinlihil. He seemed to understand her moods, if not her words, and Shandi found herself picking up a few words of Timbrali.

When Ammoss returned looking pleased with himself she thought, *He has found the village intact and they want Ghinlihil back.* She was disappointed that the child might be leaving and immediately felt guilty about it. *I should be happy that his life is going back to normal, and his people are well.*

Ammoss always took care of the horse himself; he had never hired a groom. Shandi met him in the barn. She said nothing, but waited for him to explain. It was a long wait. *Does he think I am here to watch him water the horse?* Her patience wore thin when he began brushing. "How is Foralis?"

Ammoss took some time to frame his reply. He wanted to steer her toward accepting Ghinlihil herself, that way it would not look like he wanted children. For some reason he could not let himself admit that.

When he did not reply, she asked again, "How bad is it?"

He continued brushing. "It's bad."

"What do you mean 'it's bad'?" Shandi snapped back, "What happened? I wasn't there, remember?"

"We'll have to look after the Fitheran for a while." He looked at her, to gauge her reaction. She did not react. "No one at Foralis. Don't expect there will be anytime soon. It's burnt."

"The whole town?"

He nodded 'yes' after the manner of his own people. "I'll tell Shieldmaster Roun about it in the morning. I expect he'll need some explaining." Neither Ammoss nor Shandi had much confidence in their town Shieldmaster.

Shandi left him with the horse. She walked around to the back of the house where Ghinlihil had been playing with Truck. He was standing quietly by the corner. At first Shandi did not see him in the shadow of the building. Truck gave him away by trotting over to him and dropping a stick at his feet. She watched him throw the stick for the dog again. *Ammoss will have to tell him,* she thought, somewhat relieved, *I cannot speak his language.* She smiled at Ghinlihil.

Chapter 3

Lost

"You can stay with us until it's safe to go home." *Please do not ask too many questions.* Ammoss did not know what to tell Ghinlihil, but he did not think the truth was a good idea.

"The Kutel are still attacking?" *Foralis has been attacked several times in Ghinlihl's memory. None had lasted more than a single night.*

"I don't think so. The Fitherani aren't there. They might be chasing the Kutel now. I'm sure that they will send someone for you when they're ready." *Ammoss was a poor liar, but Ghinlihil did not question him. Ammoss thought it very unlikely that Ghinlihil had any living relative, or that Foralis would ever be safe for a Fitheran again.*

"When will that be?"

"I don't know. When they get done doing whatever it is that they're doing, I suppose. How are your parents called?"

Ghinlihil had to think for a moment. He never used their real names. "Laliam Steelhand and Jilwanis Sharpeye."

"Laliam Steelhand?" Ammoss was surprised, "I've heard of him, in a song – he killed a Kutel leader and stopped half of the Kutel attack on Haafven. It must have been a big victory because there was peace for a long time afterwards." *If the song is to be believed.*

"He always said, 'Shoot for the leader if you can.'"

"Yes, it worked well that day." *Was the lightning worshiper the leader of the attack on Foralis? If so, nobody shot him. Why would he be chasing*

Ghinlihil after burning the town? He should have had more important things to do.

In the evening Ammoss asked Shandi about the song. "Ghinlihil's father is Laliam Steelhand. That name is in an old song. Do you remember?"

"'The Alliance of Haavfen,' yes, I remember it. The Kutel tried to cut off access to the sea – that is, cut off the Hollenwae in the north. The Fitherani routed one group of Kutel. Most of the story is the wizard's duel on the sea. The wizard with the Kutel actually won the duel, but had to withdraw when the Fitherani got in bow range. It turned into a massacre. Songs always exaggerate, but it must have been something because the Putnu broke free of the Kutel after that."

"I don't remember that."

"It isn't in that song. It's in 'The Founding of The Hunt.' Without the Putnu ships, the Kutel couldn't attack by sea anymore. They started coming over the mountains. The Hunt was founded to guard the pass."

"I didn't realize that was the same time."

"Both songs are by the same author. The Hunt library has both written out. The scrolls are the oldest things in town. I had to sneak into the library at night to read them. I ripped one a little – I was scared for weeks that someone would notice."

"You ripped a two-hundred-year-old scroll?"

"Just a little."

The next morning, Ghinlihil began to settle into this strange new life. Every now and then he would look down the path, hoping for his parents to come and take him home. When Ammoss or Shandi noticed, they would try to distract him. Ammoss pointed out the different plants and animals, and told their names. Shandi focused on teaching him how to speak Shield – the Tafers' language in The Shield Valley. Truck the dog was the most successful at getting Ghinlihil's attention, though. She wanted to play, or walk, or just be petted.

As days turned into weeks, Ghinlihil looked less often. *Mother and Father are going to just leave me here, out of their way,* he thought. Without a word of discussion the Tafers in Dath all agreed that Ghinlihil was too young to hear about the massacre of his people. He thought that his parents did not want him back.

***

Ghinlihil spent a lot of time in the forest around Ammoss and Shandi's house. Truck would never be far away. Ammoss and Shandi would take him into the village when either of them went to Dath and Ghinlihil started making friends with the Tafer children before he could speak Shield properly: a game of tag required very few words. He learned the language quickly, though, and soon he was asking to see his friends in Dath. Shandi would ride to town and he would sit behind her on her horse.

Whenever time allowed, Ammoss would walk with Ghinlihil and often wandered far off the trail. As they walked, Ammoss taught Ghinlihil something about tracking and the different plants and animals. Ghinlihil was not an apt student. He paid more attention to the beauty he found in the forest and heard very little of what Ammoss said. Much of what Ammoss did by hard work, study, and careful concentration came naturally to the little Fitheran. He moved quietly and easily through the woods, and it was rare for him to damage even an emerging frond with a careless step. Ammoss had to concentrate to move as quietly as Ghinlihil did and try as he might the Tafer always left at least a slight trail. They taught each other a few things about the forest.

Every week that autumn, Ammoss would go out to the ruins of Foralis to see if there were any signs of the Fitherani. There were none. When the winter rains came, he went less often. When the spring buds first started to appear, Ghinlihil waited for Ammoss to return from Foralis. "Is it safe yet? Are they back?"

"Ghinlihil, I'm sorry. I don't think they're coming back."

"Why not?"

Because they are all dead. I cannot tell him that. "I don't know why they haven't come back, but no one lives there now. No one could live there. The town is broken and burnt."

"What do I do now?"

"Well, you can stay here. We're glad to have you."

"Where did they go?"

To ashes, wolves, and crows, Ammoss thought grimly. "I don't know. When the ground dries out, I'll see if I can find them."

"The trail will be gone."

"Oh, yes, the trail is gone now. I don't know if I could have tracked them in the summer – Fitherani are hard to follow in the woods." *Which is technically true.* "I can ask at other towns, though. If they went south or east, they could have come to other towns without passing here."

Ghinlihil tossed his head, 'yes.' *That does not sound very hopeful,* he thought. *Do mother and father even know where I am? How am I ever going to find them?* He was crying.

"I'll go as soon as it's safe to ride... when the ground dries out. I promise." *What do I tell him when no one has seen any refugees?*

True to his word, three weeks later Ammoss rode to Silverport. Tafers that did business with the Fitherani usually did business there. No one seemed to know anything about what had happened at Foralis, or who might be responsible for Ghinlihil. Ammoss told the Fitherani there that there was a survivor at Dath. *What more can I do? If I try to go to Sekri Timbrali, they will likely shoot me before I get a chance to deliver the message. These Fitherani will take the news there, anyway.* The Fithern homeland was closed to outsiders.

He rode from Silverport to The Hunt. Shandi always sent a letter to her family in the spring. He took the opportunity to hand-deliver it (and took the return message, of course). Sheildmaster Talor reported that they had not seen any Fitherani refugees. He had not heard of the attack at all.

Ammoss spent most of the trip trying to decide how to explain to Ghinlihil that no one was going to come for him. His horse heard several explanations, none of which were to the Tafer's liking. *I do not even know for certain that Ghinlihil is an orphan. On the other hand, I do not know if he has any living relative at all.*

"I've delivered the messages. Now we have to wait and see who comes."

Ghinlihil was hoping for better news. "How long?"

"Until someone comes there isn't anything else to do. You can stay with us, of course." Ghinlihil stood and stared at Ammoss until the Tafer felt that he had to say something more. "It may take some time for the news to get to the right people. Someone will come." Ammoss did not know whether to believe it himself.

From then, Ammoss and Shandi effectively adopted Ghinlihil. Ammoss finished another room upstairs to serve as his bedroom. For a few years everything seemed good and perfectly natural.

As Ghinlihil's playmates from Dath began to grow up it became obvious that he did not. Noril, for instance, grew from a sandy-haired eleven-year-old farm boy to a young adult of seventeen with a young wife. He cleared his own plot of land to till next to his father's and added on to the family home in preparation for a family of his own. Ghinlihil in those same years grew from eighty-one to eighty-seven – a Tafer might have guessed that he passed from eight to nine. He was still playing the same games and making the same mistakes that he had six years earlier. Ghinlihil was the only boy in town whose clothes wore out before he outgrew them.

Shandi had no children of her own during that time. Before she met Ammoss her mother had nagged and fretted that she was wasting her youth by staying a maiden too long. At nineteen she was the last of her friends to get married. Now she was twenty-seven and her mother's words kept coming back to her. She loved Ghinlihil dearly, but she could not help wondering why her family did not include any children of her own. As the years wore on the whispers in town of a Fithern curse started to ring true. She had the argument a hundred times in her own head. Almost six years to the day after Ghinlihil came to stay she could not keep it to herself anymore. On a hot summer night as they lay in bed awake hoping for a breeze she asked Ammoss, "How old is a Fitheran when he's grown?"

"Most Fitherani stay with their parents or teachers until they're over a hundred and fifty years old, though they can take their tests at one-thirty-five." He was afraid he knew where this was going.

"How long do the Fitheressi wait between children?"

Ammoss propped himself up on one elbow so he could look in her eyes. "Who's been talking to you about Fitheressi?"

She stared resolutely at the rough-hewn beam overhead. "I want to know how long."

He gave up and let himself fall back onto the pillow. "Usually ninety to a hundred years, but some only wait thirty or forty."

"That's not what I heard. I heard that they can't have another, so long as there's a young one at home. Isn't that true?"

"I don't know. Maybe they can't or maybe they just won't. You're no Fitheresse."

"I'm no mother either. I'll be beyond bearing age before he's grown an inch taller."

Ammoss was frustrated too. He wanted children of his own as much as she did. In spite of himself, his frustration came through in his voice, "What should we do then, turn him out? You want to hand him off to someone else for a year or two? It's not his fault." He forced himself to calm down, "These things happen in homes without Fitherani too, and you know it well."

"Not in my family they don't. Has it happened in yours?"

"No, nothing like that, but what does it matter? We're not going to throw him out."

She knew him too well to argue head-on. "Shouldn't he be with his own people?" she softened. *If he keeps thinking of Ghinlihil as the victim, I will never change his mind.*

"So I should cart him off to the Silverport and foist him on the first Fitheran who crosses my path, is that it?"

It was too much for Shandi. "Well, when are you going to help him move on? We'll be old and gray before he's an adult. Another seventy years? We'll both be stone dead. We could leave him to our children, if we had any! Maybe our grandchildren could see that he's properly raised!"

Ghinlihil lay in his bed and listened. His sharp Fithern ears caught every word, even the ones that they did not shout. *Fitherani can have multiple children. When a Fitheran wants a second child, he brings his Fitheresse a bloodroot flower from the Fertility Garden. I will go get one for Ammoss and Shandi. I made the trip here in one night. I can be back tomorrow night with the flowers. I will need to be careful not to drip the flower blood on me, that's bad luck – for me or the baby? I cannot remember.* As the argument in the next room grew more animated he slipped out of bed and began packing a few things in a sheet. Five minutes later he was walking silently out the door with Truck plodding faithfully beside.

The Northeast Path had grown over in the years after Foralis' destruction. Near Dath only grasses and wildflowers grew in the way, but deeper in the forest evergreen shrubs and some young trees had reclaimed the ground. Ghinlihil began on the last ragged end of that trail and tried to follow it to Foralis. Truck walked along beside him. They moved along the path until Ghinlihil's steps started to stray and wind from fatigue as much as the undergrowth. Finally, he lay down in the ferns under an oak tree with his bundle for a pillow. Truck circled and lay down beside him.

Shandi shook Ammoss awake. "He's gone! Wake up, Ammoss, and follow him. He's gone!" *And it is all my fault!* she thought to herself, *I wished for it.* She had been racked with guilt ever since discovering the empty bed. When she had called Truck and the dog did not come, then she knew that they must be far away. Her voice was cracking with hysterical tears, "Oh, get up!"

Ammoss snapped awake and ran out to look for a track. He followed Truck's footprints to the old Northeast Path, then he ran home. He saddled a horse and then got his armor and weapons.

"What do you need those for? Nothing has happened to him!" Shandi demanded, as if saying it made it so. "Oh, tell me nothing has happened to him!"

"He's gone down the old path. I expect he's trying to go home. Truck's with him, he should be all right." Ammoss was buckling on his armor. It fit even tighter now.

"But Truck is so old!"

"She's a good dog, and she's not that old."

"Then why are you putting on your armor?"

"The Kutel have been around the ruins of Foralis. If I pass Ghinlihil in the woods, I may meet up with them." He thought but did not say, *and if they have taken him, I will have to take him back by force.*

Shandi knew him well enough. When she married him he was her hero and she would have trusted him to take on the whole Kutel nation. For eight years he had been her husband, and she worried. *If the Kutel have got Ghinlihil, Ammoss will get himself killed trying to save him,* she thought. "Be careful. I couldn't bear to lose you both."

"Nobody's lost yet. I'll be back... We'll be back for supper at the latest."

Ammoss thundered down the path to Foralis on the young, fiery warhorse that he had bought the previous autumn. The stallion was all too eager to run, even in the heat of the summer. Iron-shod hooves churned the disused and overgrown path into the air behind them. Ammoss did not try to slow the charger. He would not try to follow Ghinlihil's footprints – the Fitheran was too light and graceful to leave much of a trail. *If I look for tracks the whole way I will be too slow, he will pull away from me.* Even Truck left few prints in the hard-packed earth of the old path.

The early morning sun woke Ghinlihil from his soft, fragrant bed of ferns. He picked up his bundle and continued on his way. Truck, the loyal mutt, followed along. A small stream let them drink their fill and they shared a sausage from Ghinlihil's bundle. He did not remember the stream, or the fact that he had not crossed it on his way to Dath. They crossed it anyway and continued wandering on. Before mid-morning Truck was panting in the summer heat even in the shade of the trees.

***

A scrawny Kutel was also moving through the forest. "Cruska!" he cursed himself. He was used to everyone else cursing him, but he rarely did so himself. His name was Heust and he had stolen Lalru's sword. It was not guilt that bothered Heust: Kutel rarely suffer from guilt. He had stolen the sword and made good his escape from the settlement, but now he was lost in the forest. He knew a trader in Bur-Droo who would pay one hundred Mikenuran gold nobles for the magical sword. Heust had no idea which direction Bur-Droo was. He ran west.

"Cruska!" He was moving in the daylight and the bright, shining green leaves hurt his eyes. Kutel eyes, which see as well as a Fitheran at night and better when underground, do not adjust well to bright light. There was a stabbing pain in Heust's eyes and a throbbing pain in his ankle where he had tripped over a root. He forced himself, out of bitter self-loathing, not to favor his left leg. *I deserve the pain for being so clumsy.* Heust knew that eventually someone in Jun would notice that he was gone, probably his mate first of all. *Kilno will sell me out, stupid cow. I should have strangled her in her sleep before I left.*

Jun was a Kutel settlement built on the ruins of Foralis. Heust did not know why they built the settlement there, but he knew that he was not supposed to leave it. He needed to put as much distance as he could between himself and Jun before Lalru came after him. Most Kutel sleep when the sun is bright and Lalru usually awoke with the sunset. Heust jogged with his head down, watching for more roots, until he hit the top of his head on a low branch. "Cruska!"

Lalru the Kutel chieftain awoke mid-morning. He had drunk a cask of honey mead before the sun rose and he had vomited on himself while he was asleep. The stench woke him up. *I will throw Heust out and take his bed. He can sleep in the stink. Besides, it has been a long time since I had his mate. The ugly cow will beg for me.*

He reached for his sword, but his hand found nothing. *Where did I put my sword? No matter, I do not need a sword to deal with Heust.* He picked up his spear and stepped out into the bright sunlight. He was still drunk and swayed rather badly. He walked over to Heust's shack and was about to kick open the door when a thought caught up with him: *I will not leave the sword in the hut unguarded. Heust will steal it as soon as I turn him out.* He went back to his own hut and searched thoroughly, but he found no sign of the sword, scabbard, or belt. For that moment that was good enough for Lalru: *If I can't find it, neither will Heust.* He went back to

Heust's shack and knocked the door down (it had no hinges and was propped up in the doorway). Heust was not there.

Kilno, Heust's mate, was there, and so was their five-month-old son, Pewtle. Lalru stopped and thought, *Something is missing. Where has Heust got to?* In his dark and twisted Kutel mind, he missed the opportunity to bully the smaller Kutel. Though he did not even realize it himself, the only reason he had any interest in Kilno was to show Heust that the smaller Kutel could not stop him. One of the things he enjoyed most was making the other Kutel feel inferior and powerless.

Pewtle woke and started crying. Between the crying, the mead, and the daylight, Lalru's head was pounding. He threw Pewtle out in the dusty road, stepped into a dark corner of Heust's hut and tried to think.

Kilno ignored her own child. The maternal instinct is not strong in Kutel. She thought of it as Heust's baby and it meant nothing to her. *If I have Lalru's baby, then he will make Heust take care of me,* she thought. She was Huest's, not for any bond between them, but because he was the least powerful Kutel in the settlement and none of the other Kutel wanted to take Kilno from him.

Lalru continued to try to think. Pewtle continued to cry. As his anger rose, Lalru's hand fell to the place where his sword hilt should be. It was not there. Slowly two thoughts came together as one and he realized: *Heust has stolen my sword!* "Cruska!"

Lalru stormed out into the street and saw Pewtle crawling in the dust. Rage and hatred overcame his rush to recover the sword. *There will be nothing left of Heust!* He clawed both Pewtle and Kilno apart with his empty hands. He breathed deep the smell of fresh blood, then he took up his spear and his long knife and went to wake Nror.

Nror was a little Varro that Lalru had bought back in Bur-Droo. Nror walked too slowly and was generally a bother but Varro have a keen sense of smell. It had been said that the Varren were a cross between a Kutel and a dog. They walked erect most of the time and could speak in the Kutel language and use small tools in their clever hands. They had dog-like snouts, pointed ears high on their heads, and short fur. They rarely grew taller than three feet. Lalru knew they were not a crossbreed: he had tried to father one himself before he gave up the money for Nror.

Nror resented being woken in the daylight, but when he smelled Pewtle's blood he sat up and minded his manners. Lalru shouted, "Find Heust!" Nror snatched up his little spear on the way out the door, as eager to the chase as any hound.

Shandi stared down the empty path long after Ammoss had passed from view. Tears blurred her vision as guilt and worry addled her thoughts. She cursed herself when she realized that she was wasting time. She rode to town – straight to the Shieldmaster's house.

The title of Shieldmaster meant both "mayor" and "commander." Her father had born that title and secretly she thought that Ammoss should as well. Instead, Shieldmaster Roun ran Dath. He was too little "commander," with no battlefield experience at all, and he cared too much for the comforts of civilization to make the sacrifices necessary in a frontier town.

Shandi demanded to see the Shieldmaster. She pounded on the door to his study until he could no longer stand it. Shieldmaster Roun could ignore most of the Tafers of Dath, but not Shandi. Ignoring Shandi meant angering Ammoss, and Roun was not fool enough to do that. Sitting at his writing table, he dropped his pen as soon as he heard her voice, making a mess of his figures. He held his head in his hands and took several slow, deep breaths before rising to open the door.

Without so much as a "Good morning" she demanded that he send some armed men up the Northeast Path to help Ammoss find Ghinlihil. The Shieldmaster was shocked, though not by her manners. He was used to Shandi treating him like an underling. He was shocked because it seemed the right thing to do. He was not in the habit of agreeing with Shandi. Still, a child was missing and the Shieldmaster had a heart. To Shandi's great surprise he organized a search party at once. Before mid-morning forty Tafers followed the Shieldmaster into the forest to search for the young Fitheran.

Chapter 4

Captured

Ghinlihil found what he thought to be the path and followed it east, but the undergrowth tricked him. Instead he and Truck followed a deer run. They had been walking all morning when Truck lowered her head and began to growl. Ghinlihil at first did not pay any attention. The sun penetrated the leaf cover here, and a small stand of firs was growing in the light, making a loose green wall in front of them. Even the Fitheran could smell the strong scent of the trees in the light summer breeze. Truck could smell more than trees and she did not like the scent; not at all. Ghinlihil waved for Truck to follow. Her hackles rose and she growled some more.

Heust heard a growl. *Lalru has set Nror on me!* He had not considered that the Varro could follow him by scent. He began to run headlong in spite of his twisted ankle and in spite of the fir branches that slapped at him. He did not realize he was running toward the sound rather than away from it until he heard a dog bark. He looked up just in time to see a little Fitheran and a big dog. He threw out an elbow that caught the Fitheran in the forehead. It dropped to the ground.

Truck was too slow to jump between Ghinlihil and the Kutel when it burst from between the branches of the fir trees. When she saw it attack her playmate she jumped at the Kutel's throat. It threw up its hands and she caught an arm instead. The shock of her landing tore its left arm and pulled it out of its shoulder socket. It cried out with all of its harsh voice. It tried to draw a sword, but it stuck in the scabbard. Panicked, it flailed at Truck with sword, scabbard, belt and all. This did nothing but make the dog even angrier.

Truck let go of the arm to get a better grip. The Kutel slipped away. It stepped on the belt, drew the sword and stabbed at the dog, but Truck dodged out of the way. The big dog snatched the Kutel's other arm out of the air. This time she did not let go. She held on and shook the little Kutel until it went limp. Then she caught its throat and shook some more. The Kutel's neck snapped like a dry twig.

She went immediately to Ghinlihil and whining softly, nuzzled him. He did not stir. There was nothing for her to do but wait.

Lalru had been following Nror for hours. He was sobering up with the exercise and the afternoon air. Around noon he had heard a horse ride by. Normally he would have tried to catch it, but today he had to catch his sword. Revenge held all of his thoughts and helped him ignore the sunlight burning into his eyes. *Heust, you will beg me to kill you before I am done with you, but I'll make certain you get your whole lifetime's worth of pain before I let you die.* Now the afternoon was getting old. Nror was taking him west. *Why would Heust go west? He's not smart enough to be working for a Tafer.* Lalru could not go anywhere else. He could not follow the trail himself. Then he heard a growl.

Nror heard the growl, too. He crouched and held his spear in both trembling hands. He knew it was the growl of a big dog or wolf. The wind was wrong and he could not catch its scent.

Lalru bent to a crouch and moved forward with his spear very low. He pressed it to Nror's back. "Move, craven, or I'll cut you a new leak." Nror began moving forward again, never more than two inches ahead of the point. His hands trembled and his steps were unsure. His only hope was that he could hide under the low fir branches while Lalru fought the dog.

With no more warning the dog was flying into the branches. It was as massive as the Kutel chieftain and its jaws came at Lalru's throat. Lalru put his left foot down at the butt of his spear and raised the point. He was slower than he wished, and instead of impaling the dog he cut a wide gash through its gut. The collision brought them both to the ground.

***

Truck landed on her side and rolled to her feet. She was foaming with rage and pain. The Kutel rolled behind the Varro, sacrificing Nror for a second's respite. Truck snatched up the little Varro in her jaws and with a toss of her massive head threw it like a wet rag. It did not move from where it landed.

Lalru rose to a crouch and tried to stab at the dog while its head was turned. It was too quick and jumped at him even as it avoided the spear point. He abandoned his spear to turn the dog's jaws away from his own chest with both hands. It shook its head free and clamped vice-like jaws on his thigh. He raised his fist to punch it, but it shook him in the air as if he weighed no more than a rabbit. He landed hard on his back but the jaws did not open. He drew his long knife and stabbed down between the monster's shoulders, intending to break its spine. He hit so hard that the knife nearly jolted free of his claws. He could not break the dog's bones, but opened a gash over a shoulder. The dog put a big paw on his free leg and tore at the other. Lalru feared that the dog would pull the flesh completely off his thigh. His eyes were shut tight with pain. He stabbed blindly over and over. He might have been stabbing the dog or a tree or even himself for all he knew, pain had so overwhelmed his senses.

Ammoss discovered the Kutel settlement when the sun was high. *This should not be here*, he thought, *I should have scouted out here more often. Would Ghinlihil recognize a Kutel settlement before he was caught?* One Kutel was standing as a sentry but it was asleep at its post. Ammoss shot an arrow into the Kutel's chest as he galloped by. He rode through the little ramshackle town, looking for any other Kutel that might be stirring. He found none. He reigned in and dismounted, drew his sword, and began going from house to house.

He crashed through the door of the Kutel hut with sword in hand. He picked up the sleeping Kutel by the throat and slammed him into the hut's back wall. It was a mistake: the shoddy workmanship was not up to it. The wall splintered and broke down and they both fell to the ground.

Ammoss straddled the Kutel and held its throat in his left hand. "Where is he?" Ammoss shouted in heavily accented Kutel.

"Who, he? He who, who?" the Kutel sputtered.

Ammoss struck the Kutel in the shoulder with his sword pommel. He could feel the bone break beneath. "Where is the Fitheran?"

"There is no Fitheran. All Fitherani dead." The Kutel kicked up with its knee, intending to hit Ammoss in the groin. It missed, and glanced harmlessly against his thigh.

Ammoss rolled away, shoulder to hip and to his feet. When the Kutel sat up, he swung a two handed arc. The sword's edge slid across the Kutel's neck and blood spattered a ragged red line across the broken wall. The Kutel's head rolled out into the alley.

Ammoss leaped back in through the hole in the wall. He stabbed the female Kutel through the heart as she pretended to sleep. He then shifted his sword grip to his left hand and picked up a Kutel spear with his right. Stepping out the door into the light of the street, he saw two Kutel arming themselves and growling at one another. He threw the spear at the closer of the two. It went in and out through its gut, leaving the heavier end of the spear at the back. The Kutel grabbed the spear shaft with both hands and gaped at it in shock. Ammoss closed quickly on the other Kutel. With a stroke used more often splitting wood, he cut its right leg off at the knee. The Kutel's scimitar never cleared its scabbard. Both Kutel screamed as they died.

Ammoss moved toward the next building with nothing but death on his mind. His reason caught up before he reached the door. *If they killed him, there would be a trophy. Where is the head? Where is the evidence?* He looked quickly around and found none. *Maybe they did not get him.*

He raced towards his horse.

Kutel peering from corners and behind doors saw the Tafer turn his back. As a group they tried to sneak up behind him. None of the Kutel were particularly stealthy, and as a group of twenty-eight they had no hope of approaching unnoticed. They cursed each other for making so much noise, and for a moment paid no attention to the retreating Tafer.

Ammoss collected his horse near the burnt-out ruins of a Fithern house near the edge of town. He sheathed his still-bloody sword and mounted. Instead of retreating he drew his bow from the saddle. He loosed an arrow at the crowd of bickering Kutel. His aim was low and the arrow hit a Kutel in the thigh. The strong horn-laminate bow put the arrow in and out of the wound, leaving a cleaner wound than a lesser bow might have.

Thus reminded of the Tafer's presence, the Kutel charged at him. None wanted to be the first to reach the Tafer, nor to be the target at the front of the pack, so their advance was slowed as each Kutel tried to push another to the front.

Ammoss did not raise his aim, but waited for the Kutel to close slightly before shooting again. This arrow passed through a lung and shattered on the Kutel's spine. When the Kutel dropped two others stopped to spoil the body. The Kutel died, in blinding pain and gulping for breath in the blazing summer sun while his brother argued with his cousin over who would get the best of his possessions.

Ammoss rode out of town into the cover of the woods. At sixty yards away he stopped to take another shot. It pierced the Kutel in the shoulder. The force of the blow spun the Kutel around and knocked him off his feet but did not kill him. The rest of the Kutel stopped and backed away, leaving him unprotected. Yet another arrow came out of the woods and yet another Kutel fell. The rest of the pack ran for the safety of the town.

Ammoss turned his horse and rode away. He stopped again at the far edge of a rough clearing. The clearing was actually an area where ancient oaks provided a high canopy and left nothing growing low enough to interfere with archery but their own trunks. Ammoss waited only a few seconds. *If they are not following fast, I will get away on horseback.*

The Kutel were not following at all. They were putting on their bear hides and belting on their weapons. The smarter ones were looking for bows or spears. They soon noticed that Lalru was not trying to bully them into some type of order. They looked in his hut, but found that he was missing. Then they all hunted for his sword. When it was not found, the rumor began to spread, "The Tafer got Lalru's sword." They all began to follow the horse trail after the missing weapon of mythical power. They each hoped to be the one to recover the sword and become the new chieftain.

Lalru's knife struck deep into the dog's shoulder again and again. Eventually the tearing on his leg stopped. He used the knife to pry the dog's jaws open and he pulled the mangled leg out. With the same knife he cut a two foot wide strip from the base of his silk day cloak and used that to bind up the horrible wound. He dragged himself to his spear. He found that he could stand on his good leg using the spear shaft as a crutch. He went back to the dead dog to see how great a victory it had been.

When he broke out of the fir trees he could not believe his luck. Heust lay dead nearby. His own sword lay on a leaf bed just out of the dead Kutel's reach. Lalru quickly hobbled over to recover his treasure and pick over the body for anything else of value Huest might have. When he rose again he noticed Ghinlihil. *That is a Fitheran child!* He fought hard to resist the instinct to eat the Fitheran on the spot. *I can sell it for a fortune!* He kissed his sword pommel as it had always brought him good luck. *He even brought cloth to bandage my leg!*

He hobbled over to the little body, and prodded Ghinlihil with his scabbard point. The boy jerked away reflexively, but did not come to. *He is alive then. So am I. I am powerful. I am Lalru!* He used a tendon cord from Heust's calf to bind Ghinlihil's wrists together. He belted on his sword. He put Ghinlihil's arms around his neck. Hand over hand he climbed up the spear shaft until he was standing. Ghinlihil hung down in front of him. As he hobbled east greed and the flush of victory overawed the pain in his mangled leg.

Ammoss rode west down the Northeast Path. His mind was racing: *If Ghinlihil did not make it to Foralis, where is he? I did not pass him on the road. What if he is hiding from me? I do not have much hope of stumbling over him if he does not want to be found. Truck would come, though. She would not hide from me. She would not let him get into a town that smelled of Kutel, either. He must be alive. But where are they? He must have been going to Foralis. Did Truck make him turn away? Does he know the Kutel are out here? If he does, he will turn back to Dath, or go south. He may have never made it this far, it's a long walk.* Ammoss forced himself to stop thinking randomly. *There is no other way. I will have to try to follow his tracks.*

Ammoss galloped down the path toward Dath. He did not see the strange footprints of a lame Kutel crossing the path with a heavy burden and a walking stick. He was riding too fast.

Ammoss was still miles away from town when he drew his horse up short. A young Tafer came running toward him. It was Noril. Noril was out of breath and there were tears in his eyes, though Ammoss could not tell if the tears were from exertion or something else. He rode up and put a hand on the young Tafer's shoulder to steady it.

"We found Truck," Noril huffed. "She's dead." He was flushed and breathing heavily between words. The search party had sent him running up the path to catch Ammoss while they waited at the battle scene. "Ghinlihil's not <huff> not there." Ammoss worked his patience. He wanted to shake the young Tafer and pry him for information. *He just cannot talk any faster.*

"We didn't walk all over the ground around. <Huff> Roun said you might be able to get a track. There is a dead Kutel there <puff> and something else. Hedley called it a Varro. <Huff> There's blood everywhere." He crouched with his hands on his knees. He wavered between gasping for air and fighting nausea. Noril and Ghinlihil had been friends since the Fitheran first came to town. He knew Truck too, of course; they had all played together in the woods.

Ammoss extended a hand. Noril did not notice it for a moment, but as soon as he looked up he took it. Ammoss swung the youth up on the back of his horse. Together they rode on.

Ammoss blamed himself the whole way back. *Good old Truck. Poor old Truck! If I had stayed close and followed the track from the start, I might have heard her bark at the Kutel. A Kutel and a Varro together means a hunting party, but what were they hunting for? Could they know Ghinlihil was out here? Had he been spotted near the village? How close do the Kutel get? I should have been further out in the forest recently. I could have found their tracks. I could have taught them not to spy on Dath.*

With a little guidance from Noril, they arrived at the battle scene. Forty Tafers stood around and tried to think of something to say. No one said a word.

Ammoss could hardly wait for Noril to dismount so that he could get down and look at the footprints. He dismounted himself and handed the reigns to one of the others. The horse was lathered and beginning to shiver in spite of the summer heat. Ammoss did not notice.

The battle scene was clear to him after a quick inspection. *There are some things from the house here, so Ghinlihil was here... probably. Two Kutel had fought here, but one at a time. The first one is dead, killed by Truck. The Varro died next. Its little spear does not have any blood on it. The next Kutel came and stabbed Truck, many times.* It was hard for him to think clearly with his dog – the shaggy puppy he had bought to protect Shandi eight years ago – lying there mutilated. *The second Kutel was wounded. The blood trail stops at the torn sheet, so it made a bandage. He took the weapons from the first. One of them had a pole weapon, he used it to help him walk. It is flat on the end, not a bow. He cut open the other's leg deliberately, certainly after the Kutel was dead. What good was that to him? He needed a rope, of course. He knew where to find it. He is smarter than average. He bound something up and carried it off. Something too heavy to trust to the sheet. Ghinlihil?* What light footprints that the Fitheran had left were obscured by heavier treading. "We'll follow the trail. It's one wounded Kutel, and he's carrying something heavy. I think he's got Ghinlihil."

Even on foot Ammoss could move quickly on this trail. The Kutel was limping badly and crashing through the underbrush. The pole left holes in the soil with every step. *Wounded and heavy, he is moving very quickly.*

The tracks went west, toward the path. *He will probably go to Foralis for help. Maybe we should try to get there first. No, I tried that once, if I am wrong too often, I will lose him. I have been lucky so far.*

As they walked the Tafers of Dath began to gather clubs and staves from the forest. Many had knives and two had brought wood cutting axes. Apart from Ammoss, Shieldmaster Roun was the only one with a real weapon. In spite of his rank, the butter-soft Shieldmaster looked odd with a sword. Noril had picked up the Varro's light spear. The Tafers believed Ammoss when he said there was one Kutel, and they trusted him to fight any one Kutel alone, but in all of the stories Kutel came in hoards. No one had ever heard of just one Kutel.

Twenty-six Kutel tramped down the overgrown path toward Dath. The sun was beginning to set in their eyes. Though the light blinded them, as the sun sank and their shadows grew longer, the Kutel began to walk more proudly. They were armed and armored in their heavy bearskins and they were on the trail of a single, wealthy Tafer – even Lalru could not afford armor like the Tafer wore. Soon the sun would set. Most hoped to catch him asleep. Some few hoped that he woke up in time to kill some of the stronger Kutel, so that they could get more of the spoils for themselves. They all wanted to eat the horse.

Ammoss led the Tafers from Dath as the sun set behind them. He was both relieved and disappointed when they crossed the Northeast Path. *I could have caught them here two hours ago. At least I did not go back to Foralis. They are not going there. Where are they going?* A rough cry interrupted his thoughts. *That is a Kutel!* he thought, *Maybe we are closer than I thought.*

The battle cry was repeated by twenty-five other voices. The Kutel of Jun charged out of the evening shadows toward the end of the line of Tafers. A few shot bows. One arrow grazed a Tafer's arm. The poison was old and weak. The Tafer's blood carried it out of the wound, leaving no more than a burning sensation.

Ammoss drew his sword and war hammer then ran back to blunt the charge. A Kutel drove his spear at the warrior's chest. The iron bands of Amoss' armor took most of the force and the point only penetrated enough to prick his skin. Ammoss reached out with his sword. His long arm and long sword combined to give him the reach that he needed. The point dug two inches into the Kutel's throat. He reached out to the side with his left hand and felled another with the hammer.

Twenty armed and armored Kutel crashed into forty farmers and woodcutters from Dath. Tafers with clubs and knives fought against Kutel with maces and swords. Roun fell dead with a spear in his eye before his sword cleared its scabbard. The Tafers of Dath were pushed back by the shock of the Kutel charge. Ten were wounded, two were already dead and the Kutel were still attacking fiercely.

After the wave of Kutel passed, four black arrows shattered harmlessly against Ammoss' armor. He charged into the small clutch of Kutel archers. Two were dead before they drew another arrow. The other two ran away.

The forest helped the Tafers slow the charge, and they fought back from around the trees. Kutel and Tafers fell together on the blood spattered leaves. Tafers who had been farther off the path came to the aid of their neighbors and many of the Kutel were flanked. Ammoss attacked the rear of the Kutel. Those who turned to face him were clubbed to death from the farmers behind. Ammoss killed eight more himself.

As suddenly as the battle started, it was over. Three Kutel tried to run. Two were killed by the villagers before they got a step. Ammoss pulled a light spear from lifeless hands and threw it at the last one. It stuck into the back of its knee, taking the Kutel off its feet. Two other Tafers ran up to it and clubbed it until it stopped squirming. Ammoss looked for a long time at the light spear in the Kutel's leg. *It is the Varro's spear.* He looked down. It was Noril's lifeless hands that had held the weapon.

Ammoss looked around and saw his neighbors lying on the forest floor. Quickly he moved from one to another, checking for signs of life. He bound what wounds he could, set two broken bones, and gave everyone a silverseed from his small store to speed their healing. Eight Tafers were beyond the power of a silverseed and would never see the light of day again.

Hedley, the grizzled and pock-scarred miller, grabbed Ammoss' armored shoulder as Ammoss tied a splint to his right leg. "You were right. We should have defended Foralis when we had the chance. The Fitherani were much better neighbors." A grimace crawled across Ammoss' face. Hedley was one who had counseled against marching to Foralis six years ago. Unless he found a healer with more skill than Ammoss, he would have a limp for the rest of his life. Hedley continued, "What about Ghinlihil? How many of us can still follow the trail?"

Ammoss' voice had no spirit. "None."

"You can't just leave him!"

"A dozen or more Tafers here can't be moved right away. You shouldn't. Everyone's wounded."

"You don't need to stay with us. We'll be all right here until daybreak."

"At least two Kutel got away – two with bows and their poisoned arrows. I led all of you into this with both of my eyes closed. This is my fault. I'm not going to leave you now." Hedley started to say something, but a muscle spasm sent pain shooting up and down the entire right side of his body. He ground his teeth until blood dribbled into his prickly beard. Ammoss continued, "The Kutel with Ghinlihil, if it is Ghinlihil, has a leg almost as bad as yours. I'll see you all safely home, then I'll catch up with him." Ammoss hoped that he sounded confident. His thoughts were bitter. *What chance have I got of finding him now?*

Chapter 5

Slavers

Ghinlihil awoke feeling miserably sick. He tried to stir. He was sore all over and he could not remember why. He tried to stretch his shoulders. He could not raise his arms. He sat bolt upright, then lurched to the left and vomited on a fern. His hands were bound in front of him. It was all that he could do to keep from falling into the mess. He took a few gulping breaths as if the air itself could cure him. It did not.

He was in the shade of a large tree. The forest was bright and cheery. Birds sang and flew merrily about. He had expected to be in a dismal cave or crypt. *Why?* he asked himself. Then the overpowering stench of the Kutel sleeping nearby brought back the nightmare of the last few days. *How long has it been?* Ghinlihil could not piece the memories together. *It was daytime when he hit me.* Ghinlihil did not know that it was a different Kutel who had hit him. *There was a night when I hung from the Kutel by my arms. It is day now. Were there more days?* Most of the time he had been unconscious; the rest of the time he only wished that he was. *I will never get the Kutel stench out of my nose.*

He thought briefly of escape. A strip of cloth was tied to the cords that bound his hands and the other end was knotted to the Kutel's small finger. *If I can tear the cloth, I could walk away without waking it... him.* Ghinlihil's hands were so numbed from the tight cord around his wrists that he could not even grip the cloth. When he moved his arms, a blinding pain shot from his shoulders to his neck. He was not used to hanging by his arms for hours on end.

He tried to lie back gently, but he fell backwards. With his hands bound he could not catch himself and he hit his head on a root. He wiggled himself sideways to get off the root, and then lay still. He waited for sleep that did not come. His head throbbed both where it hit the root and where he had been hit by the Kutel. If he lay very still, the pain in his shoulders ebbed until it was only maddening. He closed his eyes as tightly as he could and cried. He did not dare to make a sound for fear that he might wake the Kutel. He did not know what the Kutel would do to punish him, and he did not want to find out. Tears dried slowly on his cheeks.

Hours of misery passed. Ghinlihil expected to wake from the nightmare at any time. Eventually he just wanted to fall into a different one. He endured three hours of pain, fear and boredom. His mind played the worst kind of tricks on him. He wondered what the Kutel might do to him. All manner of unspeakable horrors ran through his creative young mind. Sunset found him quivering with pain and fear, but sleep would not come.

As the night air began to gather in the forest, the Kutel awoke. He untied the cloth from his finger and got slowly to his feet with the aid of the spear pole. He had left the sword belted on all night. Ghinlihil could hear him grind his teeth, but the Kutel made no other sound. The Kutel relieved himself, and then reached for Ghinlihil.

Ghinlihil shrunk away from the Kutel's steaming wet claws.

"Awake at last," Lalru said in Kutel. When the Fitheran did not reply he continued in Shield, "Get up, then. You can walk on your own feet."

Ghinlihil struggled to rise without using his arms. He lost his balance and put his hands down to steady himself. Pain shot through both shoulders and he crumbled, landing hard on his face.

Lalru made an awkward swat at him. Ghinlihil was just close enough to receive a stinging cut across his back from the Kutel's longest claw. "On your feet!" the Kutel demanded. He reached for his sword.

Ghinlihil rolled away and struggled to his feet. He looked out into the forest. *I wonder how far I can run?* The sick feeling rushed from his stomach to his head and back to his stomach.

Lalru took one hobbling step and put a heavy hand on Ghinlihil's shoulder. "You can't outrun a spear. If you try to run away I'll eat you for breakfast." As if to lend weight to his words, drool fell from the Kutel's right fang. "Now walk! That way!" Lalru spun the Fitheran around until he was pointing northeast.

They moved all night hobbling, staggering and stumbling through the forest. The Kutel needed to stop for rests frequently. Ghinlihil was glad to see that the Kutel needed both hands on the spear to walk. This was not because he hoped to run away, or for any spiteful wish that it suffer pain. It simply meant that the Kutel had to keep his filthy hands off Ghinlihil when they were moving.

After midnight they came to a stream. They turned southeast to follow it. Ghinlihil walked in the stream bed. He wanted to lie down in the clear, flowing water. It was cold, but he wanted to wash so much away he would have let the stream run over him if he could. Instead he moved slowly along, keeping pace with the Kutel who walked on the gravel bank. The water washed the miles off his feet and soothed the burning that had been beneath Ghinlihil's consciousness until the water relieved it. He watched the reflection of the stars wriggling on the surface and shuffled along. Only the pain in his wrists and head kept him from falling asleep on his feet.

The dawn light was making Lalru squint when the forest split with the sound of a rough voice. "Well, well, if it isn't Lalru the Invincible?" Ghinlihil looked behind and saw that another group moving along the bank had caught up with them. The speaker was somewhat shorter and squatter than the others. One misaligned tooth stuck out past his lip. Both of his nostrils had been slit open, leaving purple gaps even though the wounds had healed years earlier. Ghinlihil thought he was the ugliest Tafer that he had ever seen. Ghinlihil did not realize that he was actually half Kutel. "You don't look invincible today."

"Korus Vet," said Lalru, "I've been looking for you."

Two Tafers with spears bracketed Korus Vet as he spoke. "Ooh, I'm sooo scared." He caught one of the Tafers by the shoulder theatrically, "Oh protect me Senlo, from the crippled Kutel."

"Later Vet, this is business. The Fitheran's for sale."

"Of course he is." Korus Vet rolled his rheumy eyes, "Senlo, Rall, kill him."

One of the Tafers protested, "But a Fitheran's worth big money!"

"Not the Fitheran, you idiots, Lalru!"

Lalru had figured out Korus Vet's plan before the hirelings. He threw his spear at the first Tafer. It broke a rib and bounced back out, leaving a sucking hole in his chest. Lalru could not regain his balance after the throw and fell to the ground. He rolled off from his sword and drew it as the second Tafer approached. Lalru fought an impressive battle from his back. He parried all the Tafer's attacks and made a few of his own.

Without reach and crawling on one arm and one leg he had little chance of landing a killing blow: the Tafer's spear was too long. Korus Vet produced a crossbow from his back. With a sort of deliberate, slow cruelty he cocked and loaded it. The quarrel ended the fight and Lalru at once.

Ghinlihil stood horrified. He had seen dead Kutel before, but he had never watched one die. Even after Ammoss put him up the tree, he did not watch the battle. Here was the end of Lalru the Kutel. *I spoke with him.* Ghinlihil was not sorry be rid of him, however his mind was not ready for the Kutel to be forever dead. *He was almost like a Tafer. A cruel, nasty, smelly Tafer? No, he was a Kutel. He would not have lived another forty years anyway.* It was not a good rationalization, but it was the best he could do with the time that he had.

Korus Vet gestured at Ghinlihil with Lalru's sword. "Senlo, see what kind of damage he did to the Fitheran."

The Tafer jogged down the riverbank to Ghinlihil. He looked the child over quickly, then he put a heavy hand on the Ghinlihil's head. He pushed his thumb into the bruise on the Fitheran's forehead until Ghinlihil saw stars. Senlo then took Ghinlihil's hands. "His skull's not broke, but his hands might be dead." When Ghinlihil heard this he was afraid it might be true. He moved his fingers to prove to himself that he could. They pressed feebly into Senlo's hand. "No, the fingers work."

"Cut his wrists loose," Korus Vet said, "He's no good to us crippled."

Senlo drew a short knife and sawed through the cords. The knife left a short cut in Ghinlihil's wrist when it went through. Ghinlihil could feel the warmth begin to flow into his hands, then the pins and needles started.

"We'll put him in second place. Give him a silverseed before you put him on the chain."

Senlo took Ghinlihil's shoulder and guided him around the bend in the stream. They had to walk past the Tafer that Lalru had killed with the spear. Ghinlihil was horrified. He was horrified to see the dead Tafer, but he was more shocked that the Tafer's companions showed no remorse whatsoever.

There was another Tafer with a spear and a line of five others behind him – five slaves on a chain. Four of them were carrying packs. Senlo went through one of the packs and dug out a small bag of bright seeds. He forced Ghinlihil to eat one of them. "It's good for you."

The five in the line were all in leg irons. Ghinlihil's ankles were locked into the chain like all of the others. Korus Vet locked the end of the chain, and checked the rings on the leg irons with the tip of Lalru's sword. When he was satisfied he walked off, back to the Kutel's body. The other two

Tafers watched over the captives while Korus Vet plundered both Lalru and the dead slaver. Korus Vet made certain that he had everything of value from the two corpses before moving on. He simply left the bodies there beside the stream. He splashed down the middle of the stream bed. The others followed him without a word.

Ghinlihil felt the weight of the chains on his legs. The slavers had just begun their march, and Ghinlihil had been walking all night. He did not bother to complain, but the fatigue would not be ignored. No matter how he walked the chains caught on rocks and plants. Suddenly his legs stopped mid-stride and he fell headlong into the water. As he was struggling to get up, Korus Vet cuffed the Taforam who was next on the chain. Ghinlihil had been so caught up in his own misery that he had not noticed the filthy, bruised Taforam with sweat-matted blonde hair. Now he lay in the stream, battered and filthy himself, he saw her shed a single silent tear. For a moment he forgot to feel sorry for himself and he was almost overcome with rage to see someone so pitiable so roughly treated. When the Tafer who was first on the chain turned around to see what had happened, he got cuffed also. Ghinlihil struggled to his feet. There was nothing else he could do.

"The whole string of ye' aren't worth the price of a healthy Fitheran! Keep him off the rocks or I'll chain the lot of you to a tree and take 'im alone."

Ghinlihil was careful not to stumble after that.

They walked all day in silence – none of the captives were permitted to speak. At the end of the day the slavers had them circle a sturdy pine tree. Korus Vet locked the beginning of the chain to the end, forming a circle around the tree. The packs were then taken from the four Tafers that carried them and set out of reach. One of the slavers took rice cakes from one of the packs and handed each of the captives two. Ghinlihil got another silverseed. The slaver also gave the captives a water skin to share. As poor as the captive's dinner was, Ghinlihil could see that his captors ate little better. They ate ten or twelve of the tasteless rice cakes and had a small cluster of raisins between them. Ghinlihil fell asleep as soon as he swallowed his supper.

Morning brought two more rice cakes, a seed, and a return to walking. The silverseeds were helping to heal the damage to his hands and his head, but they couldn't keep pace with the new wounds on his ankles where the leg irons rubbed. Stops were brief and the chains were heavy. The day ended as the last one had. Ghinlihil's legs were sore when he went to sleep. They were worse when his fellow captives woke him for breakfast. After a few miles walking the muscles unknotted themselves. Then the pain in his legs was down to a dull ache which was overshadowed by the raw pain where his ankles carried the leg irons. *I am free of the wrist cords, and they feed me, so this is better than being with Lalru.*

They had traveled this way for four days when they came out of the forest. Ghinlihil could not guess how many miles had passed, but they were not many. The captives were weak and the irons were heavy. The forest had slowed them down with rocks and roots no matter how carefully they stepped. In the open the sun beat down on them furiously, and the chain bound up grasses and small plants which they ripped out of the ground with each step, still their pace more than doubled.

It was on the plain that they met the troupe of entertainers. Ghinlihil was staring at his chains, trying not to trip, and did not notice the wagons until the slavers forced the slaves to speed up. Korus Vet decided that they might be able to re-provision from the spare stores of the traveling show, and so the captives were made to double march south to cross the path of the slow-moving wagons.

Ghinlihil had seen traveling entertainers at Dath, but not a group of this size. Their wagons had once been brightly painted, but now they were faded and patched with bare wood. Even the patches were so old that the planking was sun-bleached gray.

All of the captives were bleeding from the ankles when they closed to hailing distance. It was the troupe leader who spoke first, "Korus Vet, you worthless chunk of carrion! When are you going to lie down and admit you've been dead all these years?"

"Is that you, Fiorl?" Korus squinted at the wagon. "You stinking pussbag! What in Yultif's bright sky are you doing out here?"

Fiorl was a wiry looking Tafer with long black hair. His brown eyes were big and gentle. He was neither. "Hauling my sweaty arse out of Eastower! But you, by all means go there. The shieldmaster will probably knock your head off for sport. Do the world a favor."

"Not likely," the slaver replied. Korus Vet only now understood exactly where he was. *So, they are coming from Eastower. That puts us between Eastower and The Hunt: one more day west to a good market.*

"Anything interesting on the chain?"

"I'll sell in the market, I think."

"Not at The Hunt, you won't. The shieldmaster there is no friend of slavers. You'll have to get them to Across, and you'll have to do it without getting caught by the northerners. They're in a foul mood."

"You're goin' to The Hunt."

"I'm not a Kutel."

"Neither am I!"

"That's what your mother says, but she'd bend over for a rusty jertak."

"You go too far, Fiorl!" Korus Vet patted his sword on his hip, "I've got Lalru's sword."

"Yeah, but you've got your mother's eyes." Fiorl smiled. He loved word-games, but he had another game to play today. "Is that a Fitheran on the chain?"

"What if it is? You can't afford one."

"How much?"

Korus Vet had to stop and think. He had never sold a Fitheran before, but he knew they were worth a fortune. His slave prices were always determined by the market at auction. He never set his own prices. "Your whole troupe isn't worth that much."

"Two hundred fifty doutaks, here and now."

The slaver's eyes narrowed, "Where would you get two hundred fifty doutaks?"

"Business is good. I make people happy. They pay me for it. It's a wonderful thing. The only way you ever made anyone smile was by leaving, which you're going to do as soon as I've got that Fitheran. Tell you what, I'll sweeten the deal. Two hundred sixty for the whole chain, you won't even get that in Bur-Droo."

Korus looked at the Tafers on the chain. "Three fifty."

Fiorl almost smiled. *That would ruin it,* he thought. "No way you get that at market. I can scrape up maybe two eighty."

"You tryin' to rob me? You don't wanna do that. That's what happened to Lalru." The slaver took a few steps toward the troubadour. "Three twenty is a fair price."

"Three hundred."

"Three hundred will do." Korus Vet had never even imagined thirty doutaks. He had only seen the precious coins a few times, and only once had there been two of them together. That was at a dice game that he could not afford to join. "Take him off the chain, Senlo."

"What's this? I said, for the whole chain! You tryin' to rip me off? If you are, I'll write a new song and everyone in the Shield Valley will know who Jirad's father is."

"Three hundred for the Fitheran."

"No deal."

Korus Vet hesitated. *Three hundred doutaks is a lot of money.*

Fiorl knew he had him on the hook. Behind his smile he thought, *You greasy idiot! I could have talked you down to twenty, but that would not suit my purpose today.* "You throw in the others, and I'll give you the lockbox. It's iron with a key lock actually built in."

Korus Vet thought, *If I am going to be rich, I will need one of those.* "Let's see it."

Fiorl went back to the wagon where he produced the lockbox full of platinum doutaks. He pulled the brass key that fit it from a thong around his neck.

As soon as Korus Vet saw the pile of coins, the deal was done. He kept losing his place while counting – he was staring at the strange platinum coins. Fiorl had to keep reminding him where he left off in the count.

It should have seemed odd to the slaver that the box already had the exact amount in it in spite of their haggling. Some of the traveling band could play the flute, some the harp. Fiorl played people. He could play any tune he liked on most people and most people had no more power to change that tune than a flute does when the flautist plays. The troubadour had steered the slaver to exactly the amount that he wanted to spend. Korus Vet did not even have the wit to know he had been played.

Korus and his companions took the box and the packs. He tossed the key for the slave chain to Fiorl. Even before he turned to walk away he was dreaming of how to spend his new treasure, and how to cut his accomplices out of the deal.

Fiorl took the captives from the chain and had each take his own shackles off. After their ordeal he seemed kind and gentle, but in fact he simply refrained from cruelty. The Tafers he put in the last wagon. The door at the back of the second wagon was tied open. Fiorl lifted Ghinlihil and set him inside. Ghinlihil's eyes adjusted to see a sweaty Taforam in an old blue wool dress that strained against her over-ample curves. She was sitting on a box and sowing a patch on something. "Look after this one," Fiorl said. Sliver-gray flashed in her black hair as her head bobbed "yes." Fiorl left the door open when he walked away.

The wagon was essentially a box on wheels. The roof sloped left to right, presumably to keep the rain out. There were a number of wooden boxes – trunks – of various sizes that took up most of the floor space. Ghinlihil sat on one. The wagon started moving as he was sitting, making his landing awkward. He looked out the back door at the yoke of oxen which pulled the next wagon. *How docile they look,* he thought to himself. *They are so huge, bigger than horses. The driver has complete control over them with a couple of thin cords.*

"Where you gonna run to, baby?" asked the Taforam, misunderstanding why Ghinlihil was looking out.

"I'm not going to run." He was too tired and sore to run away. *I don't know which way to Foralis... or Dath... where should I run to?*

"Good boy." She tied off her thread and put down her work. "Aritsa will get you something to wear." She stood up opened one of the trunks.

Ghinlihil looked down at his clothes. They were barely tatters now. *Shandi bought them for me.* He thought fondly of her until he started to cry. In spite of all the horrors thrust on him since leaving Dath – the Kutel in the forest, the fighting and death, the painful chains, the cruelty of the slavers and a depth of fatigue and pain he had never imagined – what hurt the most was losing even his temporary home. *Where are mother and father? Why don't they take me home?* "I just want to go home." He was crying hysterically.

Aritsa stopped rummaging in the trunk and stared at the Fitheran for a heartbeat. She swept down on him and hugged him, burying his dirty face in her shoulder. "There, baby, it's not that bad. It's all right now. No one's goin' to hurt you. Aritsa's here." She rocked him back and forth as the wagon bounced along.

Ghinlihil had nearly cried himself to sleep when the wagon stopped again. Armed horsemen went thundering by with blue and green banners flying in the evening sun. Leather squeaked and steel rang. Iron shod hooves churned the turf into the air as they raced to the front of the column.

Fiorl dismounted from the lead wagon. *I didn't expect them to catch us until we made camp tonight.* He smiled to himself as he bowed to the knights. "What can I do for you gentlemen?"

The eldest son of the Shieldmaster of Eastpoint raised his helmet visor as his rose gray charger capered to the left. "Where is it, Fiorl?" His voice was steady, but his blue eyes flashed with anger.

"What is it? Shall we get Aritsa to look in her crystal for you?"

"My sister's dowry is missing Fiorl, and you know it well. If you hand it over this instant, I'll only cut off you left hand."

"My young lord is most merciful," Fiorl said with a genuine-looking smile. "I simply haven't got it... but wait–" he snapped his fingers as he pretended to remember "–Korus Vet – a villain of most evil reputation –

had a lockbox with him. We passed him some hours ago. I think he was bound for Across."

One of the knights pointed back down the road. "I told you – the track going south."

"Shut up! You'll not make a fool of me so easily, Fiorl."

Fiorl's mind was laughing behind his well-practiced innocent face. *You are such a fool that it's hardly an effort.* He held his hands up and shrugged.

The young nobleman did not take his eyes from Fiorl. "Search the wagons!"

Two hours later the sun was barely a nail-pairing over the plains and the lockbox did not turn up. The soldiers did not care at all about the miserable wretches in the last wagon, or the Fitheran who cried while they took his wagon apart. They were looking for coins.

"If you are quick you can still catch Korus and his accomplices in the open," Fiorl told the fuming nobleman. The nobleman and his entourage galloped off without a word. Fiorl shouted after him, "Beware! He has a deadly crossbow!" Fiorl did not start laughing until the last horseman was two hundred yards away. He had the thinnest wisp of regret, *Too bad I couldn't launder the money on something better than five wretches and a half-dead Fitheran.*

The slaves got two days' choir practice and a clean set of clothes before the painted wagons entered The Hunt. Shieldmaster Talor of The Hunt smiled and listened to the chorus. He was particularly fascinated by the clear Fithern voice and threw a couple of silver coins at the choirmaster.

That same night Ammoss returned home to Shandi after many days of searching and admitted to her that he had lost Ghinlihil's trail. As Shieldmaster Talor handed over the coins, his daughter, Shandi, wept for this same Fitheran in her home seventy miles away.

Chapter 6

The Troupe

The slaves, including Ghinlihil, were just "the new blood" to most of the Tafers of the troupe. Most of the troupe called them by the color of the hat that they were given: Ghinlihil was Blue Hat, the Taforam who had been behind him on the chain was Red Hat, and so on. Only Aritsa learned their names in the first week, even Ghinlihil did not know them all. He started calling himself "Ghinlihil Blue Hat" in Fithern fashion. They got some choral training while the wagons were moving, but any time anything needed to be lifted or carried, someone called for "the new blood." Ghinlihil's small size did not exempt him from the heavy work.

On the second night out of The Hunt, they found themselves alone around the same fire for the first time. The take at The Hunt had been good and the road stew had meat in it for the first time since they joined.

"I'm going to make a run for it. Who is with me?" Yellow Hat said just loud enough to be heard.

"When?"

"Now – as soon as no one's looking." He was careful not to look around.

"Where are you going go?" Purple Hat wanted to know.

"Back to The Hunt."

"Across is just at close, I think," Green Hat offered.

"What do you think you are going to do when you get there?" Red Hat (her name was Hafga) shook her head, "Die fighting Kutel? Are you going to learn to eat grass?"

"It beats being a slave."

"Does it? You'll wind up selling yourself to some farmer so that you can eat – work all day in his fields and sleep with his pigs, if you're that lucky."

White Hat – *Roe, his name is Roe* – scraped the last of his stew into his mouth. "You know, the last five days, this is the good life. We work maybe half of the day, sing some, and eat every day – usually twice a day. I'm not running away from this. Are you going to finish that?" He waved his bowl at Ghinlihil. *I thought it was finished.* Ghinlihil handed over his bowl and White Hat Roe began scraping even the moisture off it and stuffing it in his mouth.

Purple Hat Vir asked, "What about you? Do you know where to run to? They say Fitherani have secret cities. Can you take us to a secret city?"

"I don't even know where I am," Ghinlihil admitted. "Does anyone know the way to Foralis, or Dath?" They all looked at each other. No one had any answers for that.

"Can you get us into Sekri Timbrali? That's south, somewhere."

Yellow Hat shook his head. "Strangers aren't welcome there. They'll shoot us. You have to have an invitation."

"Not him. He's a Fitheran."

"That's not how I heard it. It doesn't matter, anyway – we don't even know where it is."

"I bet he does."

Ghinlihil shook his head. "I've never been. My father was there twenty-two decades ago."

"He's just a kid. He's not going to guide you into a secret Fithern city so you can live on pixie dust. If he did, they'd just shoot you anyway."

"I'm not going to wait all night. I'm going. Who's with me?"

Green Hat nodded.

Red Hat Hafga whispered urgently, "You're going to die! And get us in trouble!"

He dropped his yellow hat and ran.

Green Hat took one step before Purple Hat Vir jumped on him. "Stop him! We'll all get in trouble!"

Before anyone else could move, something swung out past a wagon and struck Yellow Hat in the forehead. He fell like a grain sack. Fiorl was there with two of the acrobats waiting in the tall grass outside of the firelight. Two other Tafers joined them quickly from behind the wagons on either side. Each of them had a sturdy tent pole in hand.

Fiorl pointed, "Green Hat, go get a big sledgehammer out of the prop wagon." Purple Hat Vir let him get up. Two Tafers walked with him as Green Hat went to fetch it.

The other slaves were still and silent. Ghinlihil did not understand enough to be as afraid as they were. He asked Fiorl, "You were hiding in the grass the whole time, weren't you?"

"Did you think it was luck that brought you together, by yourselves, at this one fire? The one furthest from the center of the camp?" Now that he looked at it that way, Ghinlihil could see that there was really only one direction to run. Two wagons flanked the fire. The other direction led toward the rest of the troupe. The only clear direction to run was between the wagons.

Green Hat returned with the hammer. Fiorl pointed to the prone Yellow Hat. "Break his legs."

"What?"

"Don't make me say it again."

Fiorl was the only one who did not look away when the hammer fell. The crunch was unmistakable.

"Both of them."

Again the crunch.

"He's not running anywhere now."

One of the other Tafers wanted to know, "What do we do with him now?"

"Nothing. He wanted to be free. He's free. If he ever comes-to he can crawl to The Hunt, or Across, or Sekri Timbrali for all I care."

"He'll never make it."

"Of course he won't. If he's lucky the wolves will kill him before he wakes up." Fiorl looked up. "None of the new bloods get any food tomorrow. Green Hat gets nothing until we get paid at Across."

Purple Hat whined, "I tried to stop them!"

"Only after you figured out that you didn't like the plan." Fiorl fixed them all with his gaze. "You work for this troupe, which means you work for me. You do what is best for me all the time, or you don't eat." Each time he said "me" Fiorl poked his own chest with his finger. "That includes telling me when someone else is not doing what's best for me." He picked up the yellow hat as he walked past the fire and threw it at Green Hat. "Put this stuff away!"

As Fiorl walked back past the other campfires he looked at everyone in turn. They all pretended not to see anything, not even Fiorl.

The next morning when they packed up camp, Yellow Hat was still in the same place. Ghinlihil stared when his work allowed it. *I wonder if he's dead already?* By the time they were moving again, he was wondering, *How is anyone going to find me now? Who would know where to look? Even if Ammoss follows the tracks, all he is going to see are wagon ruts. If I run, Fiorl will try to kill me. Could I run to someone who can save me from him?*

White Hat Roe seemed to read his eyes. "It's going to be a hungry day, kid, but just one. You'll be all right if you play by the rules. We make Fiorl some money; he'll forget we were even at that campfire last night." He playfully spun Ghinlihil's blue hat around backwards. The choirmaster wanted to start singing practice before Ghinlihil could say anything in response.

Green Hat was caught trying to steal food from a merchant's stall in Across the next day. The troupe never saw him again.

The traveling wagons became Ghinlihil's home. There were times when he thought of running away, but he had nowhere to run to. He was hopelessly disconnected from his former life, having no idea where Dath or Foralis was. The troupe did not visit Fithern towns, and he could expect no help from strange Tafers. Every time he thought he could ask one for directions, he found Fiorl was watching him.

Ghinlihil learned to sing and to dance. He also learned that he was expected to work all day for something to eat, and that the quality of dinner was based on the quantity of coins collected during the performances. Everyone in the troupe had to pull their own weight. Purple Hat Vir learned to be an acrobat and contortionist. Red Hat Hafga became and actress. White Hat Roe learned to love signing and eventually took over as choirmaster.

Though some of the wagons contained families, Aritsa played mother to the whole troupe. She effectively adopted Ghinlihil. One of her sons, Giril, was with the troupe also, but he had grown up by the time Ghinlihil arrived. She even made certain that Fiorl got enough sleep at night and chided him if he drank too much too often. She directed the cooking for the troupe when they were on the road. When they stopped, she told fortunes. She was fairly accurate, in spite of being a fraud. Her vast experience with the Tafers of the Shield Valley gave her good insight on what might happen.

The other members of the troupe each had their own talents that brought coins from their audiences who were always called "the Locals," no matter where they were from or how far they had traveled.

Ghinlihil traveled with the troupe to the most prosperous Tafer towns and cities. The Hunt, Across, Kingstone, Silverport, Eastower, Prefectshire, and Taferford were all on the itinerary. When they had completed the circuit of the Tafer towns they crossed the river to the villages of the Timbles. Whetfoot, Bank, and Thornhill; each had its own river and its own crowd of happy Timbles. Ghinlihil's four feet was taller than all of the Timbles he met. The Timbles joked that the Fitherani, "had once been a proper height, but then they got rolled thin and stretched long." Timbles might have looked like a small Tafer, except that they tended to be barrel-chested and, if they could manage it, pot bellied.

The Timbles worked hard on their land and produced crops that fed themselves and many Tafers who lived down river. They were not rich – none of them were. It was somehow important that none of them were, since no one particularly envied his neighbor. Few of their sod-roofed homes had bolts for the doors. Most had a sling with a few good stones handy or even lead bullets. That was enough to keep the Kutel on the other side of the Brewster River and the wolves out of their flocks.

The Timbles knew that they had less to offer the troupe than the cities of the Tafers and they were grateful for their appearance. They made a perfect audience: forgiving all faults and eager to join in. They also made a public festival of the troupe, and everyone was fed from the towns' stores. They made good beer and good songs to go with it, both of which were prized by the troupe and the real reason why Fiorl came at all. Four weeks in the Timbles' valley was the closest thing to a vacation that the troupe ever got.

Three years after Ghinlihil joined the troupe they picked up a new song from the court minstrel at The Hunt. The song made the choirmaster furious because Ghinlihil could not sing it. The lay was not any longer than others he had memorized, and the tune was slow and simple, but the Fitheran would stop in the middle and sometimes cry. Ghinlihil's voice was best for the song, but it was a long time before he could perform it. He had to practice it every hour when they were on the move.

Ammoss came unto The Hunt

The Kutel there to slaughter
and in the battles proudly fought
he won shieldmaster's daughter.

Shandi was a princess fine
born to the wooded frontier,
And Ammoss took her back to Dath.
He said, "We'll build our home here."

Together then in Dath they lived,
but Ammoss oft' would wander.
He followed print and broken twig
the Kutel paths to ponder.

Then once a Kutel troop he found
A-heading for Foralis.
He begged Shieldmaster Roun for aid,
but he stayed in his palace.

Alone went Ammoss down the path
to aid his Fithern neighbors.
Alone to face the Kutel horde,
the bravest of the Tafers.

Like reaper to the waiving wheat,
Ammoss' sword laid waste.
By twos and threes the Kutel fell.
He thinned their ranks with haste.

A Fitheran Child, he brought along
from Foralis fateful
to his own most pleasant home
and Shandi's ladened table.

But Fitheran will no Tafer be,
and ran from home and safety.
He longed for woods and brook and field;
for bushes and for great trees.

In her heart poor Shandi ached

for her ward gone missing,
and to his trail she Ammoss sent
with weeping and with kissing.

In forest glen Ammoss found
Kutel took the Fitheran
and so to them he battle brought
to win back the child again.

When the forest floor was foul
with Kutel corpses crushed,
to Lalru was the Fitheran bound,
and to Bur Droo was rushed.

Though score of Kutel him harassed,
Ammoss still gave chase.
By stream bed found he Lalru dead
with arrow in his waist.

To Bur-Droo then did Ammoss speed
with aspect cruel as steel.
For Fitheran was force marched there
with chains upon his heels.

But Bur Droo is a fortress town
with Kutel, Cral and Varr.
Yet Ammoss would have storm'd the gates
'cept Shandi's love afar.

Bitter were the Kutels' ends
who 'cross his path did roam.
But love for Shandi turned him 'round
and gently pulled him home.

With heavy heart and sagging head
he crossed his own threshold,
and through the night in Shandi's ear
his bitter tale he told.

Shandi's answer sent him back

for cruel revenge and grim.
For pots and cakes she packed a few
and traveled back with him.

She forsook her country home,
warm and safe and dry,
to stew wild squirrels in a pot
beneath a brooding sky.

And in the darkest Kutel vale
They'd made their erstwhile home
only for a week or two
and then again they'd roam.

Together the Kutel town they 'sieged
the soldier and his lady
And Kutel learned that death did walk
down in the valley shady.

A Wizard brags his Varro found
the soldier and his lady,
but Kutel know, 'tis death to go
down in their valley shady.

Ghinlihil never told why he choked on the words. Eventually the choirmaster gave up and gave the song to someone else. Ghinlihil stopped asking for directions to Dath.

Ghinlihil had never really understood how fast the Tafers lived. At Dath, he had watched his friends grow up. He watched as the troupe grew old. Many Tafers came and went so quickly that he never really knew them. Some were hauled away to meet a shieldmaster's judgment; some just left; some grew old and died.

A pair of orphans, Junneh and his twin sister Pelli joined. They sang and danced together for almost six years. At first they could hardly earn their bread, but as they grew up the crowds began to grow – especially to see Pelli. Then one night while the troupe was camped outside Silverport, the Silverport guards searched the caravan and found a strange ring among Junneh's things. They said that the ring had been stolen that evening and they took Junneh away. Ghinlihil thought this was strange because the troupe had just arrived and only Fiorl had entered the city. Shortly after Junneh went to the block Pelli became a private dancer.

The following autumn the troupe's strong man was killed by a loud drunk with a hidden dagger. Fiorl had to hire a teamster named Dond from Kingstone to run the wagons. Dond did not perform feats of strength, but he did keep The Locals away from the dancers. His voice was not for singing, but he did teach the troupe some new bawdy songs.

Joikim, the knife thrower, joined up two years later, with his wife Allod, the Taforam target. He never hit her with a knife. His hand was a different matter. After a year or so Fiorl sold the troupe to Joikim. Some of the performers would not work for Joikim and quit. It was a lean year until they picked up a new juggler and a new actor.

Pelli got pregnant and had to give up her special dancing to join the choir. Dond and Joikim had a long and private discussion about that. Dond treated Pelli's child, a boy named Litne, as if he were his own and dared anyone to say otherwise. Pelli began to apprentice under Aritsa in the "art" of fortune telling when Dond made it clear that she would no longer be a private dancer.

Ghinlihil grew from eighty-seven to one hundred fifteen years with the troupe. It was the time of the fastest growth for a Fitheran. By then he was just over five feet tall and ninety pounds. Any Fitheran who knew his age would have commented on how large he was. He was as tall now as the average adult Fitheran, though not yet as heavy. Only Arista and Lessin noticed that he had grown at all. Lessin sowed his clothes. All the while Arista told fortunes and cooked dinners. Her hair went from black to silver.

By then everyone thought of Ghinlihil as part of the troupe's equipment – only seven members of the troupe remembered his arrival at all. He was still very much a child by Fithern reckoning, but there were no Fitherani doing the reckoning. Ghinlihil grew up quickly just to stay alive. Everyone knew that Ghinlihil wanted to go home, but they could all say in complete honesty that they had only heard of Foralis in a song and they had no idea where it might be. So long as Ghinlihil had nowhere else to go Joikim could make the Fitheran sing for his suppers.

The following rainy season Aritsa caught a cold. She never recovered. They had to bury her in the mud outside of Taferford. In spite of himself Ghinlihil could not help but wonder, *How many years before she washes into the river?* Before the rain stopped Lessin took over as the troupe's "mother".

To the Fitheran, it all happened too quickly. It was like a Tafer watching a beloved pet grow old. It was hard for him. He learned not to make friends with the Tafers – it hurt too much when they were gone.

One fine day the next spring a the prop wagon broke a wheel two miles outside of Kingstone. The troupe was stuck until it was fixed. Ghinlihil took the opportunity to nap in the shade under Joikim's wagon. Heavy footfalls overhead woke Ghinlihil.

"I need more money." It was Dond's voice. "Fifteen percent of the take."

"Are you out of your mind? You just walk in here and… I can't believe it!" Joikim sputtered, "Fifteen percent! Get out of here! Go fix the damn wheel!"

"I'll take the old timers and walk out."

"What are you gonna do? You think you can run show? You gonna go singin' from door to door with your hat out? What are you gonna do?"

"I'm serious. I'll walk."

"Good, and take that crying brat of yours with you. No one else will go with you. It will be you and Pelli and her son."

"My son."

"Yeah, right, you and every other randy bastard with three stowsaw to rub together. Go fix the wheel on the prop wagon. If you want to spend your life begging on the streets of Kingstone, you can unload your crushk there. Pelli will stay on. Roe will stay on. Sure as Raiden, Hatta will stay on. You'll just be back on the street, all alone. I'll find some other slob who'll work for half your pay. There is nothing special about you, Dond!"

"I'm not one of your fragile little actors. You can't bully and goad me. I'll spend two weeks on the streets of Kingstone with your best money-makers, then we'll all be off in fresh new wagons. You can either give me fifteen percent, or you get nothing."

"If you try it…" Ghinlihil's keen hearing picked up the familiar sound of a knife sliding out of its sheath. "…who's to say what might happen."

The creaking wagon floor betrayed Dond's shifting weight. His voice was low and dangerous. "Who would cry for Joikim if he showed up face down in the harbor some morning? Not your wife, I think. I have something that you don't, Joikim: I have friends."

"You get out of here and get to work. You'll get no more from me. I know you Dond, you and your kind are all talk."

Dond exited the wagon without a reply. Ghinlihil watched him go to the prop wagon, Vir's, and began working on the wheel just as he was told.

Everything seemed to be the way Joikim said it would be until Pelli came to Dond with a drink of water. Fithern ears heard the Tafers' whispers.

"How did it go?"

"Better than I expected."

"He said yes?"

"No, but he didn't stick me with one of his knives."

"What do we do now?"

"What I said in the first place: we get rid of him. A man named Tiko will come to hear his fortune tonight. Tell him that he will soon come into a large some of money: six malstren."

"We don't have six malstren!"

"Don't worry, Hond and Roe are in on this too."

"They'll send you to the block for this, you know? Are you sure you can get away with this? They don't send murderers to The Hunt, or people who hire them."

"Tiko is the best. He'll make it look like an accident or something. Normally you couldn't get his attention with six malstren, but he's from the south end. We were close growin' up, and he owes me."

"You'd better know what your doing."

In an hour the wheel was fixed and they were rolling toward Kingstone.

Two nights later, Joikim and Allond had one of their fights. Tafer ears were sharp enough to hear every word from the head wagon, at least every one of his. She was crying. Ghinlihil cringed. He had heard these arguments before. He heard Joikim hit his wife. The sound was unmistakable. Again, and again, and again – four times the sickening sound, then it was over. In the stillness that followed, somewhere a baby cried. Ghinlihil clenched his teeth and wondered if he would too.

In the morning no one went near the head wagon. No one came out either. White Hat Roe, Hond, and Pelli kept looking at it, waiting for something to happen. Dond ignored it and packed the other wagons first. He thought it was time to leave Kingstone, though normally they stayed for at least a week.

Lessin had the courage to knock on the door of the lead wagon. There was no answer. She stood at the back of the wagon in indecision. Her imagination working with the sounds of the night before to conjure a scene in her mind. When she opened the door the scene was no prettier than her fears.

Sunlight streaming through the door showed Allond sprawled on the floor. The entire left side of her head was purple and black, and it was no longer shaped like the right side. Her chest did not rise or fall. Lessin took a deep breath and swallowed. Ghinlihil could hear her whisper to herself, "It's not as though you didn't expect it sooner or later. Maybe it's better for her this way, better than with him." The thought stirred up enough rage in Lessin to confront Joikim. When she stepped into the wagon she drew a gasp. Joikim lay on the edge of the bed in the shadows near his wife, unmoving. All of the floor between the two was a dark pool of blood and flies. One of Joikim's knives pointed from Allond's right hand into the blood, and toward the slit in her husband's throat.

As the rest of the troupe saw Lessin standing motionless in the doorway, they began to gather around. When they stood still Ghinlihil could hear the occasional drop hit the turf below the wagon.

White Hat Roe took Lessin by the hand and lead her down out of the wagon. Then each of the Tafers of the troupe in turn looked in at the scene. When Dond stepped out he said, "At least she got the bastard back, finally." Roe, Hond, and Pelli all looked at him in shock. Ghinlihil also looked with head tilted, but no one noticed him.

Purple Hat Vir packed his things and walked away before the rest of the crowd had broken. He did not even try to take a wagon. As soon as she saw him a singer was next. More members of the troupe followed her.

Dond yelled after Vir, "What are you doing?"

"Leaving."

"We've got the wagons and the props. We can do the shows without a knife thrower!"

"You can do them without me, too." He never looked back.

Two more left the assembly to pack.

A family pulled their wagon out of the troupe's circle. "Face it Dond, the troupe is done. We're not much of a troupe anymore anyway."

"Nothing's changed. We can still put on shows and make a living."

"It's all changed," Another troubadour said, walking away backwards. He was shaking.

"Joikim had the steak money," the chief musician said, "and I'm not going to rob the dead for it. Do you really think anyone believes that Allond killed Joikim? I'm not going to the block for this. If you're smart, you'll get out quick as you can too."

Ghinlihil left and packed what few things he called his own in a backdrop sheet and slung it over his shoulder. *Just like in the forest outside Shandi's home.* When he left the wagon, he saw the rest of the troupe – Roe and Lessin, Pelli and Dond, Hond and Red Hat Hafga – in a circle discussing what to do.

Dond seemed to want to go on, even as they were. Hafga was equally adamant that they should disband. Everyone else fell somewhere in between. Ghinlihil stood behind a wagon and listened.

"I guess we're leaving too," Hond said. "A couple of voices, a cittern, two actors, a dancer and a fortune teller? It's just not enough. We'd all starve to death trying to feed the oxen." Hafga began to pull him away from the circle.

"He wouldn't listen. You know, we all agreed."

Hond waved his hand at the lead wagon, "I didn't agree to this."

"What did you all agree too?" Lessin demanded. When Dond did not answer, she turned to her Roe.

He was looking at the turf. "Dond, I..." He looked at the teamster, "It's over." He took Lessin's hand without meeting her gaze. "I'll explain while we pack."

Ghinlihil snuck around outside the wagons until he could hear Roe and Lessin talking.

"You know Joikim was keeping most of the money – even more than his share. He's been lying to us about the gate money."

"We agreed to ask for a fair share. That's all, ask!"

"He didn't agree."

"Then we should have left!"

"Dond said it would break up the troupe. If we took Joikim out of the story, then everyone else could continue the way it was, only with more money."

"You thought everyone was just going to ignore the bloody murder in the head wagon and go on?"

"I didn't know he was going to do this."

"You thought Dond was going to pay someone to talk Joikim out of it? What did you think was going to happen?"

"I don't know. Not this. I thought he was going to threaten him or something."

Ghinlihil had heard enough. He turned his back on the troupe and walked into the city of Kingstone. *Maybe someone here knows the way to Foralis.*

Chapter 7

Brighteyes

Kingstone was a teeming city originally built on a bedrock promontory. The old city stood in marble majesty overlooking the ocean, home to the royal palace and all of the oldest and wealthiest families in The Shield Valley. Newer sections of the city were built in the lowlands surrounding the old city. Of the lower quarters, the marketplace was the busiest. It was always was a throng of people. When the market was rebuilt on the lower ground of the new city, the market leases were made thematically. A wealthy merchant could do business without rubbing elbows with the common rabble. A customer looking for metal goods could visit the Blacksmith's Quadrangle and find anything he needed. After years of commerce with businesses closing and opening all the time, the sections of the market no longer had much meaning. Today in the Blacksmith's Quadrangle the ringing of a hammer was hardly heard, but sardines by the pound could be had in one stall and in a counting house beside grain was sold by the ton.

In this churn of Taferdom the king's soldiers attempted to keep only the grossest semblance of order. Fighting was often ignored, as was dueling (which was illegal for persons of common birth). Fraud was so rampant that even wholesale theft was of only secondary concern. Every merchant hired guards, few of whom were as reliable as they seemed to an outsider. The force of the law depended on how far away from a soldier the crime was committed, and who was paying him more to act on it: the king or the Amada.

The marketplace really belonged to the Amada, the ruling order of criminals who were in turn ruled by their Kels. The underground union of bodyguards was wholly operated by the Amada. Their power was so pervasive that most of the market thought of them much like the government: they took out their "taxes" and spent the money on someone else. Paying off the Amada was just part of the price of doing business in the Kingstone market.

None of this, of course, meant anything to Ghinlihil as he picked his way through the crowd. Upon entering the marketplace the threat that concerned him most was that of being trampled. As he learned the flow of the marketplace, other problems began to surface in his mind. *Where am I going to get something to eat?*

Everything that The Shield Valley had to offer was for sale in the marketplace, but Ghinlihil had no coin at all; he did not even have a purse. He thought briefly of begging, but then he saw a professional beggar in the street. He was a wretched cripple, crawling and dragging his twisted and useless foot through the filth of an alley. He was so pathetic that Ghinlihil wanted to give him something himself. Tafers ignored him. *If he cannot stir any sympathy in this crowd, what chance have I got?*

Then he turned the corner to find a musician in a wide-brimmed, floppy yellow hat. He sang and played a cittern that rose bawdily above the crowd noise for a few yards. After every song or two, he doffed his silly hat and waved it before those around him. When Ghinlihil moved closer, he saw that some of the listeners put coins in the hat. It worked just like Hond had with the troupe, except that the local was not a very skilled musician. Ghinlihil had been in constant practice for twenty-eight years, and he had a hat. As quick as he could, Ghinlihil found himself a place on the street and rummaged through his bag for his cap. The feather was ruined, so he pulled it out and threw it on the street. He began to sing and pass the hat. Most people ignored him, but some few stopped and listened. Fewer still put any money in his hat. Iron jertaks and the odd brass hauger mingled noisily in blue felt. Ghinlihil began to feel that he would not starve here.

Terlak of the Gold Circle strode through the crowd unopposed. Only the bravest of fools would get in the way of a Knight of the Circle. Few even risked eye contact long enough to see that the circlet on his helmet was indeed the bright gold of a great master, and not the brass ring of a quest knight. Even the most powerful Amadan Kel did not command so much respect or fear.

Most in the crowd were genuinely afraid. Knights of the Circle were known to be honest, fearless, and violent defenders of the strictest codes of behavior. They not only required purity in their own ranks, but they expected a certain level of propriety in those around them. No one outside their ranks knew exactly what that code was, but everyone expected that it was broken every day in the market. Worse still were the soldiers who suddenly enforced the strictest letter of the law when they knew they were under the gaze of such a knight. The sword on Terlak's hip was no foil of a dandy, nor was it the rapier of a professional duelist. It was a heavy battle sword tried in combat against what kind of monsters the gods only knew. The Order of the Circle answered only to their own grandmaster. No higher authority existed. The king himself could only make requests to The Order.

Amada made every attempt to disappear. Gangs of bullies were no match for an armored knight, and creeping assassins could not penetrate their fortress compound within the old city. Once an arrogant Kel had had a knight poisoned. The Order closed the marketplace for three months, until the poisoner and his employer where both turned over to them by the starving crowd. The poisoned knight survived.

Terlak liked to walk through the marketplace from time to time. He wanted to be in touch with the people. Sometimes he went in disguise and bustled through the crowd. Today he was making the grand show, though he refused to ride his charger through the densely packed streets. *No need to put the beast through that raging sea. Besides, someone might get trampled.* He was out, ostensibly to secure provision for the fortress, but in reality he wanted to reassure the people with the show of law and order. *Too bad it is still just a show,* he thought. It seemed to Terlak a failing of The Order that they had not broken the power that the Amada held in the city. *Someday we will put a stop to that.*

He threw a silver paddiban on the ground in front of a beggar. The cripple swallowed hard and cringed even as he thanked the knight. Painfully dragging a useless and twisted foot, the beggar picked the coin up off the ground and tucked it under the filthy cloth sash that he wore as a belt. As he looked up under greasy eyebrows, he saw that the knight was still staring down at him. Quickly, he averted his eyes and took a step back – too quickly for a cripple.

Steel clad fingers dug into the beggar's shoulder like the sudden strike of a hawk. The knight tossed the beggar into a nearby wall as easily as he had tossed the coin. Dazed by the impact, the "cripple" landed heavily on both feet and took a halting step forward, showing that both feet were perfectly healthy. Without even looking at the knight, he made a dash for a nearby alley. Terlak was ready for that. He caught the retreating fraud again by the same shoulder and threw him to the ground. With his sword he cut the four inches off the villain's right foot. Terlak thought briefly of leaving him an honest cripple. *That would be too good for him and not fair to those in real need.* "A rope!" he shouted.

Someone in the crowd produced a length of sturdy rope. Terlak tied it around the beggar's ankle tight enough to stop the flow of blood. Anyone who thought this was a merciful act learned better when he threw the rope over an overhanging street sign thirty feet away. Hauling on the rope he dragged the fraud down the street and up into the air until his head hung upside down at the knight's belt. All the while the beggar pleaded for mercy. The knight tied the rope to a post, then confronted the store's tenant. "If he comes down before his head turns blue, you'll go up to take his place." He turned his back on the ugly spectacle and moved on through the market. In spite of his own self discipline, or perhaps because of it, he had a great distaste for disciplining others. *It has to be done for the common good, but I do not have to enjoy it.*

A short distance down the street he broke stride at a knot of people who stepped aside more slowly than he was used to walking. Terlak stopped and listened, standing tall to see what was causing the blockage. He could not see, but he heard a small, clear voice and the first verse of a familiar song. *I will have to clear him out of the way. He is blocking traffic.* He moved slowly toward the singer; deliberately slowly because he liked the song. *It would not do for the Order to know I like the tavern song, no, not at all.* He timed himself so that he would not enter the singer's view until the last verse.

The singer continued, undaunted by the still unseen knight.

> My love, she was fair as the sun,
> and slender as the mastwood.
> My love, she was fair as the sun,
> good fellows all did say.
> A year gone since the wedding
> and she round as any barrel.
> Some night, with luck a fool will come,
> and roll my love away.

To test the strength of her love, I hit the streets a-rovin'.
From bottle's mouth and dagger's point I never turned
    away.
Each morning as the sun did rise, I practiced all my lyin',
And took one home to my true love, to see how it would
    play.

Her sister's ugly as a frog,
and not so fair when speakin'.
Her sister's ugly as a frog,
Good fellows all did say.
She married a proud farmer,
who's happy for his cattle.
He says, "She is hard on the eyes,
but she keeps the flies away!"

To test the strength of her love, I hit the streets a-rovin'.
From bottle's mouth and dagger's point I never turned
    away.
Each morning as the sun did rise, I practiced all my lyin',
And took one home to my true love, to see how it would
    play.

Her brother is a thievin' rogue,
and ripe for any headsman.
Her brother is a thievin' rogue
good fellows all did say.
If perchance you close your eyes,
he'll steal your bloody breaches,
then sell to you a night cloak,
to keep the drafts away.

To test the strength of her love, I hit the streets a-rovin'.
From bottle's mouth and dagger's point I never turned
    away.
Each morning as the sun did rise, I practiced all my lyin',
And took one home to my true love, to see how it would
    play.

Her mother is a comely lass,

although she's pushin' fifty.
Her mother is a comely lass,
good fellows all did say.
When e'er a man comes to the door
another's out the back one.
When my true love comes home she asks,
"Who is my dad today?"

To test the strength of her love, I hit the streets a-rovin'.
From bottle's mouth and dagger's point I never turned
    away.
Each morning as the sun did rise, I practiced all my lyin',
And took one home to my true love, to see how it would
    play.

They say I am a useless lout,
and all to fond of drinkin'.
Your husband is a useless lout,
proud widows all would say.
My love she loves me rightly
for bettered or for worsted.
She says, "I saw him sober once,
and fainted dead away."

To test the strength of her love, I hit the streets a-rovin'.
From bottle's mouth and dagger's point I never turned
    away.
Each morning as the sun did rise, I practiced all my lyin',
And took one home to my true love, to see how it would
    play.

Terlak stepped forward at what he knew to be the last chorus. He had misjudged the size of the singer and could still see only the top of his blue felt hat.

The crowd roared their appreciation. The song was well known, but also well done. They all expected the hat to pass next, but the Fitheran singer continued with some new verses.

Joikim, he could throw a knife
and never miss his target.

> Joikim, he could throw a knife,
> good fellows all did say.
> And when he had one handy,
> he'd never give a pay raise.
> He'd tell teamsters go to hell
> or he'd speed them on their way.

Lyndil did not like the sound of that verse. He had been working the crowd himself, as a pickpocket. The little Fitheran held the crowd for him and distracted them, so his job was a good deal easier. He moved closer to the center of the ring as the chorus flowed once more over the crowd. Lyndil knew there had been an unauthorized job done on a Tafer named Joikim the night before. *The little Fitheran might just sing too much for his own good.* Lyndil had not seen the knight yet.

Terlak stopped where he was. The extra verse was not as good as the others, but it seemed to be leading somewhere. *I will hear what he has to sing.*

Another new verse followed.

> Dond, he grew up on the streets
> not just a humble teamster.
> Dond, he grew up on the streets,
> dark fellows all did say.
> If Joikim wouldn't pay him,
> He'd have him bloody murdered,
> Then blame it on his battered wife
> and haul the troupe away.

Lyndil moved to the edge of the crowd as the Fitheran sang the chorus. *He has said too much. How do I make it pay? The assassins will not pay me to tell them about the Fitheran, they expect it. They will kill me if they found out I heard and held back. Maybe they will pay if I shut him up.* Lyndil was not carrying a weapon. Even as frail as the Fitheran looked, Lyndil knew he could not kill him with his bare hands and escape the crowd. He began to look around for a dagger he could pilfer from a nearby belt. He found one as the next verse began.

> Tiko was a hired knife,
> and Dond, he had the malstren.
> Tiko was a hired knife,

dark fellows all did say.
He carv'd Joikim a new mouth
just underneath the old one,
left bloody knife with his dead wife
and silent stole away.

The crowd moved quickly away from the Fitheran. This was not the song they knew anymore. This was dangerous. The Amada did not suffer informants. They would murder the Fitheran and anyone else who might know too much. No one wanted to know too much.

Lyndil did not back away. He drew the dagger quicker than he would have liked, but its owner was moving away. In a single movement he sliced through the air where the Fitheran's neck was.

Ghinlihil heard the dagger come free of its scabbard and jumped back. He avoided the first swing, but he hit his back on the booth behind him. There would be no more backing away.

Lyndil was beginning to panic. He was no knife fighter and he was terribly exposed on the street. A shadow rose over him that seemed somehow wrong. He lunged at the Fitheran's heart, hoping to pin him to the wall and run away.

His knife hand met with no resistance and he staggered forward. In the split second that he had left, he saw rather than felt that his arm was missing from the elbow down. The last thing he saw was his own arm lying in the street, grasping a stranger's dagger.

Terlak drew his sword as the thief stole the dagger. He was relieved that the Fitheran was quicker than both and avoided the first attack. The knight chopped the arm off the would-be assassin before he got a second chance. He followed with an upswing that should have caught the villain in the throat. The pickpocket staggered. The steel edge cut his skull open just below his brow instead. The Tafer's skull shattered. Terlak caught the Tafer's cloak and used it to clean his sword before draping it over the gruesome head wound. Then he pointed to the little Fitheran and said, "Come you with me."

Ghinlihil took a step toward the armored Tafer before he realized that the command had been made in heavily accented Timbrali. It was all very confusing. Ghinlihil had a rough red line of Tafer blood running across his chest, but he could not think of anything to do about it. He wiped a little and smeared it into his tunic.

"You back at the fortress we may clean. Come you now with me." Terlak took the Fitheran by the hand and lead him back through the marketplace. The knight fretted: *An Amadan knife or poisoned dart could still reach him here.* Terlak wore the best armor that money could buy, though it was devoid of adornment save the golden circle on his helmet that marked his rank and order. *The Fitheran's tunic would not stop a determined mosquito.*

Ghinlihil followed through the marketplace. He had no choice. He worked hard to keep up, jogging at times beside the knights long strides – anything he could do to avoid angering this Tafer. He thought vaguely Lalru and Korus Vet. Those memories were brought back full force when he saw a fresh corpse hanging from a street sign by its ankle.

When they walked through the gatehouse of the fortress, the portcullis dropped. The knights closed off the fortress to ensure that the assassins could not follow Ghinlihil. Ghinlihil could only see it as brass bars that separated him from any chance to find his family.

Chapter 8

Knights and Assassins

The Kels' power was based on fear – the fear held by everyone in Kingstone that everyone who crossed the Kels died. Even before Ghinlihil entered the fortress with Terlak, the Amada knew of the song. Kels – for whom paranoia was a survival skill – were all very, very concerned about what was going on. As powerful as the grip of the Kels was, it would evaporate if the fear was broken. They had to make the marketplace understand that they were in full control.

The Kels no longer cared if Tiko – one of their professional assassins – had really taken a job to kill Joikim without paying the Kels their cut. They had to make an example of him to ensure that no one else thought that they could murder in Kingstone without paying the Amada. Whether he was guilty has not important, the story – the song – was common knowledge now.

The Kels also knew of the Knight of the Gold Circle, and of Lyndil's final mistake. They placed a large bounty on Ghinlihil. As an underground organization, the Amada needed to be able to operate in secrecy. They could not continue to do business if people thought that that they could inform and hide with the knights.

They needed to find Dond. No one could be allowed to hire an assassin without paying all of the right Amada. Some of the best assassins would go freelance if they could. The Kels needed to make a very public statement to make everyone in Kingstone see that Dond had made a mistake.

An army of Amada flooded the streets, collecting information and tracking down leads. Some small groups worked together, but mostly they were in competition with each other. The Kels payed for results. No one wanted to split that pay with too many other Amada.

Prenek, The Knight of the Platinum Circle, held a quick conference between the four gold knights currently in the fortress and made a decision. Knights of the Brass and Copper Circles poured out of the fortress on the same quest as the Amada: find Dond, find Tiko, bring them in for questioning. There had been no mission of worth from The Order for some months, and the knights were eager to take up the hunt.

The wiser knights waited for more information. They questioned Ghinlihil quietly, politely. They asked him to tell his story about Dond, and Joikim and Tiko. Ghinlihil was wrapped in a blanket and holding a cup of tea that was still too hot to drink. Every now and then he remembered the Tafer with the knife and shivered. He told them about the conversations he overheard, and the sight in the wagon that he never actually saw himself. Moments later, Knights of the Copper and Silver Circles came thundering out of the fortress.

It was not surprising that the Amada found Tiko first. Helkin – called The Beet because his face went red when he got exited – knew exactly where to look. He had worked with Tiko as his backup on several occasions and had held the bag for him twice. The Beet swung under the pier and landed hard on the broken rocks. He was huffing with the effort to be the first to Tiko. He spoke to the darkness where the pier met the stone, "You've been made."

Tiko thought about remaining silent. *He cannot know that I am really here. If he comes close enough to find out, I can kill him first.*

In the darkness under the pier no one saw The Beet change color. *I did not have to come alone. I could have turned you in to the Kels.*

Tiko needed more information if he was to survive. "Who said?"

"A little Fitheran. He's been named Brighteyes already, but the Circles have him."

"Crushk! What job? When was there ever a Fitheran?"

"I don't know. They're also looking for a Dond and Joikim."

"Crushk!" Tiko spat, "Crushk, crushk, crushk!" *How much to the Circles know? How much do the Kels know?* Dond was an old friend and had not gone through channels. Tiko used the opportunity to cut the Kels out. Now the most dangerous Tafers in Kingstone heard about a job that they had not been paid for, cheated by one of their own members. The assassin's worst nightmares were coming true.

"Kel Yanger wants to see you at once. He wants to know the story. You'd better get out of town, there's a reward." *Do not ask me why I am not trying to collect it.* Tiko was the only Tafer The Beet would call a friend.

A knife came out of the darkness and sank into The Beet's shoulder. The surprise, more than the force of the blow, caused him to fall backwards into the sea.

Tiko slipped out of his hiding place and climbed up on the pier. He heard The Beet rise from the water, but he ignored him. The knife was poisoned, of course. The Beet was the only one alive that knew his hiding places. *Very soon no one else will know them,* Tiko thought. *Now all I need is to pick up my backup disguise and disappear.*

The Beet wanted to scream, to call the law, or the Circles, or the Amada to kill Tiko. In reality, he croaked out a mouthful of polluted seawater. He pulled out the knife and climbed up to the stone street. His right arm was hanging limp and his head was spinning. His world narrowed to a red tunnel. He shook his head and cleared it somewhat. He was sweating. His tongue felt like dust. *Poisoned.*

He heard the squeak of leather and rattle of steel. The Beet turned and saw a knight closing on him with sword drawn. He dropped the knife, then fell to one knee. The poison was killing him slowly; the knight might kill him quickly. He doubled over. An armored boot stepped into his limited vision. "Tiko," he said as loud as he could. It came as a whisper.

The knight slung his shield and picked The Beet up by his good arm. "Are you Tiko?"

"No..." The Beet wanted to go on, send the knight after his revenge, but he could not speak. His head lolled forward.

"Where is Tiko?" The knight demanded, but The Beet could not hear.

The knight of the Copper Circle thundered into the fortress with The Beet across his forecantle. Three other knights were scouring the waterfront for Tiko. They would find nothing, but they hampered the Amada's attempts to do the same thing. Two aspirants carried away a tablecloth full of dishes to leave an empty table. The copper knight put The Beet on it. Even as he did so, Terlak and Prenek entered the common dining hall. "He may be dead, he's been poisoned. He said 'Tiko' when I found him. I think Tiko did this to him."

Terlak put his hand on the wound and spoke a prayer to Anagoth. The poison drew itself back into the wound. The spell could not stop the poison or draw it out of the victim, but it gave them time.

The Beet revived as red as ever. His first act was to roll into the fetal position and clutch his wounded shoulder. A heavy hand pushed him back down on his back. A steel gauntlet pressed his good shoulder into the hard table.

"Easy," the platinum-crowned head of The Order spoke calmly, "It is not a crime to get knifed or poisoned."

The pressure became lighter, but did not release The Beet. He opened his eyes and saw two knights of The Circle standing over him in full armor. One had a copper circlet, the other was gold. What really frightened him was the straight-backed old man with the platinum circlet on his head. There could be no question that he was within the Fortress of The Circle. He played his only card. "If you keep me alive, I'll show you where Tiko is."

The Amada had caught up with Dond minutes before the Order. A gang of ruffians surrounded him and beat him with clubs. Pelli had just stood there gaping and crying and quivering. There was nothing she could do. She was next mark for the brute squad, but she did not think of that. They beat Dond to death in front of Pelli and Litne. Then the knight came.

The Tafers were so wrapped up in beating Dond that they did not turn until it was too late. The first one to look up was spitted on a lance. The white and chestnut horse passed between Pelli and the gang. The knight drew his sword and turned around. If there had been fewer of them the gang might have run away. As it was the knight was outnumbered fourteen to one, and that gave the street toughs courage. Courage was the last thing they needed.

The knight dismounted. While he whispered in his horse's ear, the ruffians charged him. It was exactly what he wanted to see, because it drew them away from the Taforam and the child. His warhorse pranced around the gang and stood calmly between bawling Pelli and the battle.

The ruffians had no armor, short clubs, and no particular skill. The knight cut the first four down as fast as they came. Six were incapacitated before the first club struck his shield. Two more fell before they were able to circle the knight. Clubs began striking his armor. Some would cause bruises, most would not. A glancing blow on the side of his helmet reminded him that anyone could get lucky. He struck down the three in front of him and turned around. The remaining three turned to run. He hamstrung the nearest one. Four other Knights of the Circle who had seen the battle rode them down before he could remount.

A copper knight took Pelli and Litne back to the fortress.

Glinlihil was put in a tower room overlooking the fortress courtyard. A copper knight had asked him not to stand in front of the window and left him alone. The Fitheran sat on the sill, so he wasn't standing in front of the window. From there he had seen the knight bring in the other Tafer across his saddle, but it did not mean anything to him. An hour or so later he saw another knight lead Pelli and her son, Litne, into the fortress. *I wonder where Dond is?* He slipped gracefully off the window sill and walked over to try the door. He expected it to be locked, but he tried anyway. It was not. The Fitheran stepped into the hallway to try to find Pelli.

"Crushk!" Rollak cursed under his breath. He had paid a hefty bribe to the castle guard to be allowed on the wall, but it was the only place he could get a shot at the northern towers of the fortress. His good silver paid for the privilege of lying on the cold stone and waiting for a clear shot through the window.

It was a long shot, over two hundred yards of distance and twenty feet up and the window was narrow. Rollak had an excellent crossbow, and he had spent ten minutes picking out the quarrel with the perfect balance. He wound the crossbow, aimed, and waited for the wind to die. He had a line secured to the top of the wall by a hook so that he could slide quickly down the outside. *The guardsmen probably want to turn me over to The Order afterward and collect from them too.* The Fitheran simply got up and walked away before he could shoot. Rollak packed his things and left, choosing to go down the stairs by the guards instead of using his rope. *No point in wasting that trick.*

Half-way down the stairs two guardsmen stood in his way. "What's wrong, Hargus? You charge a toll to get up and down this stair?"

"I don't know what you're talking about," the guard said stiffly.

Rollak sized them up quickly. They were both sweating, nervous. *They should be, I could hand them both their heads. That would not be profitable today, though.* "It was four paddiban to get up. Four more to get down, fair enough?" He began untying his purse.

Hargus stammered, "You're not allowed up here. I don't know what you're talking about. Bribery is a capital offense." The other guard, whose name Rollak did not know, was shaking visibly. The assassin abandoned his purse string and looked around quickly. There was a sound coming from the behind, but his eyes locked on the figure that stepped out of the wooden guardhouse. The silver circlet on top of his helmet gleamed dangerously in the sunlight. "Crushk!"

Rollak jumped off the stairs onto the broad street below. The fifteen foot leap from the stairs was reckless, but Rollak was a good tumbler. He rolled to his feet and doubled back along the wall. Any other direction would give the knight a chance to cut him off, literally. As it was the knight was pounding after him only four yards behind. Rollak half smiled, *I can outrun any fool dumb enough to wrap himself in steel.*

Sir Gornet of the Brass Circle had been sent to the other end of the wall to make certain the assassin did not escape. He ran across the top of the twenty-four foot wall. As the assassin closed he timed his leap. The last thing Rollak saw was a pair of gleaming steel spurs coming out of the clear blue sky. Gornet landed with both feet on the assassin's head. It only partially broke his fall. His own legs buckled when the villain's skull hit the ground and he fell backwards. His right hip crushed the assassin's rib cage. The back of his helmet rang against the hard cobblestone street.

Sir Loro of the Silver Circle stepped around the wreckage of the assassin and slowed to a halt. "Gornet!" The other knight got slowly to one knee and recovered his sword. He was still seeing stars. Loro laid a hand on his junior companion and divine healing flowed through Sir Gornet as Loro helped him to his feet. Together they charged after the two guardsmen who were trying to sneak way. Sir Loro waived the other knight away, "Get the chargers!"

The two guardsmen began running for their lives. They cast away their spears and shields to run quicker. Neither of them entertained a thought of combat with a Knight of the Silver Circle. They were pulling away from him when Gornet returned riding an armored warhorse and leading another. Loro's warhorse came patiently to a halt when he came even with his master. The knight mounted quickly and followed Gornet after the fleeing guardsmen.

Gornet used his mace to dent the helmet of the guardsman on the left as he passed. With the added force of the speeding charger, the guardsman went down hard. Gornet continued a short way then quartered the horse across the street.

Loro clucked slightly over the use of such excessive force. *After all, we have not determined that they were both taking bribes. Still, Gornet got a nasty knock on the head. You have to make allowances.* His own charger leaped over the body in the street. When it landed, he struck the back of the other guardsman's helmet with his sword pommel. The guard crumpled. Loro shouted to the fortress for a dozen aspirants. They carried one guardsmen and led the other back to the fortress for questioning. The assassin was quite dead, but they gathered him up also, and took him into the fortress.

Pelli's life had come apart around her in a single day. Yesterday she was the fortune teller in a traveling show. *I had a family. I had Dond and he had a plan.* This morning the troupe had broken up. This afternoon, Dond was murdered. *Now I am alone with Litne to take care of.* Litne was crying hysterically. Pelli was also crying but she tried to comfort her son at the same time. When she looked up she saw a stern-faced knight.

"Your name is Pelli," Terlak began. It was not a question. "Your brother was beheaded as a thief. You have made your living as a harlot and a charlatan. More recently you conspired to kill your employer – who was himself a villain of some stature, who murdered his own wife, but I digress. Dond, the man you lived with – who was not your husband – hired an assassin named Tiko to kill the leader of your troupe, Joikim. You had full prior knowledge of this and even paid the villain yourself. All of this we know to be true."

Pelli wanted to deny it – all of it; partly because she was afraid of the knight, but mostly because she did not want any of it to be true. She could not bring herself to make up another story; she was too weak to lie now. Instead, she hung her head and wept.

In Terlak's eyes it was the right answer. *At least she has the decency to feel badly about it.* He was also greatly relieved. He would have done whatever was necessary to break her, but he would have loathed every second of it. The child greatly complicated matters for him. "You are guilty of a great many crimes, probably more than I have listed, at least one deserving death. You can not escape justice, but if you cooperate, I can see that the boy does not suffer for your crimes."

Pelli clutched Litne to her and gasped in horror, "You wouldn't...." She could not even say it.

"We of the Order will do nothing to the child if you do not cooperate, absolutely nothing. Someone will carry him outside the fortress and set him on the road. That will be the end, as far as I'm concerned. I think you can imagine what his life would be like then, and how it would end." Terlak was not sure he could bring himself to do it, but Pelli believed him. "If you cooperate, I can see that your child is given a fair chance."

A fair chance is better than I ever got. Pelli had no decision to make. *Am I already dead?* Heavy oak doors and a bronze plated portcullis separated her from the outside world. The knight who brought her in was still at the door, and then there was the one in front of her. One way or another, her life was over. *Even if I could by some miracle escape, what hope would I have outside?*

An aspirant entered with a pen, ink, sand, and a blank scroll. There was no table. He set up on the stone floor. Terlak asked questions. Pelli answered them between sobs. Some of his questions she did not know the answer to, but he did not press her then. She began to think that she could fool him, but when she deliberately held back, he knew, and he reached for Litne. Pelli gave full answers after that.

Thernas was a priestess of Feadin, the Mother of Righteousness, and as such she had dealings with the Order from time to time. Usually an aspirant with a message summoned her to the fortress. Tonight Sir Malno of the Silver Circle begged her to follow and apologized for the late hour. He had brought three Brass Knights to escort her. Thernas threw on her ugliest shawl and followed. For the first time since her wedding twelve years earlier, the crowds on the city's streets parted for her to pass.

She always felt uncomfortable in the fortress. The Order followed Anagoth, one of Feadin's favorite sons, and they were strong allies. Still, she did not like dealing with the knights. *There is just something about being the only Taferam in a stone box full of Tafers. Their vow of chastity just guaranties that they are all repressed.* She knew that she would be treated correctly, as she always had been. She had visited the fortress many times before.

At the gate the three Brass Knights turned as if to stop someone following. Sir Malno led her on a few steps, but he stopped short and spun around. Thernas looked back in wonder.

The knight on the right drew his sword and waved it in front of him in a grand semicircle. Without a word, the knight on the left picked up a ten gallon rain bucket and threw its contents in a similar arc, twenty feet from the gate. None of this peculiar behavior was what made the priestess catch her breath. Instead, it was the figure that the water struck. An unmistakable splash marked the existence of an invisible being fifteen feet from the great portcullis. Just the faintest shimmer could be seen where the moisture clung to something in the air.

Before the water had finished falling, the knight in the center jumped at the invisible follower. Sir Malno stepped in front of Thernas and raised his shield. The priestess had to look out under his sword arm to see the rest of the action.

Suddenly the spell broke. The newly unmasked Amada stabbed his short sword into a seam in the armor of the knight in the center. Perhaps thinking that he had killed the knight, the assassin turned to run. The knight was not dead, however. He caught hold of the ankle of the retreating Amada and held fast. The Amada turned and stabbed down at the knight, but the other copper knights were not idle. One knight drove his sword into the Amada's heart. At the same time the second shoved the rain bucket over the short sword to protect his prone comrade. Then he helped him to his feet.

Reflexively Thernas stepped out to heal the wounded knight, but the Silver Knight again stepped into her way. "I must ask you to enter the fortress now, please, for your own safety." As polite as it was, it was not a request. Even so, Thernas might have insisted on helping the wounded Tafer, but he was standing on his own feet now and moving toward the gate. The other two picked up the corpse and carried that in also.

Inside, the priestess was directed to the common cafeteria while Sir Malno apologized for his gruff manner at the gate. "As you have seen, the Amada have taken the most extreme steps to prevent us from questioning certain of their ranks, and others. I should never had forgiven myself if you were injured while in my charge."

Thernas was only half listening. On a nearby table was a corpse with its head and neck savagely torn apart and chest crushed. She was not used to brutality. On another table a red-faced Tafer sat holding a blood soaked bandage against his shoulder. Two unarmed castle guards slumped in a corner. One looked pitifully at her. The other was unconscious, drooling on the stone floor. An aspirant stood guard over them with a spear.

Prenek, the Knight of the Platinum Circle, personally greeted the priestess. "We are deeply grateful to Feadin and to yourself for your arrival. As you may see, things are afoot. Today we have reduced the Amada by at least seventeen." Thernas wondered if he had counted the one that tried to follow her into the fortress. She would not be surprised to learn that the chief of the Order knew everything that his knights did, even as they did them.

"We've got them this time, sister." He allowed his smile to show through. He could be a thoroughly charming old gentleman when he allowed himself to be. "We have here two guardsmen caught taking bribes, who will, no doubt provide us with a list of petty Amada, their names are Hargus and Vol. On this table we have the mortal remains of Rollak, an assassin who attempted to silence a witness under our protection."

Thernas was shocked, "One of yours did that to him? That's vicious even for your lot!"

"Now, now, you are too quick to judge. The villain was fleeing the scene and Sir Gornet was forced to jump on him from the wall. Most of the damage you see was caused unintentionally by his spurs as he landed." Thernas could hardly believe it, but she knew that Knights of the Circle never lie. After staring for a short while at the pulped Amada, she convinced herself that a three hundred pound weight falling from the wall might have done that much damage.

"And here we have Helkin, a.k.a. The Beet – as in the red vegetable. He has very wisely decided to help us capture another murderous villain in exchange for his own life. You see his best friend, an Amadan assassin named Tiko, tried to kill him this afternoon.

"I forget my manners. Wexeln, please fetch some wine for our guest." The aspirant took his spear with him when he left.

Thernas looked past him to the guards again. "And what will you do with them?"

"Send them to The Hunt if they cooperate. They are charged with taking bribes and betraying the public trust to the one with the broken head. The best they can hope for is to die in battle and perhaps atone for themselves in that way. If they do not cooperate, we may simply have them beheaded, but the heavy law calls for worse. We won't know for sure that they are guilty until we interrogate the assassin's shade."

That sent a chill up Thernas' spine. She never liked having dealings with the dead. "You don't need me for that."

"Certainly we can deal with him ourselves. It is, after all, our fault that he is in that condition. An unfortunate necessity, as I mentioned. No we, that is I, asked you here for Helkin. The wound is poisoned, and we do not have the power to stop it ourselves."

"I don't either. Not today," she added hastily. The Beet had turned sharply and his eyes were full of despair. *I should have worded that differently,* the priestess thought. "I don't have much difficulty with poisonings most days."

"So I'm dying?" The Beet was panicked. *Do I hate Tiko more, or The Order? Tiko killed me. Am I already dead?* He never had time to finish the thought.

"Silence!" Prenek snapped, "You are a prisoner here and under no consideration!"

Thernas was shocked momentarily by the sudden force of the knight's voice. She recovered and spoke soothingly to The Beet. "I can cure you tomorrow. We can keep you alive until then, don't worry."

The head of The Order turned to her and smiled quietly, "Your heart has always been soft."

"And happy," Thernas countered with equal grace. The willing tendency to forgive was what separated Feadin and Anagoth theologically. Neither Prenek nor Thernas could possibly give an inch on the subject, and both knew it. They had long ago abandoned this argument as futile.

Two knights walked in carrying the corpse from the front gate and laid him on a table next to Rollak. "Who is this?" Prenek asked.

Sir Malno answered, "He tried to come through the gate using an invisibility spell. He followed us when we brought the lady."

"Now Sir Malno, you should know better than that. She was born to be a lady, but she worked to be a priestess. That makes her..."

"The lady priestess, yes sir. Sorry ma'am." The knight bowed to both of them at once.

Thernas would have laughed, but she knew that they were serious. *I wonder what kind of penance he will assign himself for that little slip?*

Ghinlihil found a young Tafer trying to balance a tray of wine and goblets in one hand while he lifted his spear. The quick young Fitheran dashed under the tray and caught it when it started to tip. Ghinlihil remembered only bad experiences with other Tafers when wine was spilled.

The Tafer shrugged and beckoned for Ghinlihil to follow.

The Knights of the Circle were used to ignoring the comings and goings of the aspirants, much as nobles ignored their servants. The prisoners had more selfish concerns holding their attention. Thernas never ignored anyone. She disciplined herself not with the wary air of predator or prey, but rather to show empathy and respect to everyone. She was the first to notice Ghinlihil was carrying the wine platter. She thanked him as she took a goblet, then turned to Prenek, "I thought only Tafers could be aspirants."

Still ignoring the servants, the Knight of the Platinum Circle looked his guest a question. The Beet, however, was shaken from his introspection. "It's the Brighteyes!" His words carried all of the wonder he felt. Standing there, holding a platter, was the Fitheran who started it all. Half of the Amada in the city were scheming to get close to him. *I am two steps away from the richest reward in Kingstone,* he thought bitterly. *If I earn it, I'll never leave this fortress alive.*

Hargus the guard let out a low whistle. "I swear, I didn't know he was trying to kill a kid. He said he needed to see in the window, that's all."

Thernas was confused, "What does all this mean, Brighteyes?"

The Beet answered for her, "He's an informant. He saw too much, Brighteyes, you get it?"

"They want to kill him for that?"

"Of course," Prenek recovered, taking the second goblet from the platter, "They rule the streets by fear. If they let Ghinlihil get away with it, soon the honest citizens will be brave enough to start reporting their crimes."

The Beet continued, "The Kels will pay fifty malstren to the Tafer that gets 'im."

Prenek smiled again. "So you see, my dear Lady Priestess: we have a rare opportunity in the form of this poor lad. Ghinlihil Brighteyes will force all of the bravest and best of the Amada out of their hiding places. We have seen only the beginnings of this today and Kingstone is much the better for it already, no doubt."

Thernas dropped to one knee so that she could see clearly the Fitheran under the platter. He looked to be the same age as her eleven-year-old daughter, but she knew this to be an illusion. "What becomes of him?"

"We take care of him, of course," Prenek said offhandedly. "We could hardly do any less even if he were not so valuable to our cause. As it is, he will be an icon to the Amada's impotence." He grunted what might have been a laugh. "I expect that not long after my own death, no one will care who he informed on and he can get on with his life, whatever that might be. What's a handful of years to a Fitheran with all of his centuries before him?"

"All but one," Ghinlihil corrected him.

Thernas was nonplussed. The Fitheran looked like a tallish version of her daughter's playmates. She knew, of course, how old Fitherani could grow to be, but this was her first encounter with a Fitheran child. She could not make her mind accept that this child was older than Prenek or herself. Actually, he was older than both of them together.

Prenek smiled with genuine warmth. "In that case..." He took one of the two remaining goblets, forcing Ghinlihil to shift under the platter. He put the massy silver goblet in the Fitheran's free hand and took a pull from his own. "Starting today, Ghinlihil Brighteyes, we go to war against the Amada."

Chapter 9

Killer

Ghinlihil spent the night in his tower room. An aspirant had closed the shutters at sunset and he warned the Fitheran against opening them before daylight: "You'll be safe with the shutters tight and barred." Ghinlihil, in spite of all of his years with Tafers, had never developed a fear of the dark. Like all Fitherani, his vision changed when the light was low. Soon he could see the cool night air flowing through the cracks in the warm shutters. In the dark "warm" and "cool" were colors to the Fitheran that replaced the "red" and "green" that he saw in the light of day.

In the morning Ghinlihil was allowed to watch Thernas heal The Beet. He was disappointed. When he was with the troupe back flips and dancing bears were part of the everyday routine. Occasionally some trinkets were sold as magic charms with all of the mystique and wonder that the salesman could muster. The fortune tellers went to great lengths to hide the "magic" secrets of their trade from the paying public. Real magic was a topic of awe, and occasionally someone would deny that any such power existed (usually right before Dond threw him out). The priestess merely concentrated, spoke a few words, laid her hand on the wounded shoulder, then she relaxed and stepped away. The entire process took less than a minute. The Beet even asked, "Is that it? Are you sure it worked?" The knights all glared at him.

"It worked," she said softly.

In return for her help, the priestess asked for custody of Litne. She felt that she was rescuing him from a terrible fate. *Heartless fathers of noble families can condemn their sons into the Order, and I cannot stop them. This little one has done nothing wrong. Whatever his mother was, the child cannot be blamed for it.*

Prenek was quite happy to give her the child. *I cannot have children of murderers and whores cluttering the minds of the aspirants.* There was never any thought in his mind of raising the child to the level of the aspirants, who were all from respectable families.

When Litne left, so did all of Ghinlihil's contact with the old troupe. He was kept away from Pelli, and shortly she was gone. Neither was he permitted to see the interrogation of Rollak's shade. Even the Knights of the Circle knew that such things were not for young eyes. He learned something of what was going on from the stories from the aspirants with whom he shared meals and play.

The Beet led a company of knights to Tiko's hiding place on the rocky shore. They had to wait for the tide to recede before it opened. When the assassin heard the knights of the Circle had found him, he tried to bargain for his life also. Instead, he was questioned on the rack and beheaded. The information from Tiko and The Beet led more and more Amada to follow the assassin's end. So many were caught that the Amada began to carry poison vials to kill themselves rather than be brought into the fortress. Sometimes it worked, but more often the Order could keep them alive long enough to get more information out of them. If they could not be brought in alive, the knights brought their corpses to the fortress where gold knights examined their shades. In just a few months the Brighteyes got used to the muffled screams of agony that came from the interrogation rooms below the fortress.

Ghinlihil did not go to war. He stayed in the fortress. Aspirants made certain that his needs were met. Some of the knights visited him regularly. Even so, he was alone. He was never to be an aspirant to the Order, and could never be a member of the Order. In that regard he was unique in the fortress. Before long the Fitheran divined that everyone in the fortress considered him a guest and very much an outsider.

The knights did not leave Ghinlihil to his own devices. Their vow prevented them from having sons of their own, and to many that was a greater sacrifice to the Order than any other. Ghinlihil had no shortage of foster fathers. While he was not an aspirant subject to work for the knights, they still would not allow him to suffer from idleness. Instead they engaged him in such sport as they knew.

All of the games that the Knights of the Circle knew were for the training of muscles and minds for battle. Ghinlihil's favorite was the reflex game. Palms down he could get away from almost anyone. Palms up he could slap the fastest contenders. When he learned to relax during the game he was almost unbeatable. Soon none of the aspirants could best him in the reflex game. After two years in the fortress, only the quickest knights could contend with the Brighteyes.

Though his legs were shorter than many aspirants, his body was strong and light. Within a few days the aspirants learned not to race to tag the Brighteyes. In the small confines of the fortress courtyard he was too fleet of foot, and he could stop and turn in the blink of an eye. Only in thumb and leg wrestling, and putting the shot were the Tafer children more than a match for the young Fitheran.

Terlak decided to include him in the aspirant's practices and foot battle exercises, as much to keep him from mischief borne of idleness than of any need to train the child. The knight was both surprised and pleased with his natural talents. Many years had passed since Ghinlihil had failed as an acrobat, now his balance was excellent and his movements became fluid. The gold knight had expected grace from a Fitheran, but he still marveled at it. He had never trained anyone with such natural ability. Many of the tumbling and balance exercises that the clumsy Tafer aspirants failed over and over came naturally to Ghinlihil. Eventually he had to take Ghinlihil out of the tumbling classes because his natural ability was making many of the aspirants frustrated.

What surprised Terlak the most was the strength that the little Brighteyes showed. Terlak had fought along side Fitherani in the field on many occasions, and he would be first to admit that they made the finest of archers, but when the battle drew close it was always the Tafers coming to rescue them. The Brighteyes showed real strength from his stringy frame. No one else seemed to understand until Terlak picked Ghinlihil to wrestle Djun, an aspirant a full head taller and at least forty pounds heavier than the Fitheran. Most of the aspirants laughed when these two shook hands in the middle of the circle. When the initial posturing and positioning was over, Djun had corralled the Fitheran near the edge of the circle. Ghinlihil somersaulted away, but Djun grabbed his right arm as he came up. He locked the arm behind Ghinlihil's back and drew back to push him out of the circle. Ghinlihil leapt sideways into the air over the Tafer's back, uncoiling his own arm. Landing on one knee, he reached his left hand around and grabbed his own right wrist while pressing his right shoulder into the small of his opponent's back. With a high-pitched Fithern shout he twisted and lifted Djun over his shoulder, throwing him head first out of the wrestling circle.

The aspirants made no sound. Even the knights who were watching were stunned silent. Ghinlihil crawled out from under Djun's legs, half covered in the wheaten dust that made the floor of the wrestling circle. He stood, raising his arms over his head when no knight stepped forward to do so. He announced to everyone on the grounds, "Ghinlihil, son of Lalliam Steelhand, the greatest warrior of Foralis, is the victor!"

Again, for a few heartbeats a startled silence reigned. Not even the knights knew of his life before joining the troupe, none had thought to ask. Certainly none had thought that this Brighteyes might be from an honorable family. It was an aspirant who broke the silence, "Hey! No using your family name!" A general murmur of agreement rose from the aspirants who were not allowed to refer to their lives before joining the Order.

The knights were still confused, and looked to Terlak for an answer. "The Brighteyes is not an aspirant here, nor is he a member of the Order, to be bound by these rules. Even so, I think it best, Ghinlihil, that you do not use your family name on the field, for that would not be fair to the others who surrender their family name at the fortress gate."

During this time Djun had rolled to his stomach, then rose to his knees. One of the other aspirants yelled encouragement, "He tricked you by a Fitheran trick, jumping like a squirrel in the woods! That's not fair!"

Djun staggered to his feet and shook out some of the dust that lightened his shoulder length brown hair. "Ghinlihil Brighteyes won fair as day. If you don't think so, you come out and prove it yourself." He turned back into the circle and shook the Fitheran's hand again as his training dictated. The knights beat steel shod palms against their sheilds in applause, though more for Djun's honorable response than Ghinlihil's victory.

Thereafter whenever the aspirants spoke of him, they named him Ghinlhil Brighteyes, some out of respect referring to his clear blue eyes and cheery nature, others jeering at the title of the Amada.

Ghinlihil's first weapon training was with a dagger. Terlak hoped that he might learn enough to defend himself while help arrived. In spite of his obvious natural talent his progress was slow. The knight was frequently disappointed. Ghinlihil's quick reflexes made him more dangerous while attacking, but he was easily fooled with a feint and too often he allowed his opponent to get into wrestling position where his small size invited a quick end. Prenek frequently reminded Terlak that the Brighteyes had many more years in which to learn than the Tafer aspirants.

As months turned into years Ghinlihil Brighteyes grew stronger. Years of hard work with the troupe had made his muscles tough. The games that the aspirants played made them strong. For the first time since he began living with Tafers, Ghinlihil was developing quickly enough for the Tafers to notice. When he entered the fortress as an adolescent he was stronger than the average adult Fitheran. After only a few years in the fortress his muscles stood out on him as if he were a Tafer. The knights, knowing no better, thought it was all part of the normal Fitheran growing process and pushed him all the harder to develop his body.

After three years of slow progress with the dagger, Terlak began training Ghinlihil with a war hammer. At the time a short handled hammer was the heaviest weapon that the Fitheran could handle, and after the dagger training Terlak despaired of ever teaching Ghinlihil the proper use of a sword. To the knight's surprise, Ghinlihil soon showed skill with the hammer, and could ward with a dagger in his left hand. Shortly Ghinlihil joined the aspirants on the training field when they drilled with their weapons.

More years passed, and the Amada did not forget. The title of Brighteyes was a death sentence and the bounty was open until someone collected it. No one had ever survived the title, though some had lived to old age in obscurity until their past caught up with them. The little Fitheran was a tempting mark: he was easy to distinguish from the others around him, he was not particularly large or dangerous, nor were Fitherani notoriously resistant to other forms of attack such as poison or magic. Amada assassins and freelance glory-seekers frequently tried to penetrate the fortress to claim the Brighteyes bounty.

The knights, on the other hand, were resistant to almost everything. Their armor turned away physical attacks, and their devotion gave them unnatural resistances to less direct assaults. Because the aspirants prepared all of their meals within the fortress, it was impossible to poison anyone in particular. Once, an ambitious Amada tried to poison all of them by poisoning one of their provision wagons. The poison was detected and the food was magically purified. The knights traced the poison back to the source with severe results.

The most common outcome of the assassins' attacks was that the knights had another prisoner to interrogate on the rack, though almost as frequently the attacker died and they had to put the questions to his ghost. Some few even won free of the fortress with their lives, to escape into the swirl of Tafers in the marketplace. For months the Kels considered this to be the natural order of things: that eventually an assassin would come that was lucky and skilled enough to penetrate the fortress and find the Brighteyes without being discovered. As months turned into years the best and most ambitious Amada fell to the Knights of the Circle. The Kels contented themselves that these where the Tafers most likely to threaten their own positions. The bounty on the Brighteyes stood.

With all of that, the Order was not overwhelming the Amada. The armor that protected the knights also gave them away. The Amada, who could blend in with the crowd, would see them coming and melt away. In the crowded tangle of Kingstone nimble Amada could outmaneuver mounted knights.

The Amada were scoring too. Sometimes they would lead a knight into a pit or a mechanical trap. The knights' armor was not impenetrable, more than once the Amada brought down a knight by firing crossbows from the roofs around a blind alley.

The Knights of the Order were killing the Amada at a ratio over twenty to one, but no one knew who was really winning. Even the Kels did not know exactly how many bodies were at their disposal, and Knights were rare. The ranks of the knights were replenished from aspirants at the rate of two to three a year. The Amada could recruit from the masses as long as they had the coin, though they began to replace skilled operators with rabble.

In coin, though, the Amada were hurting. Knights interrupted the business of crime and that was as real a loss to the Kels as any dead assassin. Increasingly the citizenry began to think they could get one past the Amada – a thing unheard of before Ghinlihil Brighteyes. With the knights driving the Amada rank and file into hiding, fewer enforcers were left on the streets to keep the merchants and artisans in line. Kels were spending more time punishing offenders, and they were sure that many more offenses were being committed. It was well known throughout the marketplace that there was a Brighteyes in the fortress and the Amada were powerless to do anything about it. Even the punishments that insured continued compliance from the marketplace cost the Kels in lost revenue from the dead and crippled merchants. Some began to wonder how many Tafers were left in the marketplace who were neither stealing from the Amada, nor on their payroll.

"We aren't winning," Terlak lamented one day. "I always thought with an opportunity like this, we would be winning." The battle had raged for a decade without a clear winner, pausing only for a minor border war with the Manrachian Nomads to the south. Terlak began to wonder about his own health. His friend was fourteen years his senior.

"Aren't we? I wonder," Prenek said more to himself than to the other knight. "If we weren't hurting them, they would not respond the way they do. Before, when we were out on the streets they ignored us. They went about their wicked ways, so long as they were out of sight and hearing. Now they stop and watch for us. They have to. They all wonder, 'will I be the next one taken?'"

"But we're losing too many knights."

"That we shall have to look into." Prenek had thought this out earlier. "On the battle field we would have support troops. Specialists to do the things that we are not good at, and levies to fill in while we form up for another charge."

"What good will archers and sappers do on the streets? And peasant levies would be no different than the common folk of the market to begin with."

"A general levy could not be trusted, no more than they could be to hold a line of battle. Archers, however, might get us somewhere."

"The Amada would tear them apart in the narrow streets. We would loose archers at four or five times the rate we lose knights. Can we sustain that?"

"No," the Platinum Knight almost laughed, "We could not sustain that. If, however, we were to put archers in the fortress, we could free up more knights for the chase. Perhaps a third more."

"Can we trust archers to hold the fortress?"

"Fithern archers. If they knew who they were defending they would value the young one's life more than the Amada's gold."

Terlak thought for a moment. "What if we use the Fitherani to hold these walls, and use knights to hold a camp outside the city. That way we could make another secure base."

"To what end?"

"That base could be used to house troops who are not trustworthy enough to keep in the fortress. We need troops who can race with an Amada through the streets. If they can no longer make good their escapes, or move to ambush, we have the advantage."

"You want to hire mercenaries?"

"Yes. Timbles with trained dogs: keen on the chase, easy to ward. They are more nimble on the streets than any Tafer, and they have the sense to withdraw if the Amada stand and fight. I have been trying to think of a way to get them into the fight for some time now."

"And Timbles are nearly as resistant to poison as Hollenwae. I see no reason for delay. I will write up the necessary messages. Get some aspirants to copy them, and four copper knights to deliver them."

The Fithern archers arrived first. As soon as the Copper Knights arrived at Sekri Timbrali, Fitherani began to muster. The greatest archers of the Fithern city contended for the right to join the knights and defend the fortress walls. Thirty-two champion archers returned with the first knight while the second knight waited for the next round of competition.

The greatest archer of the Fitherani was Biolmi Yewstaff. Though he did not presume to command the Fitherani, he was greatly respected. Fourteen of the champions in the first group had been his students at one time. He requested and received the honor of defending Ghinlihil's own window. Of course, this made him a roommate to the young Fitheran.

"I'll be living with you now." He stepped up to the window with an arrow on his bow string and swiftly scanned the walls and rooftops below. When he was satisfied that no immediate danger lurked, he stepped back from the window and unshouldered his pack, setting it at the foot of the unused sleeping palette. Ghinlihil was sitting on the other, dressed for bed, for it was evening when the Fitherani arrived and they had listened to the plans of the knights while they supped. Biolmi looked quietly around the room, noting the youth's clothing neatly hanging from pegs on the wall. He smiled at he hilt of a heavy Tafer dagger that stuck out from under Ghinlihil's pillow, then frowned at the black iron war hammer standing near the head of Ghinlihil's palette. "They must have moved you to this room so that we could share."

Ghinlihil had not had a real conversation with another Fitheran for over forty-five years – not since Foralis burned. He spoke Timbrali with a Tafer accent now, a trait that disturbed Biolmi. "Nosir, I've been here since always."

Biolmi closed the door, more to see what might be concealed behind it than to secure the room. He found nothing. "Where is your bow?" He squinted at the blankets on Ghinlihil's bed, as if to see the missing weapon beneath. "And where are the rest of your things?"

"I haven't gotna bow. I gotta war hammer." Ghinlihil stood and brandished his favorite weapon, a short-handled war hammer just like the one Ammoss had used. *Someday I'll get a sword too.*

Biolmi was stunned. He tried to gauge Ghinlihil's age without success. The youth was a hand and more taller than his own five feet, but he knew all Fitherani began archery training between the ages of eighty and ninety unless they are apprenticed to a magician or priest. He pushed the bolt closed on the door, and after another long sweeping look, he closed and barred the shutters in the window. "How long have you been here?"

Ghinlihil shrugged, "Tenleven year."

"Eleven years?" When Ghinlihil raised his head 'yes', Biolmi sat on his bed with his own bow in his lap. "Were you apprenticed to a magician?"

"No..."

"A priest, then?"

"No. I was a dancer, and a singer."

"Dancing and singing before archery? Where are you from? And how are you called, Brighteyes?"

"I'm Ghinlihil. I'm from Foralis and Dath and all over."

"Ghinlihil Brighteyes," Biolmi repeated. *At least he has a proper name.* "How old are you?"

"Six score and six."

Raise the trees! In less than a decade he will be old enough to take his test and he doesn't even have a bow! "I don't know Foralis or Dath. Where do they lie?"

"I don't remember, exactly. Well, really I don't know at all. I left when I was young and wandered all over before coming here." Ghinlihil spent the rest of the evening explaining how he came from Foralis to Dath with Ammoss, and from Dath to the slavers with Lalru, from the slavers to the troupe, then with the troupe and Fiorl and Joikim, and finally his rescue from the Amada by Terlak. "... And I've been here everafter. I just want to go home."

"Why, you're not Ghinlihil at all, no free wind playing with the crisp autumn leaves. Over a third of your life you've been held a stranger among Tafers – and worse – bound by fate, hunger, and even chains." Biolmi shuddered at the thought of an eighty-seven year old child in the possession of a Kutel. "It's Blorfindel I call you, the Child of Bondage. Get some sleep Blorfindel Brighteyes. Tomorrow we'll see about making you a Fitheran again."

***

Ghinlihil awoke with a start. The room was dark. Night air poured in through the open window, fighting against the warmer, stale fortress air. He heard breathing close by, then realized that he was holding his breath. He slowly stretched his arm over his head and gripped the handle of the war hammer, then relaxed. *It is Biolmi's breathing. I forgot I am not alone tonight.* Glancing across the narrow room he saw the other Fitheran's heat radiating from under the blankets, the plumes of his warm breath mixing with the cold air. Suddenly Ghinlihil's grip on the war hammer was white-knuckle tight – the plumes didn't match the sound.

With his left hand and leg he threw his blanket into the air between the beds. It hung on something that had not been visible before. Without hesitation he brought the hammer around at arm's length to intersect the top of the blanket, springing up in the process. The blanket moved only slightly when struck, and sounded with a dull thud that spoke of something substantial.

The young Fitheran stepped sideways and struck again, at the same time drawing his dagger from under the pillow with his left hand. This time the hammer struck a still-invisible body before reaching the blanket.

Someone whispered, "Crushk!" Then a Tafer appeared under the blanket stabbing at Ghinlihil with a dagger of his own.

The Brighteyes was quicker. He parried the dagger with his own and whirling about struck the Tafer below the ear with his war hammer.

The Tafer staggered backwards into Biolmi's bed before recovering. He was surprised to find the Brighteyes awake, still more surprised to find how quickly he moved. The hammer surprised him too. Things were not going according to plan, but he was not about to give up now. Too many things had gone right to get him in here.

His associates had created a diversion on the other side of the fortress, nothing serious enough to wake the garrison, but something to interest the guards. Then the remaining guards had been forced to respond to crossbowmen attacking from the street. At the same time he slipped through, unseen due to an expensive invisibility spell which had lasted long enough to get him into the Brighteyes' room. He had another invisibility potion ready for his escape. The witch had been quite clear up front: the spell would break as soon as he attacked, *Some cosmic sense of fair play, no doubt.* The second potion had to wait until the job was over, but the Fitheran was not supposed to wake up.

He threw his shoulder at the Brighteyes, trying to pin him down long enough to scratch him with his poisoned dagger.

Ghinlihil braced his shoulders against the wall over his bed and, while steadying himself with the war hammer, kicked both feet at the Tafer's chest.

The Tafer was surprised by the Fitheran's strength. *I could lose this fight!* He swung wide with his poisoned dagger, cutting the Fitheran's heavy nightshirt, but no flesh. "Crushk!" *There goes half the poison!* Then he was surprised again.

Blorfindel's kick propelled the Tafer into Biolmi's bed, but the older Fitheran was not there. By now he was standing at the head of the bed with his own dagger in his hand. "Yai!" He plunged the dagger into the Tafer's neck and just as quickly retrieved it.

Ghinlihil was not a moment behind. He guided the Tafer's dagger out of the way and even before Biolmi's cry faded he cracked the Tafer's skull with the war hammer.

Anger, fear, and death seemed to blend with the mixing air. The Tafer slumped to the bed and slid slowly to the floor. Hot blood sprayed from his throat and fouled nearly everything in the small room.

Biolmi snatched up his bow and arrows and vaulted to the open window, scanning for would-be attackers.

Ghinlihil stood in amazement. He had seen many things and heard many more, but for the first time in his life he had taken a hand at killing something that went on two legs; someone who had a name and spoke a language; a Tafer with hopes and dreams. *He came to kill me. Who is... was he?* Somehow, in his mind Ghinlihil had been able to distance himself from the Amada before. The knights and aspirants spoke as if the Amada were less than people, to them they were both animals and devils. This was a Tafer dying at his feet. *Why? Why do they want to kill me? What good was his death?* Ghinlihil ignored the sound of heavy footsteps running to the door. *Was his death like Aritsa's? Like Allond's? What does that make me? Why?*

The door burst open and torchlight flooded the room. A silver knight with sword in hand framed the doorway while a copper knight held the torch. Ghinlihil was suddenly aware of how much his arm hurt. He had been wielding the war hammer well beyond his strength. The moment gone, he let the heavy weapon fall to the floor.

The rest of the evening was a blur of activity and fatigue to the Brighteyes. The knights congratulated him and asked him to tell the story over and over again, cheering every blow and parry while deriding the assassin's cowardice and cursing the poisoned dagger. Ghinlihil's goblet flowed with wine. Biolmi took no credit at all, though the younger Fitheran never excluded him from the tale.

At some point he changed his nightshirt. Ghinlihil was vaguely aware that Biolmi was angry, and an angry current ran through the knights' discussions, but never directed at Ghinlihil. He could hardly stand and needed help climbing the stairs to go to the garderobe before he finally went back to bed. Someone had cleaned up but the coppery smell made his breath catch in his throat.

When the Brighteyes awoke, Biolmi was standing in the window with an arrow ready. He jumped out of bed and reached for his war hammer again, but the older Fitheran dipped his head and said, "There's nothing." It took two or three heartbeats for Blorfindel to understand. He dropped the heavy hammer and dropped back down on the bed himself.

"You can't stay, you know," the master archer said, still facing the window, "They almost failed you last night. We were lucky, and you did well."

"You helped, too. I didn't do it alone."

"You would have won anyway. I was too slow." Biolmi Yewstaff turned to face Blorfindel Brighteyes, "I failed you. I thought the Tafer knights could hold the fortress. I never should have trusted a Tafer guard. Still, the loss is only to my pride. Things could have been much worse." Biolmi turned back to the window. "We came to protect you, and that's what we're going to do."

Chapter 10

Escape

Plans passed in secret from Fitheran to Fitheran. The knights were busy following up on the intrusion and did not notice. In four days the Fitherani did the unthinkable: they escaped from the Fortress of the Circle with a prisoner. Blorfindel Brighteyes was among his own people again.

They had not trusted him with the plan. They did not know him well enough, and they feared that he might betray them to the knights. Biolmi woke him on their fifth night together, "You are not safe here. We must go. Bring your things and come quietly."

Blorfindel thought that there was another attempt on his life and that he was moving to a different room in the fortress. Biolmi did not carry a light (the Fitherani did not need one) and none could have heard them pass.

The Fitherani archers had contrived to be the only ones watching from the south wall at this hour. It was a simple task to lower ropes and steal away. Biolmi had a gag and a short rope to bind the Brighteyes if necessary. The danger from the knights was too great to leave anything to chance. He was loathe to even carry them. He was greatly relieved that he did not have to use them. *It would put me on the long list of the child's captors.* Blorfindel – "Child of Bondage" – did as he was told.

They covered the twenty miles to Silverport before dawn. The archers broke up into smaller, less conspicuous groups upon entering the city. No one in the city paid much attention to their entrance. Fitherani were common enough in Silverport. Ghinlihil – still unaccustomed to his new name – was carried in a sack into the hold of a large riverboat. The sack ensured that none of the Tafers saw him. The Fitherani did not unpack him until they were out of the city and sailing up the river at the best speed the sail could manage.

For their part, the knights at first blamed the escape on the Amada. Precious hours were lost before they realized that all of the Fitherani were missing and there was no sign of a battle. They followed the Fithern flight and six knights were also in Siverport for the dawn. Once inside the city the trail went stone cold. The chase might have ended there except that the Timbles and their dogs arrived at the fortress that same day.

On the riverboat, the wind turned contrary during the day and the Fitherani were forced to break out the poles. Biolmi fretted, "The knights will catch us. Will we fight them from the boat?"

"If we have to, we'll keep the boat in deep water and hold them off," Ichassi, the Fithern commander, replied. "I think we'll turn up the Hollen. They won't expect that. Maybe they'll go all the way to Prefectshire before they find out they're on the wrong river. Even if they don't, we'll be able to use the sail again."

"If the wind doesn't turn again."

"We'll put ashore in groups. The first will be a decoy for the knights. Then you and I will take the Brighteyes and maybe a half-dozen archers and make for home. Then the rest can either put ashore further up, or go to Koraggen on the boat."

"No one wants to go to the Silver Hills."

"Maybe not, but they might draw the knights after them."

"Where do we get off?"

"We'll have to wait until the plateau. There's too much open country to cross until then. We'll have to let the decoys off there, too – to give them a chance to get away themselves."

"They should run, not fight."

"Of course. We don't want to make a long-enemy."

"What if they go to Sekri Timbrali?"

"The knights? That would be a mistake. In the trees we would destroy them. Besides, I don't think they want the Fitherani as a long-enemy, either."

"Where would they get the archers to fight their wars?"

"Manrachians."

Both Fitherani laughed. The Manrachian nomads were possibly the best horsemen in the world, but they shot 'like Tafers' – which to these

Fitherani meant 'like children'. *Or like the Brighteyes*, Biolmi thought sourly.

Nightfall found Knights of the Circle at the harbormaster in Silverport. Timbles and their dogs were loaded onto a boat along with one silver and five copper knights. As the crew began rowing up the dark river, twenty-three knights pounded up the bank bound for Prefectshire.

"The wind has been against them most of the day," Sir Terlak mused.

"The harbormaster said the boat was not a swift one against the wind," Sir Malno responded, "They would have to pole. Fitherani can't be fast polers."

"We could catch them tonight."

"Perhaps."

"We mustn't attack the boat. The archers would have the advantage."

"In many places the river is shallow enough to wade," The silver knight offered.

"Up to your neck. It's no way to catch a boat. We can get boats in Prefectshire and have the current on our side. Even if they beat us to Prefectshire, they can't take the river all the way to Sekri Timbrali."

"What if they turn south?"

"The Hollen? We will find out at Prefectshire either way. We can cross there and race them up the hills. It would also give us more time to catch them before Sekri Timbrali." Terkak sounded hopeful.

"More time chasing Fitherani through the woods."

"Even they can't trick a good hound off the scent."

A short night's sleep revitalized the Fitherani. They knew that the knights would not rest. They all tried to count the hours and guess the distance between them. No two came up with the same number, but they all wanted to be far away, under the trees in Sekri Timbrali.

They maneuvered the boat up the steep and rocky section of the Hollen River using the sail, poles, and ropes pulled from the bank. Blorfindel was allowed to help. He was grateful to be something other than baggage. The Fitherani were surprised and glad to have him pulling the rope. Until now they had only rumors of his strength to match his large stature (for a Fitheran). By the time the sun was fully above the horizon they all knew that the Brighteyes was the strongest Fitheran in the party. More than once a Fitheran turned to his fellow and marveled, "What is he going to be like when he grows up?" Someone might have whispered, "He's part Tafer," but none would repeat it.

The sun was high when they climbed back into the boat. Most were asleep before the wind filled the sail. Blorfindel stood on the bow and felt the wind. He had been eleven years in the rock walls of the fortress and he missed the clean, fresh air dearly. When he said as much to Biolmi and Ichassi they sat down on the bow beside him. No one knew who was the first to shed a tear.

The knights found that no boats had passed Prefectshire in days. They paced and fretted while their chargers rested. The boat carrying the Timbles crept up river against the wind.

"Our path is shorter," Sir Malno said hopefully.

The gold knight had concerns. "The horses won't take this forever. We have to save them for the last charge. Can you imagine running at Fithern archers on foot?"

"We'd never catch them. Did you ever see the Brighteyes run?"

"And they're not wearing armor. We need the horses."

Sir Malno had not worked with Timbles often. He asked, "How fast can the Timbles move overland?"

Sir Terlak just shook his head, "Our path is shorter."

"It needs to be. How far do you think they'll stay on the river?"

"Climbing the plateau doesn't get them any closer, and it would be slow. They say it can't be done in the dark. I expect they're on foot, headed west by now."

"We would catch them in open country today if we get across by noon. They have to know that, don't they?"

Sir Terlak was training the junior knight. He spoke more like an instructor than a commander, "If they went all night, they could beat us to the forest. That's what they're gambling on. They don't know that we have the dogs."

"That makes sense. They'll run to the forest and try to hide, except that it won't work. How many days can they go without sleep?"

"Not many. Fatigue catches up with a Fitheran faster than a Tafer or even a horse. A long race favors us."

"How far to Sekri Timbrali?"

"Only fifty miles."

"Where's that boat?"

The boat ferried the knights across the Eastering River under the noon sun. They struck out south as quickly as the Timbles could go. The knights could not complain about the pace: to rest the horses the knights were also on foot. Though none of them would admit it, the Timbles' pace was running them into the ground.

The sun was setting when Blorfindel, Biolmi, Ichassi, and party disembarked. They were only four miles beyond the decoys.

"We can't get caught in the open," Ichassi said, "We can rest in the forest."

"How far is it?"

"Five miles, maybe ten. I've never gone this way before." He looked at the others but none of them knew either. "I expect before too long you'll wish you slept instead of sitting in the wind, Blorfindel." *I know I will.*

"It's only ten miles. I've walked before, you know."

No one argued.

After climbing out of the shallow river valley the tree line taunted them from the horizon. It was only a black shadow in the dark sky, but it was their goal. The dark did not slow the Fitherani and the miles passed swiftly underfoot. It turned out to be only five miles. Two hours brought them under the tall trees that whispered "home" to all but one Fitheran. They set watches and went to sleep.

"They went up the plateau," Sir Malno reported. The knights had come to the edge of the forest without cutting a track.

"I can see that."

"Of course, Sir. I'm sorry."

"It's the fatigue talking. You should have slept while we waited for the boat." Terlak had to ask himself, *Why didn't I sleep?* "Since they couldn't go up in the dark, they must have waited until this morning. That more than makes up for our time in Prefectshire."

"And it makes their route longer," Malno observed.

"Yes. They're more tired than we are. We'll stay along the tree line and hope to catch them in the open."

"What if they're behind us?"

"What?" Sir Terlak was surprised by Malno's question and concerned that he had missed something.

"What if we haven't cut a track because they're out in the field waiting for us to pass before they dash for the forest?"

Then they've beaten us, Terlak thought. He gave the silver knight orders just the same, "Send two copper knights with fresh horses east to the river. They then split north and south. If they find a landing they can ride back and report. Otherwise, they can catch up with us further on."

Then we've been marching in the wrong direction, Sir Malno thought.

The knights and the Timbles had been marching well into the night when Sir Malno came to report, "The Timbles say there's a track. I can't see it."

Of course you can't, Terlak thought. Neither moon had risen yet and the Tafers could hardly see to walk. The Timbles did little better.

A Timble came to report. He sat unceremoniously on his pack in front of the two footsore knights. "It's Fitherani, awright, mebby ten – prob'ly less. Yours ain't there."

"Why split up? Are they going to set an ambush?" Malno asked.

Sir Terlak had almost expected it. "Decoy. They think they're trying to evade knights. They aren't thinking about dogs."

"Does that mean we're close or far?"

"No way to know for certain. They won't want the decoy so close as to lead us toward the real quarry. How old is the track?"

Sir Malno started to ask the Timble, "How old–"

"I heard 'im. Sun hasn't shone on it yet – so def'n'tly tonight. I half 'spected the prints to be warm, but they ain't. Call it an hour."

Malno sighed, "One more push, then."

Terlak did not think that was a good tactic. "No. Now they start getting tricky. They obviously don't know that we can track them. Now they might try your 'wait until they have gone by' strategy. It's more likely they ran for cover of the trees and they're hiding – and resting. Their watch will hear the dogs long before we can get close, and we can't use the chargers in the woods in the dark. Torches would give us away even sooner."

"I don't understand. How are we going to catch them if we don't seize the opportunity?"

"We will make our own opportunity. We will go a short distance further and wait out the night. We could all use the rest." He gestured toward the Timble who was asleep where he sat. "We will find them tomorrow, in the daylight."

Ghinlihil awoke to a light touch on the shoulder. *Blorfindel. I am Blorfindel now. I wonder what that will be like.*

The forest raised the spirits of all the Fitherani. Blorfindel ran his fingers on the bark of each tree that he passed. Ichassi had to forbid them singing. "The knights might still be following." No one believed him, but they did not sing.

***

Sir Malno reported again, "It's him. The Timbles are certain."

The sun was just creeping over the Silver Hills when the knights cut the second track. The dogs were so excited that the gold knight did not really need the report. "How old?"

"Last night." Sir Malno's voice had a little disappointment hidden under the surface.

"Don't worry – they need sleep, too. We should catch them today."

"How far is Sekri Timbrali?"

Sir Terlak's voice held some excitement, "Too far – for them. Forty or fifty miles."

"Then we're no closer than we were at Prefectshire?"

"No closer to the city, but we have nearly caught up with the Brighteyes."

Unless they walked all night, Sir Manlno thought to himself.

Late that morning Malno reported again, "The Timbles say it's a campsite. The trail leaving is much fresher. He says it was made in the dark. I wonder how he can know that."

Sir Terlak ignored the implied question. "So, they spent the night and left before dawn. We need to pick up our rate of advance. Have brass knights give the Timbles a ride on their cantles and let the dogs run."

Both knights thought the same thing: *If we don't catch them today the horses will be too spent to follow tomorrow.*

"We will be home tomorrow," Balisi told Blorfindel. "I recognize this part of the forest."

The group had stopped for lunch. *I wish I could stay here for a while,* Blorfindel thought. "The forest is beautiful here." Balisi just smiled in response.

His reverie was broken by the sound of distant hoofbeats, rapidly closing. All of the Fitherani took up their bows and listened. Blorfindel drew his dagger and war hammer. "Shouldn't we hide?" he whispered.

Biolmi dipped his head, 'no', but remained silent.

Balisi sprinted noiselessly toward the hoofbeats and out of sight. Moments later he returned with another Fitheran leading a lathered horse. It was the second Fitheran who spoke first, catching his breath in wonder.

"This is Lalliam's son. Yes, the son of Lalliam and Jilwanis – I would swear it. You were Ghinlihil?"

The young Fitheran's mouth went instantly dry. He tossed his head, 'yes.'

"I was Godiran. Do you remember me? I am Michido Lightshoe now. I ran from Foralis when I should not, to my lasting shame. Now I see that we left you. My apology will have to wait, but I am sorry."

"I remember you, Godiran – Michido. I ran away, too."

"You were a child. I was merely acting like one."

"I don't understand."

"Wait, I am not ready to be forgiven yet. Ichassi, the knights hunt you with Timbles and dogs."

"How do you know this?"

"The second group of archers reached Prefectshire just after the knights crossed the river."

"Timbles?"

"The archers said they saw them on the boat with the knights. We were afraid they might have already caught you."

"Why would Timbles side with the knights against us?"

"I don't know."

Biolmi said, "The Timbles don't really have any choice. Are they going to say 'no' to the knights? Maybe from the Timbles' side of the Brewster River, but not in Kingstone."

"They're not in Kingstone anymore."

"I wonder if the knights know that?"

"Keep the horses away from the stream until the dogs pick up the scent again." The Fitherani had gone straight across all the other streams, but the gold knight was not going to allow himself to get careless. This time his caution was justified: the dogs lost the trail. He ordered the brass knights to lower the Timbles to the ground. "Check a spot where we can water the horses, first."

Berriwallow, the Timble leader, shook his head, but did as he was told. The dogs were already drinking, but horses would foul the water. *Tafers don't understand good, clean water.* He led his best hound down stream, hoping to pick up the trail before the water got too nasty. What he found was a surprise.

"Welcome to our land between the waters – our 'Timb'," a voice whispered in his own language.

The Timble knew better than to look around. The Fitheran would be well hidden. *Maybe he'll shoot the dog first and give me a chance to bolt.* His eyes fixed on the hound as his memory flashed fondly through puppyhood. The Timble's large brown eyes misted over. *I hope he kills me first.* "It… It's a pretty forest," he said in Timbrali. His voice was only the barest whisper.

"Yes, it is very pretty, but it's easy to get lost if you don't know your way around."

The Timble tossed his head in the Fitheran 'yes'. *He wouldn't still be talking if he wanted to kill us.* He patted the hound on the back the neck absent-mindedly.

"We wouldn't want our friends to get lost. If the Timbles are friends of the Fitherani then the Fitherani are friends of the Timbles."

"To Raiden with the knights," Berriwallow whispered. *And good riddance*, he thought to himself. "We will be friends."

"Well met, friend. Your path is just north of west – straight toward the city. There you will find hospitality for all <u>friends</u>."

The Timble tossed his head again, then waited quietly for his heart to stop racing. He took a handful of muddy water to wet his mouth before speaking aloud, "The path continues here. It looks like they're headin' for the city. We should catch 'em if we rush."

The gold knight gave the order to mount. Soon the group was headed west as fast as the dogs would run.

One brass knight was late to join the group. The Timble assigned to him had gone upstream with his hound and had not returned. The hound appeared to be following another scent. The Timble called it to halt and turned back. Impatient, and anxious not to be singled out on his first quest, the brass knight rode up the stream to pick up the Timble.

The Timble was tugging frantically to get the hound to turn back. The hound was equally intent on the trail which it had found. When the brass knight arrived, he saw what had the dog so excited: six Fitherani, including the Brighteyes, were standing in the trees.

Biolmi's pinpoint aim settled on an eye slit in the knight's visor. Four other arrows were trained at his charger. The knight knew that he should raise the alarm before he died, but the young Fitheran spoke first.

"Djun," he spoke softly but he, too was armed. "What good is it? I will fight alongside my own people for my own freedom. All I want is to go home. Even if you win, you will have no Brighteyes to bait the Amada. Be quiet, follow your orders, and live. I will take your word on it."

"I swore the oath." *To die, if necessary.*

Ichassi lowered his bow. "You must choose between doing what is right and fulfilling your oath. The choice is yours, but if you betray us you have not saved yourself, and you condemn Blorfindel Brighteyes as surely as the Kels."

"Knights will die, as well as Fitherani," Biolmi said, his arrow still trained at the knight's left eye. "Our people will become enemies who have been friends since the first sheildmaster landed on Kingstone. The Timbles, too, they will get caught up in all this."

"I'd have to leave the Order."

"You'll leave it one way or another," Biolmi hissed. "I'll not wait for the others to come looking for you."

"Djun," Blorindel said, "you know right from wrong, good from evil. You said that you would rather die than do wrong."

Djun smiled in spite of himself, "Or I can die immediately after. I will not betray you, Ghinlihil son of Lalliam, though it means giving up my spurs and circle."

"Who's gonna know?" the Timble shrugged.

"I'll know. That's enough. Fare you well, my old friend. I won't forget the time you beat me at wrestling."

"I'll not forget what you did here – not for a Fitheran's lifetime."

Ichassi waived. "Go now, and quickly catch up. If they find you here it will do us all harm and no good at all."

Djun picked up the Timble and rode away.

Evening found disappointed knights. The Timbles said they were close, but when pushed for more information they gave only excuses. They kept riding into the dark in spite of the decision of the previous night. As they got closer to the Fithern homeland they abandoned all attempts at stealth. Torches flared and sputtered in the night air.

Suddenly the trees burst forth pure white light. Instinct born of long training taught the knights to rally. Before their eyes adjusted they were in formation around the gold knight.

Two hundred long Fithern spears faced twenty-nine knights. The spear Fitherani tried not to shake in their fear. The knights looked down on them in disdain. Brass knights set down torches and Timbles while the others readied their lances.

The Fitherani with spears knew that they could do little more than slow the knights if they chose to charge. The knights knew this was true.

The Fitherani knew that eight or even twelve to one was not enough advantage to defeat the Knights of the Circle – not even in the forest. The knights felt this was true.

The knights knew that for every Fitheran they could see with a spear, three more stood in the darkness with deadly arrows trained on the knights and their chargers. The Fitherani hoped this was true.

No one knew if the knights' armor was proof against Fithern marksmen.

The gold knight held his men silently in check. *If the lights go out, I charge. If they cast another spell, I charge.*

Timbles collected the torches and sat with their dogs a short way behind the knights. They knew that no matter who won the battle it would start a long and ugly war.

A voice came from the darkness behind the spears, "What brings the Knights of the Circle to our forest?"

"We come for our ward, the Brighteyes. We have guarded him against villainy these eleven years, but it is now the third night since his kidnapping."

"Kidnapping is a serious crime, and a serious accusation. In Timbrali, we use the same word for those who steal children in the night and for those who lock them away from friends and family for years on end."

"The Knights of the Circle do not bow to Timbrali law!"

"Neither will Sekri Timbrali surrender Fitherani to be locked away without cause."

"They betrayed us!"

"I meant the Brighteyes!"

The gold knight took a breath and slowed down, "He would have been murdered if he left the fortress. 'Brighteyes' is not some pretty Fithern appellation – it is an Amada death sentence."

"For his life, we are grateful. Sekri Timbrali knows the Knights of the Circle – they will ever stand against the evil that they see. For this reason Fitherani come to aid at the request of the order. It is ever the evil that you do not see – that you will not see – that mars the ways of the order."

The disembodied voice continued, "A Fitheran's freedom is as precious as his life. You who presume to take one are little better than the Kels who would seek the other."

"We do not seek to cage him, or to keep him forever. I say again: he would have died if he had left the fortress."

"He has left the fortress and yet he lives. He will live still, among Fitherani if he chooses, or return to the fortress in Kingstone if that is his desire. Would you take him by force and against his will? Is this the way of the Knights of the Circle?"

"Could I leave a child to danger – one who was in my care? Does a child always know what is best for him?"

"Is it to safety that you bring him? Has he been safe in the fortress? I hear report that it is not so. Yet I will give you leave to talk to him at length and if you abide by his choice we still part as friends."

"When the Amada come, how could you protect him?"

The Fitheran laughed. "Look around you. The Amada will not find the Brighteyes for the same reason you can't find the Amada. He will simply disappear into the crowd."

The Brighteyes looks no more like these quivering miniature spear-holders than I look like an Amada, the gold knight thought.

The voice continued, "How many Amada do you think will even try? They have to leave Kingstone and travel through the forest. They cannot go door to door in Sekri Timbrali looking for him. In Kingstone they know which window is his. Even if they were to succeed here, they would be mad to think that they could evade us long enough to collect their ransom."

"Such madness is not uncommon among the Amada. Is it less mad to seek to penetrate our fortress?" *Still, great industry is quite rare among them.* "The Knights of the Circle will not steal him away from a good home against his will. We will abide his decision if Sekri Timbrali guarantees his safety."

"We guarantee that the risks he takes will be of his own devising, as befits any Fitheran. The Kels' curse will not reach him here."

"I am agreed."

The Fithern King of Sekri Timbrali stepped into the light and solemnly greeted the gold knight. "Welcome, friend."

Timbles waived torches as they cheered and danced.

Chapter 11

A Fitheran Again

Blorfindel reached Sekri Timbrali the following evening. Michido Lightshoe caught up with him again almost as soon as he arrived. It was during Michido's apology that Blorfindel learned what had really happened at Foralis.

"I crept back to town in the morning and found all of the houses burnt. The Kutel were gone, but everyone was dead. Your parents were still together... that's how we found their bodies." For his part, Michido had thought that Blorfindel already knew. His matter-of-fact discussion of the destruction of Foralis left the young Fitheran shocked and numb before Michido realized what was happening. Blorfindel learned that there were only three other survivors from Foralis in Sekri Timbrali: Michido Lightshoe, Jehalli Quickshanks, and Leefoli Showback.

Blorfindel spent the next three weeks wandering in the forest around Sekri Timbrali trying to come to grips with what he had lost. He was used to Tafers dying around him. He had been afraid that his parents did not want to see him again. He had never imagined that they might be dead.

He was assaulted with guilt for all of the things that he never said. *What could I have done? What could I have said? I was a kid. I don't even know what I would say now if I could. I only had a minute. They would rather have me escape in silence, that I know.* For a short while he wondered if his parents would have been ashamed of him for running away. *They wanted me to run away. Father wanted mother to take me to*

Dath. I did what he wanted, the last thing he wanted. He wanted me to escape. I never understood. She wanted him to take me. She wanted him to be there, like Ammoss was, when the Kutel came. I wonder if they ever knew?

Did Ammoss know? He never told me. All those years, maybe I was too young. Maybe I still am. He knew. He tried to follow me. That's what the song was about, after all. He knew I could not go home.

Ammoss and Shandi went to fight the Kutel because of me. That is what mother and father did, too. They did not want to go with me to Dath because they had to stay and fight the Kutel. Is that what I am supposed to do? No one ever told me.

He was confused with the arrangement between the Fithern king and the knights and more surprised that the final decision lay with him. He was not used to being in control of his life. *What do I want? I do not want to go back to Kingstone. I want to go home, but home is gone. This is more like home than the fortress. What will I do, sleep on the streets?*

All three of the other Foralis survivors were very eager to have Blorfindel stay in the Fithern city. They made it clear that they would take care of him. Biolmi himself promised to teach the Brighteyes archery. Blorfindel had no idea what an honor that was.

Jerhalli had another surprise for the youth. "It was your father's. I found it when we returned to Foralis after the burning." He handed Blorfindel a long, light, Fithern sword. "It fell away from the fires so it is still strong." He thought but did not say, *Covered by Lalliam's body as if he wished to preserve it after his death.* "I haven't brought it any honor myself. I guess I was keeping it for you – though I had no idea."

Blorfindel was stunned. "You mean you're giving it to me?"

"It has always been yours. I only wish I had known that when I picked it up. We all thought you were dead. I would never have used it – well, worn it like I might use it – if I had known you were alive to make a claim to it."

Blorfindel took the sword and slashed the air with youthful enthusiasm. The Fitherani around him smiled. Then he took his fencing stance and with his father's sword and his Tafer dagger he went through a quick and precise two-handed fencing exercise on his own. The Fitherani were not expecting that.

"Time has not passed idly by him, as you can see," the gold knight said. The Fitherani were uncomfortable with the ever-present Tafer, but the king had granted him unlimited access to Blorfindel for a full month. For his part, the knight was surprised to find that the Fithern months followed the blue moon and lasted only 27 days. When he had been granted a month he expected a white moon month, at least 32 days. He was rapidly running out of time. *Who would have thought I would be rushed by a Fitheran?*

Biolmi found the Tafer almost intolerable. "Then explain to me how he learned so little archery."

"The Knights of the Circle do not engage in combat from range. We close with our enemies and crush them in the press of battle – a skill that served Ghinlihil well on one occasion, as you may recall."

Only one thing annoyed Biolmi more than when the Tafer used Blorfindel's old name, that was being reminded of how the Amada got past him to attack the Brighteyes.

"Lalliam was a great sword-and-dagger fighter," Michido interjected before Biolmi could insult their guest again.

"And Jilwanis, <u>Blorfindel</u>'s mother, was a great archer – second to Ermingo at Foralis," Jerhalli jumped in, hoping to correct the Tafer and calm Biolmi.

"Then he has a great deal to live up to, and very little time to learn," Biolmi countered. *And this delay is not helping.*

The knight was too curious to be offended, "Very little time? For what? He as a millennium to learn anything he wishes."

"He should see ten centuries and more, it's true, but he must pass his test before he's one hundred seventy-five years old."

It was Leefoli's turn to try to head off an argument. "Surely he will get an exception! He's been a captive since he was in his eighties."

"What if he were to fail – in spite of your expert training?" the knight said without a hint of sarcasm.

"He will be a non-archer. You don't understand, I see." Biolmi was instantly the teacher, "What happens to an aspirant who fails to become a knight?"

"Technically, he can continue to train until he succeeds. Usually they give up and leave the order."

"Then what happens to them?"

The Tafer shrugged, "The world happens to them. Some go back to their families. Most are not welcome. One has even become a Kel, but that was before I was born."

"The stories of non-archers are very similar. The clergy may excuse their acolytes if they wish – most do, and a wizard's apprentice must pass a different kind of test. Exceptions are made for the crippled and feebleminded." Biolmi directed this last sentence at Leefoli.

"So he has fifty years to learn to shoot a bow?"

"Yes, only fifty years left. A very good student might start at eighty and learn to be an archer by one-forty."

Jerhalli jumped in again, "Some pass the test at one-thirty-five."

"Did you?" Biolmi challenged. "I did not."

"No, but Jilwanis did."

Too bad she isn't here to teach him, Biolmi thought to himself.

The knight ignored the Fithern bickering. "Your Fitheressi must test as well?"

"No, and yes: A Fitheresse can be a non-archer. The test is only really important for them if they don't marry."

"So the Brighteyes' parents…" The knight's voice trailed off.

"Were two hundred years married when they died – side by side – defending their home!" Jerhalli was past trying to be peaceful now.

"Of course. What I meant to say is that his parentage was that of a swordsman and an archer – each of some stature. His own size is not diminished for all of his wandering. I might say that among we six I am the only one who is stronger than Ghinlihil."

The Fitherani had been trying to avoid that topic. Even Biolmi, a very fit Fitheran, was a little uncomfortable with the huge Brighteyes.

"Both Lalliam and Jilwanis were quite strong. I recognized them in Blorfindel when I saw him in the forest," Michido told the knight.

Jerhalli confessed, "Jilwanis' bow was too strong for me."

Biolmi was scandalized, "When did you draw her bow?"

"Jilwanis and I shared a set of grandparents. She taught me to shoot. This makes me your closest family, Blorfindel – that I know of, of course."

Michido bowed his head, "There were not many survivors from Foralis."

"…But one more than we thought! Perhaps there are more."

"There will be no more. I am afraid that we abandoned them to their deaths."

Jerhalli was thin-lipped and silent.

The gold knight cleared his throat awkwardly, "You were given the name 'Lightshoe' for this?"

"I took that name, and I deserve it. If there is any worse thing… to flee a battle and then return to see who died for it."

Jerhalli Quickshanks barely whispered, "We don't know. We might not have made a difference."

"Then we should have died beside them!" Michido Lightshoe responded fiercely. Tears were running from six eyes now.

"I wish every aspirant could hear that," the knight said softly with bowed head.

Leefoli Showback turned away, ashamed, "I wish no one had to hear it, ever."

The knight straightened and said, "While evil still lives in the world, we have little choice."

Biolmi surprised himself by agreeing with the Tafer. "If we run, evil catches us. If we hide, it will find us. The Kutel themselves prove this."

The knight continued, "… Build a fortress and evil will lay siege." He nodded while the archer tossed his head.

"But why is there evil?" Blorfindel asked, "Why are there Kutel?"

"The Kutel exist because like flies they breed faster than they die," the knight responded. "It's just that simple."

"But evil is more elusive." Biolmi continued, "Some say that evil exists to contrast good, that there is no good without evil."

"Bah!" the knight exclaimed, "That's just an excuse for those who won't fight, or are evil themselves!"

"But evil will always pop up, even in a good land."

"That's just because it wasn't rooted out completely in the first place. You never hear of good breaking out among the Kutel. If they are two sides to the same coin, then there could be no evil without good."

"Certainly good can come of evil. Even your Amada stab one another in the back."

"There is no good there, only less evil."

"Less evil is more good."

"If you tear a black piece of cloth, it does not become whiter."

"But the light of day can show through the tear."

The knight almost smiled but that would ruin it. "True, when evil tears at itself our fight is easier. We must fight harder then, because we have hope of doing great good then. This is why you are so important to us, Ghinlihil. You gave us the opportunity to really hurt them."

"He has to pass his test! If he isn't ready by 175–" Biolmi took a deep breath. "He must get started soon. The training is hard. The test is his gateway to adulthood, our rite of passage."

Jerhalli snapped his slender fingers, "I've got it! We will show our guest some Fitherani who have not passed, then he will understand. Meanwhile, Biolmi, you can start training without further delay. Send creditors to me, of course."

"Silver is the least of your worries, Jerhalli Quickshanks."

Jerhalli lead the gold knight along with Michido and Leefoli through Sekri Timbrali. Every now and then when a Fitheran passed nearby he would ask him how old he was when he passed his test. Though this was an uncommon and possibly impolite question, they all answered for the benefit of the gold knight.

The Tafer was beginning to wonder if any of the Fitherani of Sekri Timbrali were 'non-archers' when Jerhalli stopped in the market and bought cups of wine for himself and the Tafer. Michido and Leefoli did not stay with them, but went quietly into the alleys behind the merchants' shacks. The knight turned to the sound of a struggle, his hand falling instinctively to his sword hilt. Michido and Leefoli were arguing with another Fitheran in the alley. Jerhalli walked toward them and motioned for the knight to follow.

"We've got you, Jilin Quickhand. You just stand still and don't try any of your tricks," said Michido with dagger in hand.

The other Fitheran drew a pair of cruel-looking knives from concealment and made three quick feints at Michido, who took a step back. Jilin then turned to run away – unknowingly toward Jerhalli and the knight.

After years of fighting the Amada the knight had no difficulty with Jilin Quickhand. He did not shrink or even try to parry when the Fitheran slashed with his knives. Instead, the big Tafer let one of the knives glance harmlessly off his vambrace as his left hand closed around the Fitheran's thin neck. Simultaneously the knight drew his own sword with his right.

Jilin kicked both feet against the knight's chest but could not break the steel grip. "What do you want me for? I didn't do nothin'! You didn't see me do nothin'! We got laws in Sekri Timbrali! You can't just go around… uh…." The Fitheran's gaze stuck on the tip of the Tafer's war-sword. This was not like the knives and daggers of the Timbrali underworld, or even like the light and quick swords favored by Fitheran archers. This was a broad-bladed Tafer sword, heavy enough to crush armor and with a spear-like tip nearly as broad as the Fitheran's hand that looked destined to meet with his own heart. "You'll hang! Every one of you!" his voice was shrill now. "I've got friends, you know!"

Jerhalli was smiling, but he was also careful to stay somewhat behind the heavily armored knight. "Where did you find any friends, Jilin Quickhand? You must have bought them. Do you think your copper friends will stand up against a gold knight?"

"There's–"

"Be silent! If our guest means to kill you, then you're already dead."

Jilin was rapidly coming to the same conclusion. The Tafer was holding him off the ground at arms length with only one hand. Even if the Fitheran could find a flaw in the knight's armor, he could not reach him to exploit it. *Any second now he will stick that sword in – cruel and slow – show me my own guts and watch while I squirm.* An acrid puddle began to form on the ground beneath Jilin. The other Fitherani winced and turned away; ashamed for Jilin and disgusted to be watching this.

The knight's voice was steady and patient as if instructing a slow aspirant, "Drop the knives."

"Let me go! I haven't done nothin' to you!"

"Drop the knives or I will cut your arms off."

Jilin could not have held on much longer anyway. He could hardly breathe and his arms were getting steadily weaker. When the knives hit the ground the Tafer kicked them harmlessly to the side. Then he set Jilin on the ground, but not on his feet: he pushed the feeble Fitheran down until he sat in his own filth.

Jilin began to cry.

The knight withdrew his hand but held his sword point at the wretch's chest. "Who is this creature?"

Michido answered, "We wanted to show you a non-archer. Jilin never passed the test."

"I was cheated! Somebody stole my arrows and I had to borrow some for the test. And they were crooked!"

"All four times?"

"I could a' passed the last time! I know I could a'! And now you're gonna kill me and it wasn't my fault! Lot's o' people fail the first time. It's not my fault!"

The knight wanted to spit. *In Kingstone I would strike him down just to clean the streets of the likes of him.* "If you're trying to tell me that the Brighteyes will become like this… thing… if he fails his test, I do not believe you. He may not be a knight, but he would never sink so low."

"Never is a long time for a Fitheran," Jerhalli said. "How long has it been, Jilin, since you failed your last test?"

"Twenty, twenty-five."

Decades, the knight thought, *Fitherani talk in decades.* "More to the point: how old were you when you started your archery training?"

"Nine" Jilin mumbled.

That wasn't good enough for Jerhalli. "How many <u>years</u>, Jilin. How many <u>years</u> old were you?"

"Ninety-one! I was ninety-one when training started and that's too late! I never had a chance!"

"Ninety-one is too late to start archery training," Michido said. "I bet that's the first time he's told the truth in a century."

"So I'm supposed to believe that every non-archer is like Quickhand here?"

Jerhalli shrugged. "Go back out in the marketplace and ask. Any Fitheran who has any pride in himself will tell you when he passed his test, either for archery, or wizardry, or his religious initiation – every single one."

"Too bad you don't have a sword test."

"And if there was a whining test, Jilin would have passed with special honors."

Jilin looked up at Jerhalli through tear-streaked eyes. "Oh, yeah! Pick on poor Jilin! He can't fight back. Everybody knows he's a non-archer and he don't count! But at least I didn't run away, Jerhalli Quickshanks – run away and leave everyone to die. So just you think before you make fun of Jilin Quickhand!"

The Gold Knight swore in spite of himself, "Anagoth's beard!" *I'm in the presence of four Fitherani: three are cowards and deserters but the worst is the 'non-archer'.* The gold knight stepped in and struck Jilin with the back of his left hand. Four teeth hit the ground before the Fitheran's senseless head. "I've seen enough."

Chapter 12

Afinlia

Blorfindel never saw the knight again. The Brighteyes was used to Tafers who did not say goodbye. Everyone around him simply assumed that Blorfindel would stay in Sekri Timbrali, and stay he did. He started to settle back into the ways of his own people, though his Tafer accent persisted for years.

True to Jerhalli's plan, Blorfindel began training that day. It did not seem like archery training in the beginning, though. Biolmi was in a hurry, but he always started with an appreciation of the wood that made the bows and arrows. Training started in the wild forest outside Sekri Timbrali proper. Most of the information that Biolmi covered Blorfindel had been taught in his youth either by his parents or during his forest walks with Ammoss around Dath. Blorfindel did not tell his new teacher this. Instead, he only half paid attention and just enjoyed the forest. He had not had a peaceful walk in the woods since he was an eighty-seven-year-old child.

Biolmi gauged his student's knowledge quickly. Soon they were going over bows and discussing strings, sighting arrow shafts and discussing where the best fletching feathers could be found on a bird. Then it was target practice. Biolmi had been teaching archery for centuries and he had a lot of tricks to keep his students interested. He needed them all for Blorfindel. The young Fitheran had the attention span of a Tafer. Biolmi caught himself before he said so aloud. *Of course, he has spent the last thirty years without Fithern company.*

Many of their breaks were for fencing practice. Part of being a total archer in Biolmi's mind was to be able to defend one's self when the fighting got too close for arrows. He found Blorfindel to be further along in this regard than he expected. Biolmi had little to teach him about using the sword and dagger and became a sparring partner rather than an instructor. Still, with literally hundreds of years of practice and some actual combat experience Biolmi had a lot to offer Blorfindel in these sessions.

Also in the standard Fithern archer training were language lessons. A Fithern archer needed to be able to speak to the Fithern allies like the Tafers and the Timbles. They also needed to understand the Kutel language for spying, interrogation, and general knowledge of their primary foe. Blorfindel could speak all of these languages already. Rather than helping speed up his archery training this took away one of Biolmi's ploys to keep archery practice from getting too tedious. He taught Blorfindel the Putnu language instead which he had not used himself in many centuries and did not expect Blorfindel really needed. Blorfindel picked up the Kutel-like language very quickly.

Archery, on the other hand, was slow going. Blorfindel was too mechanical. Biolmi told him to "listen to the bow" and "feel the arrow in flight." Blorfindel got so tired of telling him, "I don't understand," that most of the time he would just got through the motions and pretend that he knew what the older Fitheran was talking about. All that did was waste more time before Biolmi realized that he was not getting through.

This was maddening to Biolmi. Days of practice turned into years of frustration and Biolmi began to worry more and more about the coming test deadline. Blorfindel had the physical skills and could be mechanically sound when he concentrated, but he did not get the spiritual aspect of archery. He could not cultivate the art within him. Even when he was hitting bullseyes the young Fitheran shot like a Tafer.

While Biolmi was growing impatient and frustrated, Blorfindel was growing impatient and bored. He did enjoy their fencing sessions and even though Biolmi would not let him use his war hammer – even tried to hide it on him – Blorfindel would hide the heavy weapon near the archery target and continued to do his war hammer exercises when Biolmi was away. Most of the time was spent on archery and archery was turning into the same thing over and over again. Biolmi would tell him to shoot something and he would. Then Biolmi would say try again with feeling. Blorfindel would act like there was some feeling involved the next time and Biolmi would yell at him for making fun of the art of archery or making light of his lessons.

Moving targets in particular were the bane of Blorfindel's archery training. He could only get a hit if the target didn't change speed or direction while the arrow was in the air. He would say that he had no more control of the arrow once it left the bow. Biolmi would say that he lost control because he was not "going with the arrow in his heart." Blorfindel would say that it was not possible and then Biolmi would prove him wrong. These sessions got more and more frustrating as both of them learned that Blorfindel was not getting any better at it.

In spite of this Blorfindel got to go hunting more often than most apprentices. This was not because he was bored, or for any special consideration of him. Instead, he was a popular hunting companion because he could and would carry more than his share of the load. Blorfindel did not mind this. He did not think that it was at all odd. With the troupe and even in the fortress he was used to working much harder than any Fitheran asked of him. He was glad for the distraction; even more so because it got him back out into the wild forest.

It was returning from one of these hunting trips that Blorfindel met Afinlia Softear. He was carrying a field-dressed deer across his shoulders at the lead of his group of four hunters. Biolmi called a rest stop. Blorfindel turned and watched Michido Lightshoe and Allicoli Greenleaf put down the buck that they had on a pole between them and sit with their backs against a tree. Michido massaged his shoulder. Biolmi sat their packs down and sat on one of them. Blorfindel did not set his burden down but leaned his back against a nearby tree, stretching his neck back against the carcass so that he could look up the tree in its autumn colors.

He was watching a bushy gray squirrel busy itself in the branches when suddenly it stopped and looked intently away. A second after the squirrel Blorfindel heard it, too: a couple of soft notes floated on the gentle breeze. For a moment he dreamed that the trees were singing, then the wind changed and stole the tune away. Only half thinking Blorfindel turned and walked toward the sound. His step was light and quiet in spite of the extra weight that he carried. He strained his hearing to try to pick up the tune again. Now the autumn leaves conspired against him, brushing dryly together in the evening breeze. Then the wind stopped for a moment and he picked up the tune again. He closed quickly on the sound, though his feet did not rustle the leaves on the forest floor. Then he stopped and drew a startled breath.

He had found the musician. She was by the bank of a small stream with her back to a tree trunk. He could see only the end of her flute and her left foot around the tree. She was barefoot. He took a step to the left and he could see her calf. Blorfindel could see just the hem of her pale green dress. The yellow embroidery trim burned into his memory as he stared at the curve of her calf and ankle. He realized that he was holding his breath, and he held it still. She played softly but he could hear clearly now. Somehow the forest, the flute and one perfect calf merged in his mind. He was afraid that if he moved it would ruin everything.

"Blorfindel! Where are you? What are you doing? I'm too tired to be chasing you around the forest!" Biolmi's patience suffered from a bit of jealousy when he had to carry next to Blorfindel. After the Brighteyes, he carried the heaviest load of the hunters, but long miles and the ease with which Blorfindel disappeared reminded him that he was a distant second in physical condition. Once upon a time the Fitheressi of Sekri Timbrali stopped to watch when Biolmi Yewstaff walked by. That time had passed, and times like this reminded him of it.

Blorfindel did not respond, except to take cover from the direction of the flautist. The music stopped after Biolmi shouted. When Biolmi moved into view he waived and caught his instructor's eye.

"What are you doing there?" Biolmi was genuinely curious now. Blorfindel did not always understand his instructions, but he was never irrational. When Afinlia stood and looked around the teacher smiled, understanding. "Ah, now I see."

Blorfindel could not see. He was standing behind a smallish fir tree trying not to be seen. He knew that the flautist had moved into the open, but he could not see her clearly through the green needles. He was torn between his curiosity and shyness. He stayed put.

"Who's there? Oh, you've been hunting." Her voice was high but soft, possibly even scared. Blorfindel's heart raced to hear it.

"And you have been playing," Biolmi replied, "I see you've charmed the ear of my apprentice. Fitherani are supposed to be more resistant than that. There must be strong magic in your flute." It was all Biolmi could do to keep from laughing. *Blorfindel has been locked away from Fitheressi for over forty years, after all.*

"Who? I'm sorry, your apprentice? You're not alone?"

Biolmi did laugh at that. "If I were alone, I'd have to be carrying my own game. I'm getting too old for that–" She frowned in disbelief, which was just the reaction Biolmi was hoping for. "–So I have my strong young apprentice, Blorfindel, to carry." Biolmi waved at Blorfindel.

Afinlia took a half step back. "You've been spying on me?" There was as much curiosity as accusation in her voice.

"Not spying, really. You were on the other side of the tree – I mean, I couldn't… see you." Blorfindel fumbled for words. *That is a lie – but I could not really see her, just her foot.* He poked his head out from behind the tree so that he could see her now. She was as perfect as her foot had seemed. Her blonde hair seemed to be wrapped in its own light as it fell carelessly to her shoulders. Her eyes seemed to change from green to blue as he stared. Her simple green dress was both worn and stained from frequent trips to the forest to play, but a cloth belt around her waist accentuated the curves that captivated the young Fitheran. "I… I was listening." He realized that he was staring and looked away. He realized that was stupid and looked back at her. Then he wondered what to do.

"You can see me now," she gestured to herself and then noticed that she was wearing her old 'forest' dress that she never wore around other people. She was instantly embarrassed and tried to smooth the dress and cover its stains at the same time. It was exquisitely awkward. "Why don't you come out?" she said in a very small voice.

"I'm carrying… I mean, we've been hunting and, well…"

"What Blorfindel is trying to say is that he does not want to meet a beautiful and talented Fitheresse looking like he just stepped out of a hunting camp." Biolmi saved him. "Very civilized of him, on the whole. For my part, I am Biolmi Yewstaff. Your mother might know that name, but not you, I suspect."

She did not turn her eyes from Blorfindel. She could see that he was tall. His sweat-soaked blonde hair hung down from under his ugly brown hunting cap. His blue eyes seemed frightened, vulnerable. She could also see the hindquarters of the deer which was still on his shoulders. *He is not even straining. That thing has got to weigh twice as much as I do. He must be strong as a Tafer.* It was a moment before she realized what Biolmi had said. "Do you know my mother?"

Biolmi laughed again, "I don't know. I don't know who she is. You haven't introduced yourself, yet."

"I'm sorry. I don't meet many people in the forest. That's why I come here to play. I am called Afinlia Softear." She curtsied. "And the spy is called Blorfindel?" She smiled.

Blorfindel had been introduced and had introduced himself many times from the stage. This part he could play from memory. He stepped out from behind the tree so that he could be seen. He nearly froze when Afinlia's jaw dropped. *I am still carrying a dead deer. I must look like an idiot.* He could hear the voice of his chorus director in his mind, *"No matter what happens, make it look like you meant it that way."* He shifted the deer carcass to his left shoulder then bowed deeply and with flourish, waiving his cap with his right hand. "Blorfindel Brighteyes, at your service." He resettled the load across his shoulders while straightening up.

Just watching made Biolmi's back ache.

"At my service? I thought you were his apprentice?"

"It's a Tafer expression," Biolmi explained, "like 'may the night wind find you under friendly branches.' People say it without really thinking about it."

"Fitherani don't say 'At your service'?"

Afinlia giggled.

Biolmi said, "Only if they want to sound like a Tafer," which was a scathing indictment of his apprentice's accent. The Fitheresse did not catch it.

Blorfindel avoided that topic quickly, "And I wasn't really spying on you. I was just listening. You play differently than I'm used to. It's nice. The music sounds like it belongs here, you know, in the trees. Where did you learn it?"

"I was just playing. I make it up as I go along. I don't really know many real tunes. That's why I come out here to play: no one has to listen."

"I used to know a Tafer who could make up music as he went. He tried to get someone to write it down for him, but no one was ever quick enough and it never sounded the same afterwards."

Biolmi shook his head. "I had forgotten that you used to be a professional musician." *I wish he paid so much attention to his archery.*

"Really? I mean, how do you do it? I come out here to play for the trees because it's fun. I could never… my parents want me to play for them sometimes but I always get so nervous and make mistakes. It sounds horrible. It's so much easier when no one's listening. You weren't really a musician. You're still an apprentice – uh, not that that's bad or anything. Everyone has got to apprentice… well, all the Fitherani do." *I am babbling. I need to just stop.* "Were you really a musician?" *There, I am done.*

"I sang with a traveling troupe for a while. And danced. I never learned to play an instrument – well, I could beat a tabor a little, just to keep time."

"Oh, sing something for me! I mean, please."

Biolmi had to call a halt, "Not right now. Michido and Allicoli are waiting, and we really should get back before nightfall." Disappointment showed on Afinlia's face as clearly as a painted sign, but Biolmi was unmoved. "Some other time, perhaps."

She leapt at the opening, "Tomorrow then? You're not hunting every day?"

"If he gets done with his training early enough tomorrow he will be free to meet with you. Whether your father wants you to meet with Blorfindel Brighteyes tomorrow evening is another matter entirely. I will not have it said that my apprentice is meeting with young Fitheressi without proper consent."

Afinlia's disappointment was not lost on Blorfindel, and he was not so resistant as the archery master. "So I'll see you here tomorrow night?"

"Evening. You can meet tomorrow <u>evening</u>. <u>If</u> you're done with all of your training exercises <u>and</u> you perform well enough I will agree, provided Afinlia's father agrees. You will, of course, be back by <u>sunset</u> so that you can get ready for work the next day."

Blorfindel deflated. *Have I ever performed well enough for him? Have I ever been done with my exercises before sunset? Why doesn't he just say 'no' and be done with it?* "Maybe somewhere closer to town, so we have a little more time?"

Afinlia, on the other hand, heard 'yes'. *How am I going to get father to let me meet with him?* "We can meet by the split willow on the edge of town – just down the stream. Thank you, Biolmi Goodyew–"

"Yewstaff."

"… uh, sorry. Thank you, Biolmi Yewstaff. I will tell my father this evening. I'm certain he'll agree."

Blorfindel could not help hoping. "I know the old willow. The crack whistles when wind is just right."

"That's the one. I'll see you there tomorrow evening."

"If he gets done in time, and if your father agrees."

Afinlia was not to be deterred, "Right, I'll see you tomorrow," and she smiled.

For Blorfindel there was no arguing with that smile. "Tomorrow. I can hardly wait." He waived goodbye. Then he turned to his teacher, "If I get everything done in time, of course." *Crushk!*

They were nearly to Biolmi's house before Blorfindel began to panic. "I don't know any songs in Timbrali. I mean, I can't just sing anything – it's got to be… I don't know, different."

"I wouldn't worry too much about it if I were you. Her father will never agree to let you meet tomorrow. He'll have to check you out himself first. Fathers are like that." *Oh no! That was a nasty thing to say to a Fitheran who lost his father when he was just a boy.* "It's… well, you'll see. No father ever thinks you're good enough for his little Fitheresse. The best you can do is try not to look too bad when you meet him. Say 'mister' a lot, they like that. Try not to mention that you spent so much time with Tafers, either. Oh, yeah, and invite him to join you. It makes them feel more comfortable, like you're not planning to do anything he wouldn't approve of. They never come – almost never. Hopefully Afinlia will tell him that it was your idea to move the location closer to town. That one will play well. He'd never have let you meet with her alone in the woods, anyway." Biolmi thought but did not say, *You will have to sneak off to do that.* "And for Ilsorma's sake, speak proper Timbrali!"

Blorfindel did not sleep very much that night. He did not eat very well in the morning – at least not compared to usual. Biolmi was hardly surprised to find that his apprentice's mind was on other things when the sun rose and training began. All through the morning the older Fitheran heard Blorfindel rehearsing under his breath as he practiced with his bow and arrows. What surprised him was that it did not seem to diminish his archery at all, so Biolmi let him sing.

Biolmi was doubly surprised when Jaico Silverfingers, Afinlia's father, arrived that afternoon. *She must have him wrapped around her little finger.* He smiled, *Blorfindel is doomed. He's no match for her. Ah well, he has got to get his first broken heart sometime.*

As always, Blorfindel continued to practice when Biolmi entertained. If he had been a little distracted that morning, his practice was absolutely thoughtless now. He was not even paying attention to how well he was shooting when he went to retrieve his arrows. All that he could think about was what to say to <u>her</u> father. He heard them leave the house. He continued to go through the motions of practice. He heard them walk up behind him. *His footfalls are faster and heavier than Biolmi's. I wonder what that means?* He loosed a few more arrows at the swinging pendulum targets. The footsteps stopped a few feet behind him, but they said nothing. *What are they waiting for?* Blorfindel continued shooting. Four more arrows emptied his quiver. He started to take a step to retrieve his arrows.

"That's it!" Biolmi's shout spun the Brighteyes around. Anyone else would have tripped, except, perhaps Biolmi himself. Instead Blorfindel stared at them with legs crossed and one foot pointed in the wrong direction. "Excuse me, Mister Jaico," Biolmi continued excitedly, "But this is a bright dawn!"

Blorfindel was confused. Jaico might have been disappointed with his first impression of the young Fitheran, but he was too confused himself. He had heard that Biolmi was eccentric, as all Fitherani of genius were said to be, but he was unprepared for this outburst. *I did not say that he could meet with Afinlia. I said that I would have to meet him myself first – that is not a 'yes'.* He did not understand Biolmi Yewstaff at all.

"Look! Six in each target! Two of them are good enough to pass the test!"

Blorfindel had not been paying attention himself. He composed his feet and turned to look back at the targets. Biolmi was being stingy with his scoring, as usual, but each target had an arrow in the center. Another arrow was touching the center marker, but Biolmi only scored arrows 'in' when none of it was 'out'. It was by far Blorfindel's best showing ever with the pendulum targets.

"I would have accused him of some trick, but we saw him land more than half of them. He's still got to learn to get them with fewer tries, and from various distances, and in the dark, and on the run, but this is a tall tree he's finally climbed."

Jaico knew from his own test that the pendulum targets were always done in good light, with the archer standing still, and from a fixed distance. He also knew that he had not come here to discuss archery. "Ahem. I have heard that Blorfindel Brighteyes wishes to meet with my daughter this evening… to sing?"

While gaping at the targets Blorfindel forgot his entire prepared speech. "Yes, Mister Jaico Silverfingers, she asked if I could sing for her, if that is all right."

Jaico smiled a little. Afinlia had not told him that it was her idea. "I have done a little looking into your background, Blorfindel Brighteyes. Jehalli Quickshanks has given a lengthy account of you. Still, it takes more than Jehalli's money to impress me, Blorfindel Brighteyes. Afinlia will not be wasting her time on a dell who was raised by Tafers. You'll learn to be a proper Fitheran if you know what's good for you. And if you ever–"

"I was just going to sing to her," Blorfindel said meekly.

To Blorfindel's shock and surprise, Biolmi came to his rescue, "Yes, he's just going to sing to her, Jaico Silverfingers, and before you get defensive about where Blorfindel spent his youth, you might remember that he and Afinlia have already met, when she was all alone in the deep woods, far away your protection. While you're chewing on that, most of his time with Tafers was with the Knights of the Circle who don't consort with Taforam, ever! So she can waste her time down by the cracked willow listening to Blorfindel sing, or she can wait in the woods by the riverbank playing her flute and waiting for the next Fitheran to walk within range. You picked an odd time to start getting protective. At least today you'll know where she is and who she's with! As for me: Blorfindel, after your performance on the pendulums today, you can take the rest of the day off. Jaico, you tell your daughter to take it easy on my apprentice this evening – if he's not fit for work tomorrow I'm going to hold you personally responsible!"

Jaico was not really expecting a threat. He might have been more prepared had it come from the giant young Fitheran. Jaico had heard the story of how the Brighteyes had already killed a Tafer in hand-to-hand combat. He certainly did not expect hostility from the master archer, but Biolmi had a reputation for backing up his threats. Silverfingers did, however, come prepared to bargain. "If it's going to be a music lesson, then you won't mind having a music teacher along. Milia Brightstrings has agreed to accompany Afinlia this evening."

Biolmi stifled a laugh. Milia Brightstrings was a Fitheresse that he knew well. *Afinlia better be careful or Milia will seduce Blorfindel and leave her in the cold. Maybe I should go along as well....* His thoughts were not purely for the benefit of his apprentice.

Blorfindel could not believe his luck. "You mean, you're going to let us meet?"

"With a chaperon, Brighteyes, with a chaperon."

Blorfindel was barely listening, "Thank you, Mister Jaico Silverfingers. Thank you very much."

The evening did center around music. Blorfindel sang, Afinlia played her flute, and Milia was very restrained with her critique. Both Biolmi and Jaico were wrong about her influence on the young couple. She was much more interested in their musical skills and intentions than any other intentions they might have or skills they might be learning. Her honest but restrained enthusiasm had more guiding effect on Afinlia and Blorfindel than a formal chaperon would have.

This turned into a habit for all of them. Jaico Silverfingers would pay the music teacher to be there whenever Blorfindel and Afinlia met. For their part, the young couple would arrange music lessons whenever they could. Milia fully understood why Jaico wanted her there, and why Afinlia did not. Over time she tended to agree with the Fitheresse and found excuses to disappear now and then.

The real restraining factor was Biolmi Yewstaff. Blorfindel could not repeat his performance on the pendulum targets the next day, or any day that month. The longer he went without a music lesson, the harder he worked to get free. Biolmi knew that Blorfindel was pushing too hard, but he could not get him to relax and just shoot naturally. "Just relax. Let your life flow through the bow staff, through the string, to the arrow, to the target." Biolmi said it so often he could almost sing it himself. He had never had a student show so much difficulty with this lesson. Blorfindel would just try harder and tighten up more. Then his aim would get worse and he got more frustrated. When his apprentice grew so frustrated that he broke an arrow shaft just drawing the string Biolmi decided he had to give in or give up.

Biolmi performed an emotional balancing act with Blorfindel. He used Afinlia to motivate him to work harder and to distract him when he worked too hard. He always said that Blorfindel had earned it, but Biolmi was more likely to let him go when he was working hard but doing poorly. When he was daydreaming about Afinlia, Blorfindel could relax and shoot on feeling. When he was trying to get free to see her again he would work harder than he had ever done in his life.

Biolmi was just allowing himself to hope again when Blorfindel brought home the cittern. It was a well worn – indeed, beat-up – old instrument with slightly frayed strings that would fall out of tune with the slightest change in the air. The sound box was both scratched and stained with wine. There was evidence of some silver inlay which was now nearly completely worn off. This cittern had the distinct look that it had been used as a weapon at least once. Its condition, however, was not what bothered the archery master. "What on Frenlias' beautiful world do you think you're going to do with <u>that</u>?"

"Milia loaned it to me. She said that since I have big hands and nimble fingers, I should learn to play."

"Did she? Did she tell you <u>when</u> you were going to get time to practice with it?"

"Well, the days are getting short, so I should have more time after sunset."

"You've got to be joking! Milia, at least, should know better. You have to be able to shoot just as well when the sun is below the ground as when it's high overhead. What if an attack comes after dark and in the driving rain? Did we take last winter off? Or the winter before? Raise the trees! You've got thirty-one years left to pass the test." Biolmi held his hands with three fingers on the left and one on the right waiving in the air, "Thirty-one!"

"But Milia said it would only take a few minutes a day, and Afinlia–"

"Afinlia! Do you know what happens to Afinlia if you don't pass the test? You'll never see her again, and if you do somehow find her she won't speak to you anyway – she'll be forbidden. If an archer comes to court Afinlia tomorrow do you think Jaico Silverfingers will wait for you? You're gone without a thought," Biolmi snapped his fingers for emphasis. "Raiden! he's probably paying for these music lessons just to make certain that you don't pass the test. All he has to do is wait and let you fail, then he doesn't have to face his daughter and explain why he doesn't like you! He can just say 'Blorfindel's a failure, now go marry some rich old dry root,' and that's that!"

"You think he'd–"

"Thorns and blood! Do you think there's one ounce of passion left in Silverfingers? He's been dead for a century, just nobody told him so he keeps walking around. Look, he cares about things that jingle, sparkle, and shine – that's all that matters to him. The only hope you have with his daughter is to pass your test and get your cousin, Jerhali, to teach you how to make a whole lot of money. Until then you're just a way for Jaico to get Afinlia to stop whining at him because he isn't tough enough to say 'no' to her."

Blorfindel looked pathetically down at the battered cittern.

Biolmi softened just slightly, "I don't give two dry leaves in the autumn wind what you do with that thing: play it, burn it, break it over Milia's head for being such a fool. Understand this: you have no chance with Afinlia, or any other respectable Fitheresse, until you pass your test. If you reach seventeen and a half and you haven't passed the test, you can just forget about all of it. You can go play your cittern for Tafers somewhere and live in your own private hell for a millennium. Maybe I'll learn to play the harp and become Biolmi Longface, since I'll be too ashamed to stay in Sekri Timbrali and take on apprentices.

"You're it, Blorfindel Brighteyes. You're the only son of Lalliam Steelhand and Jilwanis Sharpeye. You're the only son of Foralis with any shred of honor left. For millennia now some Fitherani – Fitherani like Silverfingers – have been saying that we should all retreat to our safe cities: Sekri Timbrali and Sekri Tao – if the Tafers haven't swallowed that up yet. They said Foralis was a mistake, and more and more Fitherani are agreeing with them.

"You can give up, and run away, and prove them all right. You can pass your test, settle down, and show them that a good Fitheran can be born in a place like Foralis. Or you can do one better. You can take it to them – take it to the Kutel that murdered your parents and stole your childhood. You can show the Tafers that they can't bully the Fitherani and teach them the respect that you never got. You can prove to the puffed-up Fithern cowards like Silverfingers that a real Fitheran can fight the world, and win."

Blorfindel looked up from the cittern to his master's eyes. He was shocked to see tears flowing freely. When the Brighteyes started crying himself, he did not really understand why.

"We're dying out, Blorfindel Brighteyes. Fitherani like Lalliam Steelhand, Ermingo Coldheart, and Biolmi Yewstaff – and yes, like you, I think – we're dying out. Jaico Silverfingers thinks that's a good thing. We scare him. He doesn't understand that once we're gone there will be no one left to save him and his strong box when the Kutel come, or the Tafers. They already think we're weak, you know – the Tafers. The Kutel just hate us, always have, always will. They're both afraid of our arrows. That's all we have to stop them, Fithern arrows and maybe the legend of Fithern magic, though I haven't seen any battlefield magic for many centuries. The test is important, not just for you but for all of Sekri Timbrali.

"That's why I do this, you know? I don't need the money. Normally, I'd take on six or eight apprentices at a time to keep the ranks filled with some talent. I left a class – sent them off to different masters – so I could go to Kingstone and meet you. When we came back I knew it would be hard to get you ready in time. I didn't know if I could do it, but I knew no one else could, so I tried.

"But this is it. If you fail, I fail too. I am the toughest archery master in Sekri Timbrali. The only reason Fitherani let me put their children through this is because I get results. All of the best archers of Sekri Timbrali were once my students. If you don't pass your test, the legend of Biolmi Yewstaff is over."

Blorfindel's voice was a cracked croak, "What will you do?"

"What? I'll go back out into the world and do it myself. Take it to the Kutel, show the Tafers, prove to Jaico Silverfingers what it means to be a Fitheran. I've done it before. I thought I could make a bigger difference by teaching. I knew that I couldn't breed a hundred of us, but maybe I could teach a hundred.

"We haven't failed, Blorfindel. We still have thirty-one years. Then it's really up to you. If you want to be a rich merchant like Jerhali, marry some proud Fitheresse – Afinlia or whoever holds your heart at the time – and play the cittern and raise little ones that's no disgrace, and no harm done either."

"I want to pass." Blorfindel voice was so clear and loud that he surprised himself. "I don't understand, Biolmi. I'm sorry, but I don't. I don't understand what you mean about a 'real Fitheran,' and I don't understand what I'm doing wrong all the time. I'm trying. I really am. It's like I'm bound to fail. When I was with the troupe I was too clumsy for acrobatics. At the Fortress I learned too slow with my weapons training and all. Now I can't learn to be an archer. I'll probably never play the cittern either." He dropped the cittern noisily on the floor. "Even when I was a kid I was always in the way. The last time that I was with my parents they were fighting – and it was my fault. Now I'm ruining your life, too."

Biolmi tried to laugh, "You're a tough Fitheran, Blorfindel Brighteyes, but you've got a lot of work to do before you're tough enough to ruin my life." He took a deep breath and wiped his face on his broad sleeve. "I don't know everything about you – about what happened or when you might have failed. I do know that you're not a failure. You learned enough to survive in that troupe, to be a musician – at least well enough to con Milia out of a cittern. You couldn't be an acrobat? You could be now, I guarantee it. I've seen squirrels clumsier than you are. You didn't learn your weapons fast enough? I've never had an apprentice so skilled with a sword and dagger. Children get underfoot. Parents fight. It's not about you. You're a survivor. You've succeeded where it counts. Do you know how many Fitherani could have done what you've done? When you told me your story I was amazed that you were still alive – that you hadn't lost your mind and tried to become a Tafer. When the assassin came to get you, you fought back – and won! He had every advantage but he's gone and you're still here. You can still pass the test. You can take your life back. You'll probably learn how to play that stupid cittern, too!"

This time Biolmi really did laugh. They both laughed. They needed it.

Blorfindel went back to work. He understood that everything he wanted now was on the other side of passing his archery test. He still met with Afinlia as often as he could. He practiced with the cittern for one candle's length every night, though some nights it seemed that it took that long to tune it. He still practiced with his father's sword and his Tafer dagger, and even snuck away to drill with the war hammer when he could. Before, after and in-between, however, he practiced his archery.

He practiced in daylight. He practiced at night. He practiced with stationary targets. He practiced with the pendulum targets. He practiced combining archery and stealth by hunting any time he could. He practiced with light arrows and heavy. He practiced in calm, in wind, and in rain. One year it even snowed in Sekri Timbrali, and while all the other Fitherani were admiring the pretty flakes Blorfindel practiced his archery.

Still, as the years flew by the icy knot in Biolmi's stomach grew tighter. Blorfindel was getting better, certainly, but not great. He really thought that Blorfindel could be great. He still had a problem with the pendulum targets. Only one time in three could he shoot well enough to pass that part of the test. It was even worse when he was nervous or trying too hard, and Biolmi knew he would be nervous and trying too hard during the real test. They were down to just five years and Biolmi had a lot more to teach before the test. *If he had started at eighty-five, he would be doing just fine. His progress is good. He is not slow. He just got started too late.*

Then it happened: Afinlia had a new suitor.

It was very rare that Afinlia could not join Blorfindel when he got free. In fact, she only did it to toy with him from time to time. This time, however, Milia met Blorfindel by the split willow, half of which had fallen into the river only a month earlier. "Afinlia can't come today. She's busy. Her father said that something came up." He had actually told Milia that she would not be required for this evening, maybe not for some time. The music teacher felt that she should tell Blorfindel herself rather than just leave him standing there.

"Something came up? Is she all right?"

"She's fine – well no, not really fine. She'd rather be here, I'm sure, but she's not sick or anything."

"I can probably get free in two weeks. Do you think she can be here then?"

"Ah, no. No, I don't think so."

"Then when?"

Then she told him. There was another Fitheran. He was older, well-established, an archer, of course, but not a musician. "I'm sure she would rather be here with you. I know it. It's just that Jaico likes this guy, and she's Jaico's daughter. You'll see, Afinlia has her ways with her father. She'll be back. He's a stiff. I mean, he's probably a nice Fitheran and all, but no style. She'll be back as soon as she can get rid of him."

Blorfindel was not listening. His world came crashing down around him. He could not even remember his rival's name. He did not remember saying goodbye to Milia. He turned and shuffled towards home.

Milia really liked Afinlia and Blorfindel. In her romantic heart she wanted Afinlia and Blorfindel to fall in love and stay together. She wanted to watch a real love story unfold. *Afinlia is a princess who needs a hero and he is so heroic with his gallant sword and his powerful strut.* Milia always felt very small around the Brighteyes. She was a petite Fitheresse and nearly a foot and a half shorter than Blorfindel. She had to look up to check his fingering when he played the cittern. Now, as he was walking away he looked crumpled and broken. She wanted to run after him and give him a hug or something. Instead she stood there shouting encouragement.

Chapter 13

The Test

Blorfindel did not go straight home. On the way Biolmi's voice echoed in his mind, *If an archer comes to court Afinlia tomorrow do you think Jaico Silverfingers will wait for you? The only hope you have with his daughter is to pass your test.* He took a detour into the heart of the city. Many Fitherani would have advised him not go downtown alone, but Sekri Timbrali had no evils to frighten Blorfindel Brighteyes. Today, they could not even penetrate his mood. The non-archers in the back alleys wanted no part of the giant with sword and cittern – both of which looked like they had seen more hand-to-hand combat than the street toughs were ready for.

Blorfindel was not looking for trouble, however. He was looking for, and found, the militia registrar. "I need to schedule my archery test."

"Your master is supposed to put you on the list. <Sigh> Who's your master?"

"Biolmi Yewstaff."

The registrar stopped and looked up. "You're that Brighteyes? Blorfindel, right?"

Blorfindel looked darkly with a mix of emotions that even he could not define. "That's right. Do you want to try to collect the bounty?"

"Hey, relax. We're all friends here. There's just a bet in the office, you know? Some people didn't think you would make it. Just so you know, my copper's on you. They say Biolmi's the best there is. He's probably told you the test for this year is in three weeks. Biolmi's students are never late, but the judges are not obliged to wait for you if you can't be there on time. I'll just put your name down and you're on the list. I'm not on the staff this year, so I won't see you there. Good luck, and don't worry, if Biolmi says you're ready, you are ready."

"Thanks… um, really, thank you."

Biolmi was surprised to see Blorfindel back so soon. There was still an hour of daylight left and he was much more likely to be late than early. The younger Fitheran's heartache and nervousness were easy for Biolmi to read. "Big fight?"

"What?"

"Oh, you're back early. I just wondered if you had a lover's spat or something."

"She wasn't there."

"You waited a long time for her, then. At least you're learning patience."

"Milia told me she wasn't coming." Blorfindel braced himself.

"Then what took you so long?" Biolmi was genuinely curious. *Did he really stay for a music lesson?*

"I put myself on the list for my archery test."

Biolmi did not explode as Blorfindel expected. A number of his apprentices had done this in the past. It was the price he paid for not putting them on the list himself: the registrars could not know if an apprentice was lying. "You'll fail, you know. You're not ready."

"I have to be." Blorfindel poured out his story in one jumbled mess. "So if I don't pass, I'll lose her."

"If you lose her that easily… Never mind. The test is in three weeks. Think of this as a practice run. You're not ready and I can't make you ready in three weeks. I don't think we can do it in three years. You won't pass. Just accept that and you have a chance of learning something. Maybe you won't be so nervous when your time comes."

"I will be ready."

Biolmi did not bother to argue. "Don't worry about the Fitheresse. If you've got a chance, she'll come back. If not, well, you had some fun. You learned a few things, too. This happens, you know? After three or four times you start to get used to it."

Blorfindel, of course, was not listening.

For the next three weeks the days flew and the nights crawled. Biolmi did not bother to try to teach anything new; they just went over the basics.

The day before the test they did not even shoot. Instead, Biolmi had Blorfindel check all of his equipment, especially his arrows, for the test.

"Are you certain you don't want more arrows that that?"

"I don't want them to rattle during the stealth test."

"You can take an extra quiver and put it down before making your approach."

"I always lose them when I do that. It would be too embarrassing during the test."

"It's up to you. It is possible to complete the test with what you've got." *And next time you will know better.* "At least swap out the one with the odd fletchings. You want to have a matched set if you can."

"Oh, right, good idea."

The morning of the test was bright and sunny with a very light breeze. Biolmi watched as Blorfindel checked his gear. "At least the weather will be easy."

Blorfindel started out without a word then stopped after a few strides. "Aren't you coming?"

"You got into this alone. You can get through it alone, too. Just try to remember where your problems are so we can work on them later." *His problem is the pendulums. He will never get past that test, anyway.* "Oh, and the judges are likely to be the same Fitherani next time, so be nice to them, even when you fail."

Blorfindel spent the whole walk to the testing grounds telling himself, "I will not fail."

There were seven other Fitherani testing with Blorfindel. All of them were younger than he was. After forty-five years in Sekri Timbrali he was used to being taller than those around him, still he felt out of place and uncomfortable. The others were friendly, though they were all nervous.

The judges were used to that. "I am called Lalegdo Gingerhair." He was somewhat taller than average height and very sensible-looking. He had a smile which he hoped was reassuring. "I will be leading the testing today. First, let me tell you, that if you do anything that I consider to be unsafe – either to yourself, another apprentice, or any of the staff, you fail immediately and I will send you home, if you're lucky. Does everyone understand?"

Blorfindel was the first to say, "Yes, judge!" All of the others had less demanding teachers and were not used to the call and response. They followed suit in their own ragged fashion.

The judges just smiled. "Linchia Faircandle and Eresi Silkenrobe will be your other judges today." Linchia was a Fitheresse, which surprised Blorfindel. Eresi looked striking with his red silk robe shining in the sunlight. "If there are any scores in question we will decide. We do not need to hear you arguing your case. The rules are quite clear and we know them better than you do. Do you understand?"

Two more voices joined Blorfindel. "Yes, judge!" The others followed.

Lalegdo Gingerhair continued: "All archery judges have sworn an oath to administer the test fairly and correctly. All three of us really want you all to pass. Try to relax, and if it doesn't work out for you there is always next year." He tried not to be seen to cock an eyebrow at Blorfindel.

"The first test is the stationary target. Each contestant will loose two arrows from fifty yards. Then we will all move back and each contestant will loose two arrows from one hundred yards. We will then move back again, as a group, to one hundred fifty yards for your final two arrows. You will each have your own target. All targets are the same, there are no good or bad lanes. Lanes are assigned in the order that you appear on the roster." He walked over to one of the targets and slapped the three-inch diameter black dot in the center. "This is the bulls-eye. The other rings on the target are just traditional and do not count for this test. You must put five of your six arrows in the bulls-eye. It does not matter what range they come from, you are allowed only one miss. If you have clearly missed twice, you may go, or continue to watch the rest of the test. If there is any question, please continue shooting normally throughout the test. I will not stop the other contestants to check for you. Do not ask. Do you understand?"

"Yes, judge!" All of the young Fitherani had heard the rules before.

"Then let us take our positions at the fifty yard mark."

Blorfindel was somewhat surprised to see that the shooting ranges were exactly marked. Biolmi had made him move his shooting points and angles every day when he practiced on the stationary target. He had expected the ranges to be approximate, possibly minimums. These lanes had obviously been used many times in the past and were well worn. There were twenty lanes so the last twelve would be empty. Blorfindel found that when they called the names he was last.

Linchia stood in the lane next to him to watch. "You're Biolmi's apprentice, right? We can always tell. Yes, this is exactly fifty yards. Yes, we use the same lanes every time. And yes, we know you're here without his permission." She smiled. "He always comes if it's for real. Don't worry: you got on the list so if you pass the tests today it still counts." She paused to let them all shoot their first two arrows. There were no misses. "If I were you, even if I passed today, I'd go back to Biolmi and finish up. There is a big difference between 'good enough' and 'the best you can be'." They backed up to one hundred yards. Each contestant shot two arrows. There were some that the judges were going to have to check, but none clearly out. They backed up to one hundred and fifty and loosed the last two. "Oh, and the <u>official</u> rules say that any hit is in, even if it is just touching the bulls-eye. Biolmi just likes to be the hard knot."

None of Blorfindel's arrows were clearly out. Four arrows from other contestants were, from the farthest range, but no two from one contestant. They all had to wait for the official decision from the judges. The contestants were silent, hardly breathing as they waited for the call.

The judges moved from one target to the next as a group. Blorfindel's target was last. In the stillness he could hear them debating.

"These two are out."

"What are you looking at? That one is almost completely in and the other one is touching the bulls-eye." Blorfindel recognized Linchia's voice.

"That one, I might debate, but it is not important – the others are clearly in. He passed."

"He is Biolmi Yewstaff's apprentice. Biolmi does not count halves. He would call them out."

"Biolmi Yewstaff is not a judge here today. He has not ever been a judge that I know of. The rules say this is in, so it's in. Do you agree?" From the gestures Lalegdo was speaking. Blorfindel could see that Linchia agreed.

Lalegdo Gingerhair waived to the attendants. The attendants, in turn told the contestants to approach the targets, but leave their bows.

Blorfindel found himself eyeing Eresi Silkenrobe carefully as he walked to the target. The flamboyant judge seemed to notice but said nothing. Blorfindel could hear Biolmi's voice, *Be nice to them.* He tried to concentrate on his arrows.

When all of the contestants were close enough that he did not have to shout, Lalegdo announced, "You have all passed the first test."

All the contestants exhaled at once. The few spectators applauded.

As Blorfindel recovered his arrows he realized that the judge had been correct. Two of his arrows were touching both in and out of the bulls-eye. Biolmi would have failed him right here, and this was not the test that he was worried about.

"The next test will be the pendulum targets." The contestants looked surprised. "I know, the stealth test usually comes second, but the rules say I can change the order if I want to, and you may get some more clouds later." Lalegdo smiled that smile again. Some of the spectators applauded. All but one of the contestants smiled. Blorfindel had been hoping to have the other two tests put away before he had to shoot the pendulums.

"The pendulum targets are moving targets. You may loose six arrows. At least one must hit the bulls-eye on each pendulum before the targets disappear behind their trees. It does not matter how many bulls-eyes you score, but you must have one in each − not two in one. Do you understand?"

"Yes, judge!"

The judges walked the contestants over to the pendulum targets. Blorfindel noticed immediately that they were different from Biolmi's. The targets themselves were smaller, but the bulls-eyes looked larger. They were also attached to wooden pendulums. Biolmi's were on weighted ropes and tended to spin.

Lalegdo continued: "These four trees close the shooting lanes. If any of your arrows goes outside these four trees it will be considered unsafe and you are disqualified. I must stress this again, two staff members will be downrange to set and release the targets. This is very serious, Fitherani have been injured. That will not happen today, but if it does you are responsible for the harm your arrows do. Is that clear?"

"Yes, judge!" Again, everyone knew how it worked. The pendulums were hung from the two outermost trees, in the back. The judges did not need to make a judgment call on whether the pendulum stopped moving, because when they stopped moving they would be behind the trees. Less than half a yard separated the middle two trees, which were at the maximum distance the pendulums would swing in and in front of their path, so at the top of their arc − when they were the easiest to hit − on the first swing the pendulums would be concealed behind the inner trees. In general, each target was only visible for six or seven swings so the archers had to start early if they expected to get all six arrows off before the targets stopped. Biolmi's training targets had hooks that held them in place at the middle two trees. Blorfindel would pull a rope to release the hooks and start the swinging, or Biolmi would do it for him. Here two Fitherani stood on stumps to the outside of the shooting lanes. At a sign from a judge they were to release their pendulum from the designated height, which was marked by a pole in the ground. From where he waited Blorfindel saw that it was Eresi, not Lalegdo, who gave the go sign. The judges stood behind the contestants during the shooting. Contestants were allowed to shoot at any time during their turn.

Since he was last on the roster, Blorfindel had to watch nervously as the other contestants each took their turn. He noticed that the boards that had been put up to shield the staff members down range were somewhat short. They had to duck after their release in order to get behind them. From this range he was not certain that the boards were sturdy enough to stop an arrow completely, anyway, but a tester would have to miss very badly indeed to put them at risk.

Blorfindel watched one of the other contestants fail out. He hit the targets, but only one bulls-eye. The other contestants rallied around him, though Blorfindel was too nervous to say much. Someone from the audience shouted, "Don't feel badly about it, Damachil! No one passes the test at thirteen and a half!"

When Blorfindel's turn came at last he knocked his first arrow before he stepped up and drew as soon as he was at the line. Instead of letting the targets drop, as they had for all the others, this time helpers threw them and ducked quickly down. This made their flight more erratic, as Blorfindel immediately saw. It also meant that they would go farther than they were supposed to, past the inner trees. Blorfindel held his shot, hoping to get an easy early hit. The targets not only came past the inner trees, but they were going to collide. Blorfindel loosed his arrow. In their irregular paths, the targets passed each other. Blorfindel's arrow struck. All onlookers were stunned. Blorfindel's bow – with a much heavier pull than most contestants – put the arrow well through the left target and pinned the right one to it.

Blorfindel drew his second arrow while the targets settled.

Someone shouted, but Blorfindel was not paying attention.

He loosed his second arrow at the left target, then drew his third. The arrow was a clear bulls-eye on the now-stationary target. Again he waited for the targets to settle.

He could hear Lalegdo behind him. "This is most irregular."

Eresi said, "Let him finish the round. The rules say he has to hit both bulls-eyes. They don't say he can't pin the targets together."

"They don't say that because it's not supposed to be possible!" Lelegdo countered.

Linchia said, "The second bulls-eye is stuck behind the first target now. How is he supposed to hit it?"

"Then perhaps he should not have pinned them together," Eresi said.

"He should not have pinned them together because they should never have been that close! You hired these Fitherani. Didn't you explain to them how it's done?" Lalegdo was fighting to keep his voice under control.

Eresi said, "Good help is hard to find. Now please, we're not supposed to distract him during his round."

The targets had settled. Blorfindel loosed his third arrow. It hit well to the right of the bulls-eye on the exposed target. Once again he drew an arrow and waited for the targets to settle. The crowd was whispering feverishly, as were the other contestants, but the judges remained silent. Blorfindel loosed his fourth arrow. Twice more he waited for the target, twice more he loosed an arrow. The final three arrows formed a neat triangle, each two inches away from the third.

Eresi remarked at the end of the round, "If he can't do any better than that, perhaps he doesn't deserve to pass anyway."

Blorfindel stiffened but continued to stare at the targets.

"That was uncalled for," Linchia rebuked.

"I'm not so sure..." Lalegdo was walking toward the targets.

"He's not supposed to deride the contestants!"

Lalegdo was looking intently at the targets now, "That's not what I meant. Come and see."

"See what? Five out of six arrows are clearly out," Eresi was walking downrange nonetheless. Linchia followed silently. Many of the spectators also went to see what the judge was talking about. They could all see that only one of Blorfindel's arrows hit the bulls-eye. The other five were all to the right.

Lalegdo was standing directly under the targets now. "I think we can all agree that one of Blorfindel's arrows has pierced the bulls-eye on the left target."

"Yes, yes, but he has to hit both! You know that."

"He never had a chance from the start. He should get another attempt to do this properly."

Lalegdo turned to the Fitheresse. "I am sorry, but you are mistaken. What happened here is irregular, and should never have happened, but it does not change the rules. I will register a complaint, of course," – he looked pointedly at Eresi – "but the rules state that he must put at least one arrow into the bulls-eye of each target."

Eresi continued for him, "Which he clearly has not done, so he fails."

Lalegdo transfixed the flamboyant judge with his gaze, "Again, you are mistaken. Blorfindel Brighteyes has put two arrows into the bulls-eye of the right target. Come and see." He pointed up without releasing Eresi from his gaze.

It was true. The spectators saw it, too, and awe turned into inspired applause. None of the other contestants' bows were strong enough, but each of Blorfindel's arrows had passed through the first target and into the second. He had to guess where the bulls-eye was but by judging from what he could see and his spread pattern he took his chances. He had two undeniable hits.

"That can't count! He was shooting at the other target."

Linchia smiled and replied with artificial innocence, "The rules don't say anything about that. I suppose he could shoot through the trees if his bow was strong enough." She lowered her voice, "I don't know how much you stand to lose if he passes today, but we're not going to let you cheat him, either. You'll never judge archery again, I promise you that."

Eresi smiled and waived. Many of the spectators heard it all.

Lalegdo spoke up for all to hear, "The judges have decided, there are hits on both bulls-eyes. Blorfindel has passed, and very well done to all of our contestants." The crowd cheered again.

"After that bit of excitement, I think we'd better go directly to the stealth test." Lalegdo whispered to Eresi, "You'd better hope that he wants to be an archer more than he wants revenge, because you make a beautiful target in that red robe. You know he's already killed a Tafer."

Eresi swallowed hard, but said nothing.

The judges moved the group to a large circle of the forest roped off for the stealth round.

"This is the stealth test. In the center of the circle is a single, blue-painted stump. If there is any question in your mind whether you are looking at the right target, you are wrong. It has been freshly repainted this morning and it is unmistakable. Each contestant gets only one arrow for this test. That arrow must strike the stump before any of the judges detect the contestant within the circle. We will be moving around. We will be looking for you. We have all done this before – we're better at it than you think." There was some laughter from the spectators. "The rules do not state that you must shoot from any particular range. You may loose your arrow whenever you are ready, but remember you get only one arrow. At the beginning of each round each judge will begin at their particular station. It is not possible to see the starting area from any of our stations, so we can not watch you enter. Does everyone understand?"

"Yes, judge!"

"Now, all three judges will be out there. If you think that you have a hope of ever becoming an archer after wounding a judge, think again. Be very careful what you shoot at. None of us is wearing blue. I am in white, Linchia Faircandle is in gold and white, and Eresi Silkenrobe is, of course, in red. Do any of us look blue to you?

"No, judge!"

"Good! Now all spectators and waiting contestants will remain here, behind the orange wall. Does that orange wall look blue to anyone?"

"No, judge!"

Some of the spectators laughed, but Lalegdo looked deadly serious. He made certain that everyone was completely behind the wall before continuing. "Now, I know that you all want to see what is going on. Do not attempt to watch this event. First, it is unsafe to do so. Second, if the contestant is good enough there won't be anything to see, anyway. Third, if you did watch a contestant you might lead a judge's eyes to that contestant, and that would not be fair to the contestant, now would it? Normally, I would have our two helpers make certain that you stay behind the orange wall, but since they have proven themselves incapable of simple tasks I don't want them anywhere near this event and I have sent them home." Eresi looked surprised to hear that. "I will take your word that you will not attempt to watch this event. Now, will you stay behind the orange wall?"

Even the spectators said, "Yes, judge!"

Again the contestants had to wait their turn, and Blorfindel was last. For the most part the contestants spoke quietly to one another about the event. There were a number of important skills for the event. Stealth, of course, was key. The sun was bright, the wind was low, and there were only a few puffy white clouds. It was perfect weather for the other events, which meant it was dreadful for stealth. There were tactics to be discussed, though they had all been over this thoroughly in advance. How to find the target without being detected? Do you take a long shot and chance a miss or try to get close and risk detection? Most candidates favored the long shot today, but out here the contestants would have to find their own shooting lanes and an odd branch could easily ruin their only shot. To creep or dash? Almost everyone said creep. Can you help yourself by throwing a stick to make a distraction? It was a high risk ploy, only to be used in desperation.

One by one the contestants entered. After their turn they were kept away from the rest so they could not pass any information. With each contestant a group of spectators shifted from the "before" to the "after" staging area. When his turn came Blorfindel was completely alone. Time seemed to crawl. He rechecked that the rag he had stuffed into his quiver prevented any rattles. He already had his one arrow out.

At the starting whistle Blorfindel made a dash, not toward the center but along the left edge to the first piece of cover that he had picked – a double-trunked maple tree. *I will be exposed for a long time, but the judges probably will not close fast enough to see it. I will be clear of the entrance when I begin.*

He was in position behind the maple when he heard the first judge. He did not look. *It must be Eresi. The footfalls are too heavy for Linchia, anyway, and it sounds like a robe. He would be the one to save his energy with the other contestants and sprint after me, anyway.* The sound was heading for the orange wall. *You think that I started creeping from the start. Too bad I can not disqualify a judge by pointing him out.*

Blorfindel made another dash to the next piece of cover – a large pine this time. If Eresi had stopped and turned around he would have seen him clearly, but he was running for the wall. *You are too late, but where are the other two?*

Blorfindel smiled and made another dash into a thick bush. Getting in silently was difficult, but it would be nearly impossible for the judges to see him. He waited. *Of course, getting out of here could be tricky as well.* He drew his dagger and began cutting branches and leaves. Part of them he made into a sort of a door for his exit, the others he wove into his clothing. *Look at me. I am a bush.*

The faint breeze brought him a scent. *Candle wax and vanilla bean? Linchia Faircandle, how close are you?* He moved slowly to avoid drawing attention, first sheathing his dagger so that the bright blade did not give him away. Then he turned his head, ever so slowly. There she was: fifteen feet away and looking in the wrong direction.

He heard Eresi return. Linchia turned to face the other judge but they did not speak. They exchanged hand signals. *You have no idea where I am, and now I know where two of you are. You think you are hunting me? I am hunting you.*

Linchia held her position perilously close to Blorfindel as Eresi maneuvered again, but came no closer. *If the wind shifts, can she smell me? She should smell the fresh cut bush by now. Too much vanilla for you, Linchia.*

Eresi stopped. Now Blorfindel could see him from the corner of his eye. He was gesturing again, but not to Linchia. *That is Lalegdo, then – unless Eresi has hired spies. No, it must be Lalegdo. How far away?*

Eresi gestured again. *He has found a footprint, too late.* Linchia moved to examine it herself. *She's quiet. I should have heard that. Even so, it is a mistake for them to be so close together. Where is Lalegdo? I can get by him if I can find him. He must be within sight of the target! He's keeping watch there while they sweep.* Blorfindel looked around for more cover. He found another bush of the same type. This time he kept low. Linchia and Eresi were on the other side of the bush he left. *Now, if I just keep something between me and the center, Lalegdo will be covered.* He was behind the new bush in a minute or two.

That is it! That is the target. Blorfindel could see a flash of bright blue in the distance. *No, it is a bird. That is not the right direction anyway.* He looked back at the judges. They had spread apart, but they were much farther away now. They signaled again. Rather than try to read what they meant, Blorfindel watched for Lalegdo's response. *That shadow! That is not the wind. He is on the other side of that oak. I have you all, now!*

Lalegdo can see the target. What can he see from there that I cannot from here? Wait! He can see the target, but he can also see the best shooting points around the target. That is what he is looking for. He does not even have to see the target. He checked the other way. Eresi was at the first maple looking down at footprints. Linchia was looking the wrong way.

Blorfindel broke cover again. This time he covered more ground than even on his first sprint. He kept good cover between him and the judges and he was not worried about being spotted. *So long as they do not hear me, they will never see me.*

Three minutes later he was breathing heavily but noiselessly. He had traveled three quarters of the way around the roped off area. Now both Linchia and Eresi were looking in the wrong place and Lalegdo was looking in the wrong direction. Blorfindel smiled.

Eresi was at the first bush. He held up a cut branch and waved to Lalegdo. He did not know that he was signaling Blorfindel as well. Lalegdo made a quick search of the area and then began to stalk similar bushes. *If he is looking there first, then the target must be... There!* Blorfindel saw it. It was no bird this time but a blue stump as plain as could be.

Blorfindel watched Lalegdo stalk another bush. It was all Blorfindel could do to keep from grinning. Again he dashed. As he passed by the target stump he stuck his arrow straight down into the top by hand. *I have won! Now for the good part.* He did not stop running at the target, but continued on to the first bush Lalegdo had searched. *He will not check here again.*

Blorfindel waited there until he had caught his breath and re-acquired the location of all three judges. Then he disappeared again for one more stalk.

Clap! Blorfindel's hand slapped down on Eresi's shoulder. The Brighteyes was standing behind the judge, and Eresi had no idea he was there before the hand struck him. "I'm finished!" The young Fitheran grabbed and did not release his grip. He could feel the judge try to jump, then go weak in the knees. Steelhand's son held him in place with as much pressure as he dared to apply to an archery judge, careful not to break his collarbone. "I'm sorry! Did I scare you!" Blorfindel was grinning like a madman now.

Linchia stared at them with her mouth open. "But, what are you doing? You've been spotted now. It's over. Why?"

"My arrow is in the target. I thought I ought to let you know so you can stop searching now."

"But, we would have heard it."

"He right." Lalegdo's voice was incredulous. "His arrow is in the stump. How did you ever get it to hit strait down? Oh, you were standing right here, weren't you? You had to be. Yes, there are the footprints."

Blorfindel was grinning too hard to speak. *That might ruin it.*

Eresi took one slow breath. "You can let go now, please."

Blorfindel let go and took a step back. When Eresi turned around his eyes fixed, not on Blorindel's laughing eyes or his goofy grin, but on the heavy-bladed Tafer dagger on his belt. Blorfindel thought to himself, *That is right, you Kutel's son, I could have finished you here. The other two would never have seen me.*

Lalegdo returned with the arrow. "Most contestants are content to shoot the target. As we have seen in the past, Biolmi Yewstaff's students sometimes have higher standards. We should join the others, if my fellow judges are ready?"

Two contestants had failed during the stealth round. One was caught when he broke cover for a long shot. The other sneezed. None of the contestants left and they found themselves lined up in their original order, without any prompting, when the judges joined them.

Lalegdo gave the official results of the stealth round, which everyone already knew, then he put on his smile and continued: "With three tests behind us we move on to the obstacle course."

Blorfindel immediately sunk from the self-satisfied heights to the depths of panic. *What obstacle course? Biolmi never said anything about an obstacle course!* This was true. Just as he did not start Blorfindel on the pendulum targets or the stealth round until he had a good showing on the stationary targets, Biolmi did not want to introduce the obstacle course until Blorfindel was better prepared for the other events. Of course, any Fitheran who grew up in Sekri Timbrali knew all of the events on the test long before he was eligible. Foralis had been a small town and there were far fewer children, well spaced out in ages. They did not need to hold the test every year, or in fact, every decade. Blorfindel was only forty-eight last time he saw a test. He spent most of the time fighting boredom and trying to get his mother's attention. One hundred twenty-two years had passed since then and Blorfindel did not remember even being there. *This is why Biolmi knew I would fail. Maybe he was right. Maybe I can at least learn something from this test.*

Fortunately for Blorfindel they had a short walk from the staging area to the actual course. He had about two minutes to pull himself together before Lalegdo repeated the rules. Blorfindel was the only one in attendance who had never heard them before. "There are four targets to the sides of the obstacle course. Two on the right, and two on the left. They are both clearly market by the fences that you see now to either side. You will not be able to see the targets until you have progressed a certain distance through the course. You may shoot at any time it is safe to do so. Each contestant must put one arrow in the bulls-eye of each target. If you are unsure of whether you have hit the bulls-eye, I recommend you shoot again. The judges will not be scoring until after you complete the round, so don't take chances."

Blorfindel looked down at his quiver and checked. He had seven arrows left. He had left the six that he used on the pendulum targets. *Biolmi said I should take more arrows.*

"You may use as many arrows as you like on this test but remember: One, you need to still have enough arrows left for the fourth target, so don't use them all on target one." The spectators laughed. "Two, you will have to carry your own arrows through the course – and you may not leave any arrows in the lane. And Three, this is a timed test. Don't waste all your time on the first three targets and not leave yourself enough to complete.

"You will be timed using special candles made by Linchia Faircandle. Needless to say, the candles are fair." Again, the spectators laughed. "Your round begins when the candle burns to the first mark. If the candle burns down to the second mark before you have completed the course, you fail.

Linchia will tell you when to start. You don't have to stare at the candle. When you are on the course, you will not be able to see how much time you have left. Don't bother looking, and no, we won't tell you if you ask.

"You have all heard this before, but I must clarify some things. The course has two lanes, an outbound lane and an inbound lane. The outbound lane has all of the obstacles in it, you can't get them confused. You must remain in the outbound lane for the complete outbound part of the test. All shooting must be done from the outbound lane. If you exit the outbound lane at any point, you may not shoot again. The inbound lane is for your convenience only. The inbound lane is the fastest return trip from the end of the course. I recommend that you use it. Remember, your test is not complete until you return here. Do not stop and celebrate when you hit the fourth bulls-eye; your candle is still burning.

"Also, as I mentioned before, you may not leave arrows anywhere on the course except in the targets. If you dump a quiver full of arrows in the middle of the course, stop and pick them up. If you can't recover the arrows from within the outbound lane, be certain to get all of your shooting done before exiting the lane to retrieve them. Linchia will not extinguish your candle while you have arrows on the course. If we find one of your arrows on the course after the candle is extinguished we will have to disqualify you for this year. Do you understand?"

"Yes, judge!"

Once again the contestants would test one at a time, and this time Blorfindel was glad to be last. He stared anxiously at the obstacles. The outbound lane was about twelve feet wide and quite straight, so he was not concerned about accidentally stepping out. The course itself did not look too bad: a sixty yard sprint across a field of loose river rocks to a swath of thick undergrowth; then up a rope to the top of a sixty foot tower that was really just four posts, some bracing, and a platform; descend the tower back into the undergrowth; a short swath of grass; then a thirty foot log wall; more grass; and another, shorter tower. On the other side of that tower the undergrowth looked savage – a brier thicket of some kind. Then the course went into a stand of low fir trees. He could not see much in there. On the other side of the trees was a swampy area that led to the river. A rope was strung across the river and on the other side the outbound lane was easy to spot as two blue-painted lines ascending a twenty-foot rock face that climbed out of the river. The fencing to the left at the top of the bluff clearly marked the last target. The inbound lane made a sweep to the right (as Blorfindel viewed it) and re-crossed the river on a wooden bridge, then it was all easy footpath. *I can handle that, but how much time do I get?*

One of the other contestants, Hadilbel, broke Blorfindel's concentration, "You must be confident. You're only taking seven arrows?"

Damachil, the first contestant to fail out, joined in, "Seven? I wouldn't go with less than a score!"

Hadilbel asked, "Didn't have more arrows when we started?"

"Yes," Blorfindel looked unconsciously at his quiver, "I left six in the pendulum targets, like a fool."

Damachil offered a quiver full of arrows, "Take mine, I'm not going need them this year."

Hadilbel dipped his head, "It's not allowed. You can only use the arrows that you brought. Besides, yours would be too short for him anyway. What's your draw length, Blorfindel, twenty-eight?"

"Thirty."

Damachil belted his quiver back on, "I can't get near that." He pantomimed drawing his bowstring back well behind his head. Even Blorfindel had to laugh.

Then it was time for the first contestant to begin. They all watched in silence, each going over course in his own mind as the contestant was going over if for real. He took three shots to the left from the first tower. *That makes sense. The first target must only be visible from the top of the tower. If you did not have to shoot from up there, why would you ever climb?* The log wall slowed him down a good deal. Again, from the second tower he sent three to the right. Five arrows came out of the fir trees and flew to the right. *They look low.*

When the first contestant got to the river Blorfindel realized how long the crossing really was. His angle did not give him much perspective, but it had to be forty times longer than the Fitheran – about two hundred feet. He went quickly across, hanging from his hands and feet. The rope did not sag or sway too badly. The rock cliff gave him nearly as much trouble as the log wall, but he made it up and put three arrows into the final target. He turned and sprinted down the inbound lane, but he made a detour after getting past the swamp. He raced over to the base of the log wall and picked up two arrows, then back to the inbound path and across the finish line.

Linchia smiled, "You made it."

Lalegdo said, "As soon as you've caught your breath, we can go score your round."

Blorfindel and all of the others had to wait for the judges to walk to each target and check his score. They did not walk the outbound lane, of course, but they still seemed to take forever. When they returned, Lalegdo announced that he had passed. He actually had at least two bulls-eyes in each target. "Very wise," Lalegdo said, "Take no chances that you might have a near miss. You had me worried there for a moment, though. I was afraid you might not have noticed that you dropped those arrows."

Blorfindel counted arrows, *Three, three, five, three, and two dropped; that's sixteen, and he still had some when he finished.*

For the next contestant Blorfindel watched the timing. Linchia unwrapped a new candle and placed it in a special holder, which was in a special box. The candle itself was red at the bottom and at the very tip, but white in the middle. She lit a taper from an oil lamp, also in the box, and used that to light the timing candle, then she put a glass and copper tube over the candle. They all waited for the candle to burn down to the white and Linchia said, "Go!"

Again Blorfindel counted arrows: *Five, five, eight, three. She brought three times as many arrows as I have and she used them all!* The candle had so much white left when she got back that she walked across the line.

She passed as well. "That fir stand is tough. The bulls-eye is low and there is no room for your bow's limbs to move in there." Blorfindel eyed her bow. It was easily six inches shorter than his own. Her draw was short, too. *Space is going to be tight in the firs, as if I needed something else to worry about.*

The next contestant got a very bad start. He lost his footing in the rocks and went down hard. He got back up and continued, but his limp was painful to watch. The spectators and contestants debated where the injury really was. Most thought it was his ankle. He seemed to get over the wall and up the towers without too much trouble, though every landing had to be punishing to his injury. He looked good shooting, though. The river crossing was a bit scary. He went over using just his hands, and his fingers must have been tired for the last target. He took a long time there and shot seven arrows. Blorfindel looked at the candle when he started the return leg. *He is going to make it!*

Linchia noticed him watching. "You shouldn't stare at the candle. You'll ruin your eyes for your own run."

The contestant's limp got worse as he tried to run back. The candle was in the red when he crossed the finish line. He did not make it in time. The crowd was crushed. Everyone had been rooting for him. Three of them helped him to the river to clean up his scrapes and soak his ankle.

Blorfindel heard himself say, "You'll make it next time, no question."

The judges walked around and scored him anyway – they had to get the arrows out of the targets for the next round. His shooting was good enough, he just could not beat the candle.

Hadilbel was next. He was a little afraid of the rocks at the start and went slower than usual. His pace picked up nicely as he moved along.

"Blorfindel! Arrows!"

Blorfindel turned away from the course to see Damachil waiving a handful of arrows.

Linchia heard him, too. "I'm sorry, but the rules are clear. Contestants may only use the arrows that they bring to the test."

"But these are his! We pulled them out of the pendulums!"

Blorfindel stared at the arrows in disbelief as he accepted them. "Thanks Damachil. I… um… weren't there six?"

"We only found five in the targets. We didn't stop to look around. I was afraid that we wouldn't get back in time."

"You know, five is a lot better than none. Thanks a pile, Damachil. I owe you for this."

Linchia was not satisfied, however. "Let me see those arrows." She made a quick examination to see that the fletchings matched the rest of Blorfindel's arrows. "And give me the rest."

Blorfindel dutifully handed over all of his arrows. The judge compared their construction, weight and length. Blorfindel thought, *It is a good thing Biolmi got me to bring a matched set!* She then took one of the spent timing candles and rubbed some of the red wax on each of the shafts. The color was faint, but there would be no denying the dozen arrows that she had examined.

They all watched the rest of Hadilbel's turn. He was tired and slowing down at the end of his run, but the candle was still in the white when he crossed the line. He doubled over completely and panted. "I… <puff> thought that rope was going to kill me. <Huff> It's too big around for my hands. <puff> You should be fine though… <huff>, Blorfindel. <puff> You've got big hands. <huff> How does anyone… <puff> do that in the rain?"

Linchia answered, "We use longer candles in the rain."

His score was good and Hadilbel passed.

Blorfindel waited at the starting line. He looked ahead at the rocks, trying to gauge which ones he should trust.

"Go!"

He was gone. The rock field gave him no problems at all. He felt slow through the thick undergrowth, and he was especially careful not to get his arrows caught on anything. The sixty foot rope climb was no trouble at all but as he swung up onto the tower his quiver nearly tipped over. Blorfindel froze for a couple of heartbeats and then carefully recovered.

He stood on top of the tower looking at the first target. It was nearly two hundred yards away. There was a tall wall in front of it that would have obscured it from the ground, or even for most of the way up the tower. He realized that he had not even looked this way until he was on top of the tower. He took a couple of deep breaths. *It is a long shot, and the tower changes things. The target is higher than the base of the tower, but by how much?* He visualized the flight of an arrow in his mind. It missed low. He corrected and tried again. This time his mental arrow hit. *Now I have to do it for real. Four targets, twelve arrows, that is three arrows for each target, but I need to save some extra for the firs.* He released the first arrow. *That is hit! Do I dare trust it? If I am wrong here then the rest of the course is a wasted effort. If I run out of arrows...* Blorfindel's second arrow looked good as well.

Rather than climb down the rope like the other contestants had, he used it to repel down one of the corner posts of the tower. He ran out of rope about ten feet short of the ground. The undergrowth helped break his fall but also held him tangled for a while. He lost more time trying to reorient himself, but eventually he broke out of the brush and three running strides later he was on the wall.

The logs were worn and a bit slippery, but there were cracks between where he could get his fingers in. Climbing down was slower and he actually slid the last four feet. He skinned his right knee and his right palm on the way down.

He sprinted to the next tower. This one did not have a rope. He scrambled up the bracing and onto the platform. *I think that was faster than the rope. I should have done that last time.* The second target was similar to the first, though it was lower than the base of the tower and the obscuring wall was higher. Blorfindel shot an arrow at it without thinking. It looked like a hit, anyway. *Once more.* Blorfindel rested, took careful aim, and missed. The arrow was clearly out to the left. *Crushk! I do not have enough arrows to waste like that!* He took slow and careful aim. Then he closed his eyes, relaxed the string, opened his eyes, took a deep breath and shot his next arrow. *That might be in. It must be in.* He looked down at his quiver. *Seven arrows left – thank you Damachil!*

He climbed down the tower and trotted across the swath of grass. He was looking for the best path through the briars. *They are thinner at ground level.* So he got down on his stomach, stuck his nose in the dirt and crawled. He had to keep his bow and quiver ahead of him to keep them from getting caught. Thorns caught and tore his clothes and he was working dirt into his wounds, but he got through.

He was in the firs. He was somewhat surprised to see how clear it was at ground level. He did not attempt to stand up, but crawled until he could see the third target. He had to crawl a bit more to get a clear shot and he saw what had given the other contestants problems. There were small trees standing dead among the firs. Their tough branches interlocked with the fir boughs to make an effective web. Down on the ground he was below most of the fir boughs and all of the dead branches.

The target was odd, as well. Instead of the usual concentric rings they were broader at the top and narrower at the bottom, moving the bulls-eye into the bottom third of the target. Mercifully, it was not far – only twenty yards away. Blorfindel turned his bow sideways and drew an arrow, then he relaxed. There was a small bump in the terrain – nothing that would normally concern anyone, but it would be in the flight path of the arrow. Rather than try to raise up he shimmied awkwardly along under fir boughs until the target was clear. His first shot still missed high. His second arrow skimmed off the ground and bounced up a bit, striking the target even higher than the first. For the third he was angry and frustrated and the arrow missed right.

Blorfindel forced himself to stop. *This happens every time! I get angry and I push and I can not shoot well enough to hit a wall from inside the house! I have come so far! How much time has it been? That does not matter! I have to hit the bulls-eye. If I cannot get the hit, then the time does not matter.*

He drew another arrow. *I might as well shoot.* This one was on target and clearly in the bulls-eye. From this range he did not need another arrow to be sure. *Three arrows left for target number four.*

He crawled out of the firs. Even before he was free of them his hands were in the swamp water. He rose and began leaping from one tuft of grass to another. Only a few would hold his weight, but he did not stop and they did not sink fast enough to topple him. He was quickly approaching the river and the rope. *How much time have I lost so far?* It had seemed like an eternity in the firs. *I crawled through the briars; that had to be slow, and I have been taking a long time with my shots. I got lost in the brush at the bottom of the tower – that was stupid.*

He ran to the rope and kept on running. With his bow out for added balance and his eyes fixed on the knot on the other side, Blorfindel Brighteyes ran. Forty-one running strides on the thick hemp rope and Blorfindel was across the river.

The rock cliff was not as steep as it had appeared from the other side, and unlike the other contestants, Blorfindel had not fatigued his hands on the rope. He scrambled up easily and steadied himself for the last target. *It is about one hundred yards away and slightly below where I am standing. I have three arrows to get one bulls-eye. This should be easier than the first test.* He took his shot. Zzcrack! The arrow fell uselessly to the ground at his feet, split nearly in half by the string.

Blorfindel laughed. It had happened so often in practice through the years that he was used to it. It was the most familiar thing that had happened to him all day. He was still laughing when shot his last two arrows into the bulls-eye. He stuffed the broken arrow into his quiver and started down the inbound path. *I wonder if there is any candle left?*

As he ran his legs picked up their rhythm. By the time he touched the bridge he was at full speed. *Next time, I will bring more arrows. Next time I will be ready for the obstacle course. Next time, I will pass.* He was still running hard when he crossed the finish line. He ran through the knot of spectators before circling back to the judges.

"We've come to expect things to be a little different from Biolmi's students," Linchia was saying. "Blorfindel, we don't keep records of elapsed times on the obstacle course." She held up a candle that was still half-white. "I've seen maybe a dozen contestants walk the rope. Lots of them get a good run off the start and at the end. A few get over the walls and up the cliff with ease. You got all of that, and a great time through the briars; quick shots from the towers and a quick descent!"

Lalegdo was more formal, "As soon as you are ready we can go score your round."

"I'm ready! Let's go!"

The first target had two bulls-eyes. The second had only one. His last shot was not as good as he thought, but the first was good enough. The target by the fir trees had one bulls-eye and the two arrows in the last target were not only centered, but touching each other.

"It looks like you did it!" Lalegdo congratulated him as Blorfindel stuffed the last two arrows into his quiver. *Eleven arrows, plus the broken one; I will have to keep these.*

Blorfindel, Lalegdo, and Linchia were halfway back to the start when Eresi emerged from the fir trees waiving an arrow. "I'm sorry Blorfindel, you had a brilliant run, but you dropped an arrow."

Lalegdo sighed, "Oh, my."

Blorfindel frantically counted his arrows again: *Eleven plus the broken one. I have all of my arrows.*

Linchia spoke before his head came up, "Let me see that arrow."

Eresi strutted over and handed it to her. "It is clearly Blorfindel's: none of the other contestants use arrows that are so long or heavy, and of course, the fletchings match."

Blorfindel had to admit, "That is one of my arrows. I just don't know how…" His voice trailed off.

Lalegdo was genuinely disappointed. "I am very sorry, Blorfindel, but as you know, the rules state that you must not leave any arrows on the course – only in the targets."

Linchia's voice was firm, "Blorfindel didn't leave this arrow on the course."

Eresi said, "It's his arrow – he admits it himself. I just picked it up in the fir trees. He has to be disqualified, that is the rule."

"No," Linchia persisted, "the rule is, he may not leave any arrows on the course."

"But he did, in the fir trees."

"No, he did not. Before he began his obstacle course test, when I heard that Blorfindel was missing an arrow, I marked all of the arrows that he had with him." She drew one of the arrows from Blorfindel's quiver. "You see this red mark? Your arrow doesn't have a red mark, Eresi. Blorfindel didn't leave this arrow on the course because he never had it with him. He left it in the pendulum targets. You remember the pendulum targets? The ones that your servants couldn't handle properly?" She slapped his robe with the arrow's fletchings for emphasis, "except that they seem to handle them just fine for all of the other contestants."

"Are you accusing me–"

"If she isn't, I am." Lalegdo's reassuring smile was gone now. "You broke your oath today."

"But this–"

"It doesn't matter now. You'll get your day in court, I suppose. Falsifying an archery test is a court-martial offense, and I think you will find that it is still taken very seriously."

"Listen–"

"I don't want to hear it. In any case, Linchia and I officially agree that Blorfindel has passed this and every test. You are out-voted. There is nothing more to discuss.

"I knew there was a lot of wagering going on surrounding Blorfindel's late training, and quite frankly it disturbed me. I never dreamed that it would influence an archery judge. We will be a century regaining the trust of Sekri Timbrali. A century when your name will be remembered, I assure you.

"Today, however, there are three Fitherani and a Fitheresse who deserve better than to wait for us. They have passed their tests and will be named archers at the ceremony. Eresi, legally, you may attend. I recommend that you do not. Personally, I think it would cheapen the event for those who deserve to be there, specifically the new archers. Since you don't seem very concerned about what these youngsters deserve, you might consider this: you can count yourself very fortunate that Biolmi Yewstaff has not taught his legendary temper to this apprentice–" Eresi's eyes flashed down to the dagger again. "–and I think it would be in your best interest to avoid an encounter with Yewstaff."

Eresi Silkenrobe crossed the bridge and took the long way home, avoiding the onlookers and the city center.

Lalegdo, Linchia, and Blorfindel walked silently back to the starting area. Lalegdo had his happy face on when they arrived. "Blorfindel has passed." There was a mix of cheers and murmurs from the onlookers, but the other contestants seemed thrilled.

"I was concerned about your <u>hands</u> on the rope! hah!"

"It never even occurred to me that you could run on the rope. I feel like an idiot!"

"Almost nobody can."

"How did you get over the wall like that?"

"How'd ever get an aimed arrow out of the firs? I though <u>my</u> bow was too big!"

"I couldn't see how you went down the tower so fast. Weren't you afraid you'd fall?"

"You must have run the obstacle course for years!"

Blorfindel tried to have an answer for everyone. No one believed that this was his first time, of course.

Lalegdo waived them back to order. Contestants always celebrated at the end, of course, but he had to get them home in time to clean up for the ceremony. "Sekri Timbrali has four new archers to answer the call when danger threatens. We will all welcome them to the ranks this evening at the Archers' Hall. All archers and family are welcome, of course. Our tests today have taken a bit longer than usual, quick times on the obstacle course not withstanding, and I know that you all want to get a bath and a change of clothes before the ceremony." *Frenlias help you if you do not.*

"To the four other contestants, well done. You are not far from the mark and I have no doubt that you will be joining us in your own time."

Blorfindel shook Damachil's hand. "You saved me. I would've had no chance without the other arrows."

"Eresi had the sixth one, didn't he?"

"You could see that from here?"

"Everyone saw it. Only a few of us knew about the red wax, though."

"You figured that out from watching us? I almost didn't get it myself, and I was there."

"You were under a lot of pressure."

"Yeah. Hey I've got to go clean up. I think I'm still bleeding under this mud. Good luck Damachil! You'll pass next year."

"I don't think I'll try again for a while. I was kind of hoping to break the record today."

"The record?"

"I turned one-thirty-five last week. I wanted to take a shot at being the youngest ever."

Blorfindel laughed, "I was afraid I was going to take a shot at being the oldest ever."

On his way out Blorfindel made a point of finding Linchia Faircandle. "Thank you, judge."

"Don't thank me, you did the work. You passed on your own merit, Blorfindel Brighteyes."

"Maybe, but that wax thing, that's not in the rules, is it? I mean, if you hadn't done that..."

"It's our job to make certain that those who can pass the test become archers." She smiled. "You did very, very well today. Many Fitherani would have been less well composed. You know, when you snuck up behind Eresi, you had us all frightened."

"You knew I was there?"

"No! Make no mistake, if we could have caught you out there, we would have. It is also our job to see to it that no one becomes an archer who doesn't earn it. What I meant was, well, you've probably noticed that Biolmi sometimes gets a bit excited. Some of his apprentices pick up that trait as well, and after the pendulum targets you had a right to be a little upset."

"You know, I was afraid of the pendulum targets. He probably did me a favor."

"Go get cleaned up or you'll be late for your own ceremony. And good luck with the Fitheresse."

"You know about Afinlia and me?"

"I've been an archery judge for six centuries. When one of Biolmi's students sneaks out to test early, there's always a Fitheresse in the woods."

Chapter 14

Celebration

Fatigue, abrasions, soreness, mud, and even Eresi's attempt to cheat him could not dampen Blorfindel's pride and excitement on his way home. *I have done it! I can get Afinlia back. Her father will let me see her again now that I am an archer. Biolmi was wrong. I passed. He said I did not have a chance, but I passed!*

Biolmi was not waiting for him when he got back. Blorfindel changed out of his muddy clothes and started bringing in buckets of water for a bath. Biolmi found him emptying his third trip. "You stayed for the whole thing, then? I bet you learned something today. How did you do? You did get a chance to try the stealth test? That's got to be your best event."

"Actually, the obstacle course was my best."

"They didn't make you start on the obstacles? That's just stupid! The ones who passed would have to go through the other events all torn up. That's just stupid!"

"The obstacle course was last."

"Last for you, I expect. Look, I wasn't trying to keep it from you, it's just that you have to build on what you know, and you still struggle with the pendulums. I just want you to be able to focus. You'll pick up the obstacle course really quickly, I'm sure of it."

"I already did. I passed."

"You passed the obstacle course? You didn't even bring enough arrows for the obstacle course."

"I had twelve left, and that was enough."

"You really passed the obstacle course? Don't fool with me, I know all the judges."

"I passed the test. I passed all the tests. I passed." Blorfindel was grinning again. As he ran back out to refill the buckets he was singing, "I passed, I passed, I passed the archery test..."

Biolmi stared out the open door in disbelief. "What is Sekri Timbrali coming to when <u>that</u> can be an archer?" His tone was cynical, but he was so eager to hear the story that he helped his apprentice carry water.

"So you got a perfect weather day. You just skimmed by on the stationary targets. You got through the pendulums on a technicality. You had one good event: the stealth (beautiful, really – I've got to give you credit on that one). And you got through the obstacle course on dumb luck and a lot of help. It may make you a defender of Sekri Timbrali, but it doesn't prove you're ready for it." Biolmi stood up, "Come on, get dry and get dressed. You'll be expected at the ceremony, just don't get you're hopes up."

"I passed the test. That makes me an archer, right? They can't take it back?"

"You're an archer. They won't take it back. You'd have to be some kind of criminal. The ceremony is a waste of a perfectly good evening, though, and the food's horrible." Biolmi stopped to bite a stale walnut-cake. "Horrible.

"On that topic, Eresi is going to take some looking into. I always knew that he could be bought, but only to help some fool pass. I never heard of him trying to keep someone out. Where's the money in that?"

Blorfindel was toweling off in front of the fire. "They were betting that I wouldn't make it."

"Who was betting?"

"I don't know. The registrar said that there were bets in the office."

"Eresi isn't fool enough to risk his reputation over an office bet. Do you know how much archery judges get paid? Maybe he would quibble a little about whether a shot was in or out, but to rig the pendulums <u>and</u> plant an arrow on the obstacle course? He's not that foolish."

"Lalegdo and Linchia both said–"

"Lalegdo and Linchia live by the rules. If the rules said the Kutel were allowed to move in next door they'd help them unpack. What do they know about the real world? Eresi is a dirty judge who loves fancy clothes and admiration. Somebody dumped a big pile of coin on him to risk all of that."

Blorfindel did not know what to say. Biolmi never talked to him like this before. He had been patient, teaching, condescending, even bullying, but never thoughtful. Blorfindel could hardly remember Biolmi asking a question unless he already knew the answer.

"So who wants you to fail badly enough to buy a judge? Ha! Just think, if you had failed, whoever-it-is would have to buy a judge again next time! You could have bled him for a couple more years.

"As soon as you're ready the tea is hot and the walnut cakes are cold and stale. It's still better than your going to get at the ceremony, so eat something. Eat one of the Frendlias' Gift seeds, too – it's good for your wounds. And don't forget your father's sword, you might remind someone that the archers of Sekri Timbrali are supposed to be warriors." Biolmi was putting on his own boiled leather armor and belting on a well-worn sword. *He should get some armor, too. Someone who would buy a judge might be willing to... Amada?*

The ceremony was everything Biolmi knew it would be. A small group of regular archers, two judges, the four new archers and some friends and family gathered in the Archers Hall to officially celebrate. The hall was supposed to be big enough for all of the archers of Sekri Timbrali. It was not that big, but it still made their little party seem pathetically small. The food was bland, the wine was cheap, and the cups were stingy. Blorfindel grew tired of it almost as quickly as Biolmi. The archery master was the only person there for him, anyway. He felt very awkward and a bit lonely.

Each new archer was given a small wooden talisman. It was supposed to look like a drawn bow with an arrow ready, but it was really little more than a stylized "x". Biolmi brought a leather thong so that Blorfindel could hang it from his neck, everyone else did. Shortly after they were handed out Blorfindel asked Biolmi, "How long are we supposed stay?"

"We can go whenever you want."

On the way out they both got a surprise: Milia was on her way in. "I just heard! I came as soon as I could, did I miss the ceremony?"

Biolmi answered, "You didn't miss much."

"You're such a kill-joy! This is Blorfindel's big day! Congratulations! You're an archer!"

Blorfindel shook her hand. "Thank you... and thanks for coming. Ah, we were just leaving."

Biolmi smiled crookedly. "I was going to take him up to The Canopy for some real adult refreshment. You're welcome to join us."

"I don't know, you two have your own little celebration."

Biolmi said, "I'd like you to join us," at the same time Blorfindel said, "I'd like you to come."

Milia smiled, "How can I refuse?"

The Canopy was full of Fitherani eating, drinking, singing, and generally having a good time. The fire was bright and warm. The crowd recognized Milia as soon as she stepped inside and practically demanded that she play for them. She was whisked away to the corner as Biolmi and Blorfindel joined a long table near the fire. A waitress put two flagons of dark red wine in front of them before they even spoke. She disappeared again just as quickly. The music was cheerful and wine was very good.

"Biolmi Yewstaff! How come I only see you here after the archery tests?" A well dressed Fitheran pounded the archery master on the shoulder. "It wouldn't kill you, or your apprentices, if you got out more, you know?"

"Linxico Oldgrape, I'd like you to meet Blorfindel Brighteyes."

Blorfindel stood and extended his hand. Linxico was still talking when he shook it, "So you are The Apprentice? Congratulations! Hey! Your hand's all skinned up."

"I slipped coming down the log wall."

"I'll mix you up something for that."

Biolmi snorted, "Can you still remember how? When was the last time you mixed up something?"

"It's been a long time, hasn't it? But a good wine isn't any easier than a good poultice. Oh, and the quail is very good tonight. I'll have one sent out to get you started, but the wine is a little heavy for quail, isn't it? Chalise! Bring out three cups of the special golden for my friends in Biolmi Yewstaff's party!

"Do you ever think about going back out, Biolmi? You do, don't you? The Kutel are massing again. There is a strong leader in Shonu now. If The Shield Valley wasn't in the way they'd already be cutting down our forest."

"I can do more good here teaching. How about you? Do you miss pulling our sorry asses out of the fire? You know, Blorfindel, Linxico used to be the most useless baggage all the time on campaign, then we'd get into some tight spot and, poof! Out would come Linxico with something none of us had ever heard of. Once, he poured this sticky, gooey mess on some rocks, and they started arguing with each other! Rocks! The Kutel are probably still staring at them."

"I hope not, the potion only lasted for a couple of minutes." They both laughed.

"I'll be back in a few minutes with something for that hand." He dropped his voice to a hoarse whisper, "Oh, and stay away from the almonds, there not very good." Linxico fought his way through the crowd toward the kitchen.

"Who is he?"

"He's an old friend – the last one left from my glory days. The Tafers and the Hollenwa have grown old and died. He owns this place, that's why I wanted to come here. He spent his cut of our treasure to set himself up. He's got his own vineyards and special farms for the things only he can get. You won't find better food or drink in Sekri Timbrali. In fact, the only way you'll ever do any better is if a Timble invites you to a guest-dinner. And Linxico's wine is better."

The guest next to Blorfindel said, "They say he brews magic in it."

Biolmi laughed. "I guarantee it! Linxico doesn't take a drink of water without putting a spell on it."

Milia rejoined them in time for the second round of drinks and the quail. It was marvelous. They all said so when Linxico came back with the poultice. "It is pretty good, isn't it? Too bad I can't get more of them, but then people would get sick of them. Variety! That's the key! Except for Biolmi, he does the same thing over and over all the time. But not you, eh? You must be just about bubbling over – just passed your test, young and in love! Ready to go conquer the world and lay it at her feet."

Milia explained, "Linxico knows everything about everyone – at least everything he wants to know. He's got a steady stream of guests and a hearty flow of wine; the result: a river full of information."

Biolmi laughed again. "The crystal ball doesn't hurt any, either."

"Hey! That's supposed to be a secret!"

Blorfindel remembered Aritsa's crystal ball. "Do you tell the future?"

Linxico put the back of his hand to his forehead dramatically and said, "In the future, I predict Blorfindel Brighteyes will learn the difference between real magic and a showman's trick. The future is a hard nut to crack, and in general you're better off not knowing. Keeping your mind on what you're doing right now is tough enough. I will give you one prediction, though. The word is that they are not only going to take Eresi's talismans, they're going to banish him, too."

"He's got too many friends in court."

"Ah, but not in the court martial! His friends are in the wrong high places. You see, justice will be served! Love conquers all! And your garden fish are here, I better get out of the way." The waitress placed an overflowing platter of colorful vegetables and small, glittering, marinated fish between them as Linxico disappeared again.

Milia stared at the place where he had been standing, "He can move faster through a crowd that I would have thought possible."

"That silver-green robe is magical. It makes him slippery as a fish." Biolmi waived a fish for emphasis before tossing it in his mouth. "It saved our lives more than once. I never thought he'd put it to work here, though."

Again Milia explained for Blorfindel, "Fitherani like Biolmi and Linxico go off on their adventures and come back with all this amazing gear, just to make us all feel inadequate and plain."

Biolmi was laughing a lot tonight. "You let me know the next time you feel inadequate and plain, Milia Brightstrings!"

"Why Biolmi Yewstaff, are you going to make be feel special?" The crowd called her away for another song before Biolmi could respond.

Blorfindel was still thinking about the magic robe. "Did you bring back a lot special stuff, magic and stuff?"

Wine is not good for his vocabulary. "What's a lot? Listen, Blorfindel, for the most part people just do their jobs all the time. They're never going to see things like Linxico and I have. Do you think Jaico Silverfingers has ever seen a sunrise from above cloud level? Never happened. If you want to be special, you've got to go out there and do it. As for the stuff, well, your average Kutel likes gold and silver as much as anybody, except maybe a dragon, and when he's dead there's no reason to leave it with him. Most Kutel carry more money than it costs to kill them, so if you're willing to put your life on the line, eat hardtack and sleep in the rain, you can make big money and do the world a favor at the same time. Now someone like Linxico, he's always got his eye out for the good stuff. The trick is to keep them alive long enough to tell you is this worth money or is it junk, or is it something really special like his fishy robe." He paused to munch. "And sometimes you do a favor for someone – like rescue his daughter or something – and they do something nice for you – like give you a magic belt buckle that's been in their family for generations." Again, he paused to eat. "Or something like Lalliam's sword, if your cousin hadn't found it some Kutel chief would have it now, and you would have to remove him from it to get it back." Biolmi pantomimed drawing and releasing an arrow.

After his third flagon of wine Milia pulled Blorfindel up to sing. The night seemed to fade away from that point. He could not remember the next three courses, but Blorfindel remembered being a very popular and a very welcome with the guests of The Canopy.

Chapter 15

The Shapetaker

Blorfindel awoke to a knock on the door. He sat up and braced himself for the hangover to pound his head. It did not. *Feadin bless you, Linxico Olgrape, you are a genius and a saint.* Still, his stomach was moving fast and his feet were slow as he moved to the door.

"Good morning Blorfindel Brighteyes. You and the master are required at the Archers Hall as soon as possible. I will escort you."

"I remember you. You're called Balisi, right?"

"We climbed the Hollen River together. They tell me you passed your test yesterday, congratulations. But the judges are waiting, you should wake Biolmi."

"I'm awake, I just don't want to be." Biolmi looked a lot better than Blorfindel felt.

"I'm sorry, you know it's not up to me."

Biolmi threw a bucket, hard, and Balisi had to be quick to catch it. "If you want to speed this up, go get some clean water from the stream." Biolmi waved in the general direction.

"I remember where the stream is, master Biolmi."

The water made a huge difference. They each had a long drink before they washed in the cold water. Still, anxiety was churning Blorfindel's already uneasy stomach. "What do they want us for?"

"They probably just want to apologize for Eresi. They think they're being nice by doing it first thing." Biolmi put on his full kit, including his armor, his favorite bow, two quivers of arrows, a sword and dagger. Blorfindel followed suit, though he had no armor. He also hung the black iron war hammer from his belt. Biolmi frowned at that. He had wanted to throw the hammer away many, many times, but he was not going to steal it from his apprentice. "You look ready. Let's go."

The Acher's Hall looked bigger in the daylight. Lalegdo and Linchia were there, and another judge whom Blorfindel did not recognize. There were also a score of archers around the hall looking solemn. Biolmi was just as surprised as Blorfindel to see Linxico there. He handed each of them a small vial of syrupy purple liquid. "Drink this," he whispered.

Blorfindel looked at the vial and started to ask what it was. Biolmi was already returning his empty to Linxico. "Do as you're told." It was handling the glass vial that Blorfindel noticed that his hand had healed completely. He drank the potion. As soon as it was down his stomach settled. He could feel the magic radiating out from the middle of his body and soon the effects six flagons of four different wines were gone.

The third judge began without introducing himself, "We brought you in to discuss the events following yesterday's test."

Biolmi had been whispering something to Linxico when he snapped his head around. "What? Following the test? What business is that of yours?"

"Eresi Silkenrobe is dead."

Biolmi's anger rose instantly. "We went out to celebrate at The Canopy. He had too much wine and we were peacefully sleeping it off when Balisi woke us up. For the love of Iamdoor! If Blorfindel wanted to kill him he could have done it during the stealth test! Even if he was the kind of Fitheran to take revenge himself, Eresi Silkenrobe would be at the bottom of a long list. He's been beaten, sold into slavery, held in captivity, his parents were killed and his village was burnt! He's a Brighteyes! He's had more assassination attempts than you've had straight arrows! Eresi Silkenrobe was a villain, but he's not villain enough to qualify for revenge! Not for this archer, anyway!"

"He's been dead for weeks. We sent someone to hear his side of the story after the official complaints by Lalegdo Gingerhair and Linchia Faircandle. The investigator overstepped his bounds a bit by investigating the house. Eresi's body was in the basement–"

Linxico cleared his throat, "Ahem, he was packing last night. I warned the Hall that he might be trying to escape justice. That's why I didn't come back to the table."

"But he was there for the test yesterday?" Blorfindel looked around for someone to tell him what was going on.

"All of the flesh had been pealed from his head. His skull was cracked open. His brain was gone."

Biolmi shuddered. "Shapetaker."

Linchia broke in, "We're not here to accuse you, Blorfindel. We're here to warn you."

Blorfindel was thoroughly confused. "Could someone please tell me what you're talking about?"

Linxico was the first to respond. "A shapetaker is a creature that impersonates people. Eresi Silkenrobe was already dead. The creature that you met yesterday was an impostor."

Lalegdo interrupted, "It is somewhat of a comfort that it was not a real archery judge that displayed such despicable behavior."

"Some comfort!" Biolmi snorted, "I don't suppose the shapetaker has been caught?"

Linxico continued as if he had not been interrupted, "A shapetaker is like a doppelganger, in fact many people don't know the difference. The doppelganger mixes shapeshifting and mind reading powers to make itself look and act like someone its victim knows. A shapetaker takes the form of a dead person, and absorbs all of their memories by eating the brain. It is a lengthy, grisly process, but the result is much harder to spot or trick out than a doppelganger."

"What has this got to do with Blorfindel?" Biolmi wanted to know.

The unknown judge answered, "The shapetaker did not want Blorfindel to pass his test. Doesn't that seem remarkable to you?"

"I had just assumed that it was following through Eresi's plan. I've told you before that he is... was corrupt. I mean, why would a shapetaker care whether he passed?"

Linxico resumed, "I did a reading on the skull this morning. Eresi was killed two days after Blorfindel's name was added to the roster."

"How did it happen?"

"I couldn't tell. I think he was surprised. That's the normal way, anyway. Shapetakers are great impersonators, but remarkable cowards for all their abilities."

One of the archers spoke up, "He had… the body had a hole in its back. Probably from a dagger. His robe was covered with blood."

"But why fail him? Why not just kill him? That's what they do, after all."

The judge answered, "I don't think it had the chance."

Linxico took over again, "Shapetakers need to get close and attack when the victim isn't ready, generally from behind and when they are alone. How could it do that? Blorfindel spends most of his time with you, Biolmi, and you never go anywhere."

Linchia spoke up, "He might have had a chance during the stealth test, but Blorfindel surprised him... it. You remember, Blorfindel, he kept looking at your dagger? It was desperate enough to take a chance, but you were armed and on guard."

Lalegdo continued, "After the obstacle course it was really desperate and it almost took a chance with all three of us. It kept looking at the dagger. It's afraid of you."

"It still doesn't make sense," Biolmi objected, "Why fail him? It draws attention. If it had just played the honest judge we still wouldn't know it was around."

Linxico explained, "I think it wanted to fail him just to keep him from leaving – so it could continue to stalk. I think it had another lead."

Linchia asked Blorfindel directly, "There is someone else who could catch you alone and off-guard, isn't there?"

"Afinlia!"

Linxico was already trotting towards the door, "Let's go!"

Biolmi, Blorfindel, and Linxico raced through town to Afinlia's home. Blorfindel pulled away from the other two and knocked on the door. The peephole opened and Jaico Silverfinger's eye appeared on the other side.

"I need to see Afinlia!"

"Afinlia doesn't need to see you. Go home." The peephole closed.

Blorfindel pounded on the door with the flat of his hand as Biolmi and Linxico approached. Jaico's voice came through the door, "You're not helping, you know. Go home and cool off!"

Biolmi tried the door handle. It was locked. He shot a quizzical look at Linxico.

"I haven't got anything on me. You'll have to do it the hard way."

Biolmi slapped Blorfindel on the shoulder, "Break the door down."

Blorfindel took three running steps and shouldered the door. Both hinges pulled free and sent him falling into the room. He caught his fall on his left hand and flipped forward onto his feet.

Biolmi was already through the door and had an arrow pointed at the stunned Silverfingers. "Sit! On the floor, you idiot! And put your hands on your knees where I can see them!"

Linxico's entrance was much more restrained, "Is that really necessary?"

Biolmi kept his arrow trained on Jaico. "What makes you think this is really Jaico?"

Blorfindel asked, "Where's Afinlia?"

"If you think I'm going to help you kidnap my own daughter–"

Linxico interrupted calmly, "Jaico, there's a shapetaker in town. It may be trying to take the form of your daughter."

Jaico's eyes went wide, "Afinlia! Come down here right now!"

Biolmi relaxed his draw. *It is really Jaico. The shapetaker would not be surprised and would not be concerned for Afinlia's safety.* He put the arrow back in his quiver and offered Silverfingers a hand up. "You're not the shapetaker."

Linxico said, "Of course not. The shapetaker can't use Jaico's form. It can't be both Jaico and Afinlia at the same time, can it? It's got to use a different contact to get to her, one that might not be missed for a little while."

Jaico was even more pale than usual. "Why Afinlia?" He was starting to shake.

Linxico just pointed to Blorfindel.

Afinlia ran barefoot into the chaos.

"Thank Feadin, you're all right," Blorfindel breathed.

"Wait! We don't know it's really her!" Biolmi cautioned.

Linxico shrugged. "Kiss her." They all turned to him, slack-jawed. "The shapetaker can impersonate her form and steal her memories, but it can't <u>be</u> the Fitheresse. If it's not really her, he'll know." There was an awkward silence while Blorfindel tested his theory. Once Linxico was satisfied that she passed the test he ignored the young couple. "So, who's the next jump?"

Jaico wasn't paying attention to him, "What?"

"The next jump: if the shapetaker is trying to get at Blorfindel through Afinlia, who is it going to use to get to Afinlia? It can't be you, or anyone that would be immediately noticed when they disappeared. Who would be alone with Afinlia long enough for it to make the change?"

"The music teacher, Milia Brightstrings," Jaico replied, then to Blorfindel, "Enough! You've proven the point!"

"Milia was herself last night," Biolmi said.

Linxico raised an eyebrow, "You tested her yourself, did you?"

"Very funny. She played last night. The shapetaker would remember the songs, but it wouldn't have the talent. Who's the other Fitheran?"

"What?"

Biolmi explained for Linxico, "Afinlia has another suitor. What's his name, Jaico? Could he be the one?"

"He is called Glimbel Goldbranch, but they have never been alone together."

"Of course not, if they had it would have already... taken Afinlia's form." Linxico did not want to panic the young Fitheresse.

Biolmi was headed for the doorway. "We should go find him!"

Linxico held up a hand, "Wait, wait. When was the last time you saw him? When was the last time anyone saw him?"

"I don't follow him around. He was here a few of weeks ago to present his credentials."

"When, exactly? The exact day is important."

Jaico closed his eyes to think, "Twenty-two days ago."

"That's the day Blorfindel put himself on the list for his test."

Afinlia had not followed what they were talking about, but now she spoke up, "You took your test?" Blorfindel gave her waist a squeeze and drew out his talisman. She practically squealed, "Oh, Blorfindel! You're an archer!"

Biolmi interrupted, "Come on, we've got to go check on Goldbranch."

They got quick directions from Jaico and they were off. Linxico detoured them on the way. "We should check on Milia, anyway. Even if she is still herself, she's in danger of being the next target. Besides, this Glimbel is probably already dead."

Milia was practicing on a lute quietly on her front porch when they got there. It was obvious that she was a genuine musician. When they explained the situation she was panicked. "What am I supposed to do now?!"

"Just relax."

"You relax! There's a monster out there somewhere who wants to eat my brain!"

Biolmi gently took her lute out of her hands and set it on a chair inside the door, "You'd better come with us. It won't attack you unless it gets you alone."

The four of them arrived at Glimbel Goldbranch's residence. It was dark and quiet. Biolmi knocked but there was no answer. He tried the door. It was unlocked. "Blorfindel and Milia, you better wait out here." Linxico nodded and followed Biolmi in. It seemed like a long wait, but it was really only a few minutes later when Biolmi emerged, "It's empty. You might as well wait inside. Linxico is mixing something up."

A few minutes later Linxico came out of the kitchen. "It hasn't been here in a long time. Three weeks or so. The timing works out."

"Goldbranch?"

"The shapetaker was here for more than a month. Do you think it was a guest?"

Milia started shaking. Biolmi put an arm around her shoulders, "We should go now."

Without making any spoken decision they were walking toward the Archers Hall.

"Who's next?" Biolmi wondered.

"Well, either it gave up and ran away, in which case we're all safe," Linxico paused to look at each of them, no one believed that it had given up, "or it's looking to create a new chain. So, we're back to where we started. It can't get to Biolmi because he never goes anywhere. Blorfindel spends time alone with two Fitheressi – lucky dell – and I think we can assume that Jaico will have Afinlia under guard day and night until we sort this out, that leaves Milia."

"I know!"

"Take it easy. We're not going to let anything happen to you. I'm just going over the situation. If it knew about Afinlia, and knew that Blorfindel had put himself on the list for the test, it must have been watching you that day. It has to know that you met with Milia."

"So now I'm the next target! I get it!"

"No, you're not the next target. You're not going to just walk away to some secluded place with Eresi Silkenrobe, are you? It has to find a way to get next to you. Who could it use? You give private lessons, don't you?"

"My students! This thing is stalking my students!"

Linxico held the Fitheresse by the shoulders and looked in her eyes, "I can't use you like this. If you don't calm down, I'm going to have to give you something to calm you down. Do you understand?"

She nervously tossed her head, 'yes'.

"It's got to find out who spends time alone with you. Shapetakers learn from their victims, but they don't know everything. Yesterday it was Eresi all day. Milia, you were at the restaurant last night and Eresi wasn't, so it probably did not follow you there. Eresi and Glimbel didn't know who your students are, did they? So it's got to find out who you're with. How is it going to do that?"

"It can watch the house."

"Not as Eresi, it can't. He is too public. Even if it doesn't know we are on to it, if Eresi steps out the door wearing something that isn't loud and flamboyant all his neighbors will notice. It needs another form, but to stalk you, it can use almost any form so long as it doesn't stand out."

Biolmi offered, "As Eresi, it can get to any one of a dozen Fitherani – probably more. All it has to do is drop a hint that Eresi is going to tell the judges that he falsified their archery test."

"Too bad for them. We can't save them. It has probably found one by now anyway. If it did not take one over last night, it will tonight. How many students do you have?"

"Ten… eight not counting Afinlia and Blorfindel."

"That's too many. We can't protect them all."

"But they're my students! We can't just let it–"

Biolmi put a gentle finger on her lips, "Linxico is just thinking out loud. We're not going to let it get your students. He'll think of something. That's what he does."

"We have to catch it spying on you."

"How are you going to do that? There has to be a hundred places it can hide!"

Blorfindel thought about that. "Not really. There's only a few good pieces of cover, really. I mean, it has to be able to see who comes to see you, but it can't be seen watching by anyone. It's just like the stealth test. We just have to hunt the hunter."

"This isn't a game! You don't get to try again next year after that monster eats my students!"

Linxico liked the idea. "We don't have to play by the rules, either. Blorfindel, how confident are you?"

"I caught it during the test and it had two judges backing it up." He brought Linxico and Milia up to date on his stealth test. "I'm sure I can get it again."

Linxico smiled, "Especially if we cheat. Milia, go straight home. Don't worry, it won't just jump you. Don't take any of your students in, though. Tell them you're sick or something."

"Tell them you have a hangover," Biolmi suggested.

Linxico shoved Biolmi, "You'll ruin my reputation." Then he turned back to Milia. "Tell them whatever you want, just don't open the door for anyone. Blorfindel, you do your sweep, just be careful. It probably isn't ready, yet, so just be patient. Biolmi, you come with me, I'll mix some things up so we'll really be ready tomorrow. Oh, and Blorfindel, if you do find someone stalking try to capture it alive."

Blorfindel tossed his head. He walked with Milia until they got a quarter mile from her house, then he disappeared into the trees. Milia rushed home and locked the door.

Blorfindel spent the rest of the day moving carefully from one place of concealment to another around Milia's house. He did not catch the shapetaker there, but he did notice a Fitheran who walked by on the path fairly often. Four students came to Milia's but she turned them away as directed. When the fourth student turned down the path towards town the suspicious Fitheran was forty yards behind her.

It could be a coincidence, Blorfindel thought. *The path is a public way. Maybe he just has a lot of business to do around here. I could follow him, but then I would be leaving Milia.* The Brighteyes watched Milia's student walking carelessly down the path. She was a little Fitheresse, probably only in her eighties. *I should stay and follow the plan.* Milia's voice echoed in his memory, *"You don't get to try again next year after that monster eats my students!" All right, Milia, I will follow her home.*

He followed from concealment until the houses started to get closer together, then he waited until they were out of sight and stepped boldly out into the lane. *It is a public way, after all. It should not be unusual for me to be walking down it, either.* After a very short distance he realized something. *She walks very slowly.* Blorfindel had to find an excuse to pause from time to time to avoid catching up with them. *He should be catching up with her, too. If he is not following her, then he should have walked by her long ago.* Blorfindel waited on the side of the path and checked his gear. He was as heavily armed as he had ever been. The Fitheran that he was following might have a concealed weapon, but certainly nothing to contend with his long bow, sword or war hammer. He took a deep breath, loosened the sword in his scabbard, and followed.

Soon the path ended at a road. The Fitheresse turned left and so did her follower. *That is just too obvious.* Blorfindel cut the corner, moving quickly from concealment to concealment and had a position up the road where he could not be seen. The Fitheresse went by. The Fitheran went by. Blorfindel waited until he could get out into the road without being seen. He had to wait too long ʝand his quarry was out of sight when he was finally on the road. He forced himself to walk normally. *I am catching up to them at this pace. I must not seem to be chasing.* He went a long way without catching them. *I should have caught up by now. I have lost them!* He was getting ready to check the cross streets when he heard a voice, "My lesson was canceled. Mistress Milia is sick. She thinks it might be catching."

Blorfindel slipped into cover again and closed on the sound as quickly as he could. The student was having a conversation with another Fitheresse. *That's probably her mother.* Then she started practicing on a harp. The sound was not loud, but distinct. Blorfindel found the house. *She did make a turn!* He found a good hiding place and almost forgot himself. *Where is the mystery Fitheran? If he is stalking the student, where will he go?*

Blorfindel moved away from the house. The suspicious Fitheran walked by on the street but kept going. *That is no coincidence. He will be back.* About an hour later he was back in a slightly different costume. Blorfindel was surprised when he walked boldly up to the house and knocked. The Brighteyes took a chance and dashed closer to the house, taking quick cover within easy hearing range.

The suspicious Fitheran was already talking, "…I'm sorry to say. I think you'll agree this is very serious."

"But there must be some mistake," the older Fitheresse responded, "Chessadel was with her aunt Meresa until her music lesson."

"I'm sorry, but I have reports that she was down by the river–"

"This is silly. Chessadel was with her aunt all day. She does this every week, the same thing. If you don't believe me go check with Meresa."

"And where can I find this aunt Meresa?"

"She lives at…"

You sneaky Kutel's-son! So now you go to the aunt, who might be alone, because you can not attack the little Fitheresse here. Blorfindel got the directions and left before the stalker. *I have you now!* Blorfindel had to remind himself that this was not fun. He ran through the streets until he reached the aunt's address. Once again he concealed himself and waited.

All was quiet for a very long time. The aunt did indeed seem to be alone. Blorfindel had started second-guessing himself when the stalker came down the lane with a wheelbarrow. Inside the wheelbarrow was an expensive-looking tall stone vase filled with long-cut flowers. There were four steps to get to the front door. He left the wheelbarrow at the bottom and knocked on the door.

"Hello?"

"Good afternoon. I'm looking for Meresa."

"That's me. What do you want? I'm not buying any flowers. I have a whole garden full out back."

"I have a gift here from a Chessadel? A vase to put your flowers in."

"A gift? She shouldn't be getting me gifts."

"I guess I can take it back if you want."

"A vase? Is it very expensive?"

"I wouldn't know about that. It's very heavy, so if you'll just send your husband out to pick it up, I'll be off. It's getting late. My wife will be wondering where I've got to."

"He's not home."

"Well, I can't wait long. My wife will have my head if I'm not home before the horizon covers the sun. When do you expect him?"

"Not for hours, I'm afraid."

That is just what he wanted to hear! Blorfindel started moving toward the house, keeping concealed all the way.

"Listen, why don't I just drop this off inside and you can have him move it around when he gets home?"

"If you're going to carry it in anyway, could you just set it over here at the end of the cloak-pegs?" She walked inside and to the right of the door. The stalker picked up the stone vase and followed her in. He left the door open.

Blorfindel gave up trying to stay hidden and made a run for the open doorway. He heard the vase touch down on the floor. Then he heard, "Just take a look and make certain that's where you want it." Blorfindel could just see the stalker's shoulder through the doorway.

Blorfindel dropped his bow at the base of the stairs next to the wheelbarrow. *It is not going to do me any good in there.* He vaulted the stairs and landed inside the cloak room. The Fitheresse had her back to him, looking at the vase on the floor. The stalker was behind her. He pulled a knife from within his tunic and clapped his other hand on her mouth. His back was to the door.

Blorfindel grabbed the stalker's knife-arm at the wrist and drew his own dagger with his left hand. His momentum carried him into the wall and spun the stalker around. He spun free of Blorfindel's grasp and they stood facing each other. Meresa fell to the floor.

Blorfindel looked it in the eye. "Do you remember me? Of course you do. I'm the one you're really after. I know what you are. I'm ready for you. Are you ready for me?"

The stalker shifted a bit, as though contemplating trying his luck in a knife-fight.

Blorfindel drew his war hammer. "What's the matter? Do I scare you?"

Its eyes flashed toward the doorway.

Meresa screamed.

It bolted for the doorway.

Blorfindel threw his hammer. The iron head struck between its shoulder blades and knocked it off its feet onto the wheelbarrow. It rolled and got back up, losing the knife in the process.

Blorfindel followed, drawing his sword as soon as he cleared the doorway. Blorfindel was faster. He cut its right ear open with a flick of the sword. "Are you ready for me? Are you ready to die?"

"Mercy!" It kept running.

"I am Blorfindel Brighteyes, son of Lalliam Steelhand! You live by my will or die by my hand."

"Mercy!" It was running down the street.

Blorfindel was easily faster than it. He laid his sword edge against its neck. "Stop."

It came gingerly to a halt. Blorfindel let his sword rest against its neck.

"Mercy." It was quivering now.

"You keep saying that. I wonder what you'd do if I were the one begging for mercy? Not this, I think." Blorfindel struck it on the back of the head with his dagger pommel. It dropped.

Blorfindel ran off to collect his bow and war hammer. He brought the wheelbarrow back as well. A crowd had started to gather when Blorfindel returned. He let Meresa do the talking when they asked their questions. She did not know the whole story, of course, but she knew that she had been attacked and that Blorfindel came to her rescue. That was enough to satisfy most of them. He threw the unconscious stalker in the wheelbarrow.

"What are you going to do with him?"

"I don't know. Linxico Oldgrape said I should bring him back alive, if I could." Blorfindel wheeled the senseless stalker away.

Blorfindel did not know where to go. Eventually he settled on Milia's house. *They will come looking for me there.* Linxico and Biolmi were there when he arrived.

"I told you he wasn't here," Linxico said to Biolmi. "What have you got there, a new friend?"

Blorfindel addressed Milia, "He followed Chessadel home and then tried to attack her aunt Meresa."

Milia covered her mouth with her hand but did not reply.

Linxico met Blorfindel in the lane and examined the body. "Well, it's still alive. It's not a Fitheran. I think you've got our shapetaker." Biolmi and Blorfindel took the body out of the wheelbarrow and set it on the ground, face down. Linxico examined it before rolling it over. "Shoot!

What did you do to it? I can understand knotting its skull, but it's got broken ribs, and maybe a broken spine?"

Blorfindel gave them a quick description of the battle.

"If I knew it could take this kind of punishment I would not have left you alone with it. It got up and ran with two broken ribs and a broken back?"

"It was pretty slow."

"I don't wonder! I don't suppose you've ever had a broken rib? Never mind, it's here now. Normally I'd tie off the cut ear, but that would put pressure on the skull. It won't bleed to death, anyway." Linxico drank one of his own vials and motioned for Biolmi and Blorfindel to roll it over. Then Linxico smeared something dark orange and unpleasant onto its upper lip. The smell made Blorfindel gag from six feet away.

Biolmi was careful to stand further back. He had his bow drawn and an arrow pointed at the shapetaker's chest. It coughed and flopped on the ground in obvious pain. Blorfindel cringed and Milia turned away. Linxico put a foot on its shoulder that kept it from rolling around. "Did you have a nice nap?"

It took a few quick shallow breaths through its mouth and whispered, "Mercy."

Linxico held up a vial of clear liquid. "I have your mercy right here. I can make the pain go away, or I can make it worse." He ground his heel into its shoulder. "But maybe we should check with Glimdel Goldbranch or Eresi Silkenrobe before we grant mercy, eh?"

It did not respond. The panic in its eyes was clear to see. Its breath continued in shallow, irregular, and painful gasps.

"If you want mercy, you're going to have to buy it with information."

Its voice as still weak, "Yes, information."

"What are you doing here?"

"I don't know where I am."

Linxico ground his heel in a bit more. "The next time you give me an answer like that, I'm going to have our oversized friend test your kneecap against his war hammer," Linxico nodded toward Blorfindel. "How much do you want to bet your bones lose?" His smile was most unpleasant.

It did not respond.

"Why are you in Sekri Timbrali?"

"I have to eat."

"You eat brains," Linxico replied, "Fithern brains don't taste good, do they?"

Biolmi broke in, "I'm disgusted that you know that."

"Have you forgotten how this works? I ask it questions, it answers, or Blorfindel hurts it. If it does anything stupid you put an arrow in it and I have to summon its ghost and examine it with a spirit wrack." He looked down at the shapetaker, "You didn't know I could do that, did you? If you think this hurts, imagine how bad it gets when I put the screws to your soul."

"Pig brains. I eat pig brains."

"I wondered who bought those. All I could ever do with them was make a sauce for acorns or truffles – you know how pigs love truffles? Well, if you get the right part of their brains in the sauce with a little empathy magic it really brings out the flavor. But that's not the point. You're here to kill someone. Who is that?"

"No one. I eat pigs."

"Break his kneecap."

"No! Mercy!"

"What's his name?"

"Son of Lalliam, Ghinlihil, Blorfindel, the Brighteyes." It looked at Blorfindel, waiting for the hammer to fall. "But not anymore."

"Did you give up before or after he beat you senseless? Never mind. Why Blorfindel?"

"I don't know why. I don't!"

"So you just had this overwhelming urge to travel to Sekri Timbrali to kill one Fitheran in particular? You're going to have to do better than that."

"Curse. I have a curse. I used to eat Kutel. Nobody cares if Kutel die, right? But I got caught."

"I always wondered, are Kutel smarter than pigs?"

"Pigs' memories are sweeter, but Kutel remember more."

"So a Kutel put a curse on you?"

"No. It was the Kutel Wizard-King."

Biolmi raised an eyebrow. Linxico said, "The Wizard-King isn't a Kutel, I suppose that's no surprise. What is he?"

"He looks like a Tafer, but he isn't. I don't know. His skin is all wrong."

"Not a skeleton, though? Tafer Wizards do that to themselves sometimes. I guess you can't become a great wizard if you die of old age at a hundred."

"No he has skin, but it looks older than the rest of him."

"Name?"

"The Kutel don't use his name."

"So the Wizard-King put a curse on you to kill the son of Lalliam. Did he know his name?"

"No, I found the name."

"Who did he tell you to kill, then?"

"The son of Lalliam. I must kill… he said I must kill the son of Lalliam."

"Why?"

"He didn't say why. He said I could accept the curse or they would whip me to death. That's all I know."

"Who do you report to?"

"The Wizard-King said if I come back, they pay me. I won't go back. After I kill him I will be free of the curse, but now I will never be free."

"Where were you when the Kutel caught you?"

"Shonu."

"Why would the Wizard-King know Lalliam's name, and why would he want Blorfindel dead?"

"I don't know. I promise, I don't know."

"You must have found out something. How did you find Lalliam's son?"

"He heard that not everyone died at Foralis with Steelhand, but Foralis is gone. All Fitherani come to Sekri Timbrali, so I came here to look first. Everyone knew about the Knights of the Circle and the Brighteyes from Foralis. Biolmi trains the Brighteyes, but they live like hermits."

Biolmi laughed bitterly, "Was it just last night you told me it wouldn't kill me to get out more?"

Linxico answered matter-of-factly, "Yes, it was last night." He turned his attention back to the shapetaker, "When were you caught? How long have you been cursed?"

"Last fall. I have been on the trail for five months."

"He told you something else, didn't he? Or he said something when he didn't think you were listening? No… one of the Kutel whose brain you ate had heard something, hadn't he? Tell me what it is. Maybe we can get some sort of revenge for you – for putting this stupid, dangerous curse on you."

"A prophecy. The line of the Steelhand… I don't know. The Kutel was stupid, he didn't understand."

"What was the prophecy? What did the Kutel remember?"

"A steel hand slapped… him… in the face, but he bit the hand off. Then a chip from the hand caught in his throat. That's all he remembered. That's all I know."

"How did the Kutel know about the prophecy?"

"The Kutel worked in the palace. Scrubbing floors, that sort of thing. The Kutel was listening when he should not have been. The Wizard-King was telling the dream to someone, or something. The scrubbing Kutel was afraid, but he could not remember why. I remember the name, Lalliam Steelhand, but I don't know why. It was a stupid, floor-scrubbing Kutel."

"How did you get caught?"

"The floor-scrubbing Kutel, I don't know... the Wizard-King knew I wasn't the floor-scrubbing Kutel. I don't know how, but he recognized me. Please, I've told you everything."

Linxico opened the vial and poured it into the shapetaker's mouth. "I guess you've earned this."

It closed its eyes and it relaxed. The pain seemed to go away. Then it lay still.

"Now what do we do with it?" Blorfindel wanted to know.

"We find an out-of-the-way spot to bury it."

"Bury it?"

"We can't just let it rot in Milia's yard, can we?" Blorfindel looked to Biolmi for an explanation. Linxico continued, "The vial was poison. We can't have shapetakers stalking around can we? It's not painful, just like falling asleep. Compared to what it did to Glimbel and Eresi, and whoever it is now, that is mercy."

"What about the prophecy?"

"What about it?"

"The chip from the steel hand gets caught in the wizard's throat."

"Well, if you have a lot of faith in the prophecy, and you're ever in the presence of the wizard who rules the Kutel, you can try to jump down his throat. Maybe you'll get caught."

"What?"

"Listen, Blorfindel, remember what I told you about predicting the future? Just forget about it. Yeah, the prophecy could have been talking about Lalliam Steelhand, but it also could have been a knight, right? A steel hand – a gauntlet. Maybe you're the chip off the steel hand; maybe not, maybe it's his sword, or an arrow, or a bone fragment or some idea that he told someone before he died – if the prophecy is talking about your father at all. Maybe the wizard just spends all of his time and effort trying to hunt you down instead of paying attention close to home and someone puts a knife in his back." Linxico gestured toward the shapetaker's body, "He never said why he took the form of the floor scrubber, did he? I expect he wasn't in it for the glory. It got him pretty close to the wizard, though, before he got caught.

"The best thing to do with prophecies is ignore them. If they are going to come true you can't stop them. If not, then it's nothing anyway. Almost no one really figures a prophecy out before it gets fulfilled, then they say, 'Oh, that must be what the dream was about.' Don't waste your time. It's probably just some paranoid nightmare anyway. Megalomaniacal wizards suffer from those all the time."

"What kind of wizards?"

"Never mind. It's not important. Just forget about the prophecy. The point is that there is a wizard who rules the Kutel in Shonu who is afraid of you. He doesn't know who you are. He doesn't know where you are. The shapetaker was under a curse, and a powerful one, but because the curse was what drove him, there probably isn't anyone following him. The only other thing would be, was he scrying you?"

"Scrying?"

"Looking for you in a crystal ball or something. The answer is no. He isn't. I checked before we started the interrogation, no one was scrying. So you can add this far-away wizard to the list of people who want you dead. Personally, I'd be more concerned about the Kels. They're much better at this assassination thing."

"But the Amada haven't even come close since I came to Sekri Timbrali."

"Exactly, so don't worry about it."

"But the shapetaker–"

"Shapetakers are rarer than patient Kutel. This one got unlucky and got caught by someone who cared. If he said the wizard was breeding shapetakers to hunt you down, then I would be concerned. There won't be any more coming."

Biolmi put his arrow away. "We should take it to the Archers' Hall. The judges will want to see it."

"Morbid fools, what good will that do?" Linxico shrugged, "You're right, though."

The judges at the Archers' Hall were satisfied that they had killed a shapetaker. Since Sekri Timbrali had never had problems with shapetakers, they accepted that this must be the one. The last form was indeed from a Fitheran who had tested with Eresi. They found his mutilated body in a shallow grave under his home.

Biolmi went with Blorfindel to Meresa's house where they gave her all the information that she could stand. The archery master decided that there was no real reason to alarm Chessadel or her mother, since they were in no danger now.

Blorfindel and Biolmi went home, ate standing, and went to sleep. It had been a very long day.

Chapter 16

Exit the Hero

The next morning Blorfindel was woken by a knock on the door.
Not again. This morning he was only hungry and stiff. He slung his sword
belt over his shoulder before answering. There were two Finterani at the
door, one adult and one child. They were surprised and slightly afraid
when Blorfindel opened the door. The little one said, "He's still here."

"Hello?" Blorfindel's hand dropped to his sword hilt. *Who are you and
how do you know I was supposed to get killed?*

The older Fitheran took a deep breath. "Good morning. I am called
Haomin Darkleaf. This is my son, Galron. We, that is, I had heard that
master Biolmi Yewstaff was without an apprentice. You must be the one
called Blorfindel Brighteyes?"

"That's me. Good morning."

"I don't mean to be rude. Didn't you pass your test this year?"

"This year? The day before yesterday, yes." Blorfindel took his hand
off the sword.

"So, does master Biolmi have an opening?"

"I'll go ask him." Blorfindel turned to get the archery master. *What if
he does? Am I really done here? What do I do now?*

When Blorfindel returned with Biolmi there was another father and son
pair coming down the path. Blorfindel was lighting the fire under the
morning tea when another arrived. By the time Blorfindel and Biolmi had
finished their morning tea (the new apprentices were all too young for

tea), there were four new apprentices and Biolmi had to start turning Fitherani away.

Blorfindel lead them out to the stream to show them where to draw the morning wash water. They all looked very, very young. *I passed my test. I am done here. They all know it. All of Sekri Timbrali expects me to move on with my life. What do I do now?* All of his plans for after the test had been vague, romantic notions. Now that the time had come he could not think of the next step.

Biolmi was busy with the new apprentices as soon as they came back in. Blorfindel went out to think. He spent some time with the pendulum targets. The archer's talisman around his neck did not magically make him better at hitting them. He only shot one round good enough to pass the test.

One of the new apprentices came out to get him. "Master Biolmi says you're supposed to come in now." Blorfindel absentmindedly followed.

Biolmi handed Blorfindel a message. "Take this to Jerhalli Quickshanks." He handed another message, "On the way, drop this one with Milia Brightstrings, but don't dawdle." The apprentices laughed. Biolmi looked at them sternly. "You need to talk to your cousin as early as possible." Blorfindel started towards the door. "Wait! Take your full kit, especially that Tafer skull-cracker of yours. I don't want any of these youths getting any stupid ideas."

Blorfindel armed himself as quickly as he could. *He is throwing me out.* The smiles on the new apprentices disappeared when Blorfindel came back looking grim with sword, dagger, bow, two quivers full of arrows and that black iron war hammer. *That's it, I'm out the door. He is sending me back to Jerhalli. I should want that. I can learn to be a Fitheran like Jaico wants for Afinlia. I can make money and get married and be a father... like Jaico.* Blorfindel felt sick thinking about it. Three weeks ago all he could think about was being with Afinlia. Now all he could think about was 'Blorfindel Silverfingers.'

He arrived at Milia's house looking shocked and dazed. He knocked twice and the music stopped. "Oh, hello Blorfindel. I'm with a student."

Blorfindel handed over the message roll. "Message for you."

"Blorfindel? Are you all right?"

"Yes, I'm all right. Why wouldn't I be all right? I just became an archer."

She took a step back from the door. "Sing."

"What?"

"Sing." Her hand reached behind her and grabbed the stem of her cloak rack. Her knuckles went white even as the color started draining out of her face. "Sing!"

Blorfindel sang the first verse that came to mind.

Milia slumped against the wall and exhaled. "You scared me. You aren't yourself this morning, and after yesterday..."

"I'm sorry. I guess my mind is on other things."

"It's all right. I should have expected it, really. Fitherani like Biolmi and Linxico, they act like it's no big deal – like we're supposed to just get over it. They've done it so often, I think they forget what its like for the rest of us."

"I should have seen it coming."

"Don't be silly. How could you have known? Listen, I am with a student right now, but if you want to talk later–"

"I have to go see Jerhalli. Maybe I can set something up with Afinlia later." His voice was flat.

"You should do that. Just remember, Jaico had a hell of a scare yesterday, too." She giggled, "You broke his door down."

Blorfindel could remember the terror on Jaico's face when Biolmi pointed the arrow at him. *How long before I am just like Jaico?* He did not laugh.

"Don't worry about it. You did him a favor yesterday. You saved his daughter. I guess you saved me too. In all of the excitement I forgot to thank you." She smiled up at him, "Thank you, for my life."

Blorfindel had never been more proud in his life. "You're welcome. I'm glad I could do it before... How old is Chessadel?"

"Too young. She's seventy-nine. What would we do without you?" She had to pull him down a bit to kiss his cheek. "Thank you."

Blorfindel walked to Jerhalli's home with his mind swirling. His door was open and he was doing business in the front office.

"I don't care if it is the first shipment of the year. Five paddiban is too much. We both know that it will be less than two in month."

"Not for Conjinese silk. You'll have to buy from the Kutel to get a price that low."

"Oh, right, and you can prove that your silk wasn't made by slave labor?"

"Just look at the seal on the crates."

"You can get crates anywhere. Two paddiban, that's it."

"Four."

"Go ask Eresi if he wants to pay four. Oh, yeah, he's dead. Two."

The seller turned to storm out of the office. He was not expecting Blorfindel to be in the doorway. Blorfindel was not expecting him to be a Tafer. The Tafer's hand went to the hilt of his Manrachian scimitar. Blorfindel was faster. He jumped back and drew his sword.

"So this is how you keep your prices down? First you eliminate your competition, and if I won't sell at your price, it's down to steel?"

Jerhalli was as surprised as any of them. "What? Blorfindel, what's going on?"

"He went for his sword."

"You snuck up on me. You scared me." The Tafer held his hands up with palms facing Blorfindel. Blorfindel sheathed his sword. The Tafer walked away quickly, cursing in his own language.

Jerhalli waived Blorfindel in. "That was exciting. I do believe you rattled him. Good. He keeps trying to act like a big bad nomad. Maybe he'll be a little more pliable next time."

"I have a message for you." Blorfindel handed over Biolmi's message.

Jerhalli did not open it immediately. "I heard that you passed your test this year. You should have told me, I would have been there. Too bad it wasn't really Eresi, I heard you rattled him, too."

"You know… knew Eresi?"

"We both do business in silk. It's purely professional. He liked people to think he was more trustworthy because he was a judge. Hah! He was as dirty as a Kutel. Too bad about the thing, though, the whatever-it-was. I hear they're dangerous. You were involved with that, too, weren't you? Don't look so surprised. I knew the first silk shipment was coming soon and I was keeping track of Eresi." He stopped to read the message. "Oh. Well, I guess I should have expected that." He picked up his yellow cloak. "Let's go."

Blorfindel did not ask. He fell in behind Jerhalli. Jerhalli Quickshanks was perhaps the only Fitheran who could walk faster than Blorfindel. Blorfindel tried to keep up without running. He was surprised to see him enter an armorer's shop. The armorer was busy with another customer. It was the Fitheresse who had passed her test with Blorfindel. He could not remember her name. She was trying on a shirt of mail.

"The mail shirt is very popular. It offers good protection, especially from the slashing weapons that the Kutel favor, without slowing the wearer very much."

"It's heavy."

"You get used to it, though you can expect to get tired more quickly than usual. There is no way around that. With the extra weight you might weigh as much as a Taforam. You can't expect to just ignore that."

"I feel fat with all the padding and the mail."

"You look great," Blorfindel blurted.

"Really?"

"Um, yeah. Before – you know, during the test – I didn't know you were so pretty."

Her father said, "Armor is going to be bulky and heavy. The important part is that you don't get hurt."

The armorer disagreed, "Well, it's kind of a balancing act, really. Like I said, the mail shirt is a good compromise, but she won't be as fast on her feet, there's just no way around it. On the other hand, look at the knights' armor. It's easily twice as heavy, and it is very good protection, but very restrictive."

Jerhalli smiled, "And then there's the price."

"That's true, you'd be paying maybe forty times as much for armor that isn't twice as good. Still, it works for the knights – they're in close all the time. With mail you can shoot and move. That's the key. Don't let them get close to you. That's why everyone likes the mail shirt. I sell five shirts for every set of leggings."

She was still frowning at it. "Isn't it loud?"

"Walk around. Yes, it makes some noise, but again, it's a compromise. Now we could try to get you in something quiet, like a leather armor, but you're giving away a lot of protection, and you still have to spend a lot of time on it to keep it quiet."

Her father dismissed the idea, "We won't be giving up the protection."

Blorfindel remembered from his years at the fortress. "The knights would just charge their enemies. Most weapons couldn't touch them."

The armorer disagreed, "That's not really true. Part of it is armor, part training, and part is up to the person doing the attacking. No, you're not going to put an arrow through the center of a heavy breastplate, but there are joints and visor slits and that sort of thing."

"What about the mail shirt?" Her father wanted to know.

"Mail is sort of hit and miss against arrows, if you understand my meaning. These rings are smaller than an arrowhead. That, combined with the padding, will usually stop an arrow, but if the bow is strong enough a link can break. You can go with reinforcements here and there, or we're talking about plate again."

Blorfindel remembered Ammoss' armor, "What about bands? Little rectangular plates?"

"What, were you raised by Tafers?"

"Is there something wrong with that?"

The armorer started to say something, but bit it back. He was used to being the biggest Fitheran in the room and Blorfindel worried him a bit. "Metal bands do provide more protection against arrows, but it's a lot more weight and you still can't cover everything. If a Kutel shoots it doesn't have to hit anything vital because they use poison. Most archers just count on being better archers than Kutel, which isn't hard. You hit, they miss, no more problem. It's when they get close you want the armor to protect you until you can win free."

"Except they don't always miss, and you can't always win free."

"Who _are_ you?"

Jerhalli introduced him, "He is called Blorfindel Brighteyes. His parents were killed by Kutel in Foralis." Tears were running in Jerhalli's eyes. "He's right. I was there. Sometimes the Kutel win. There is more to coming safe from a battle than armor."

Her father asked, "You made it. What's your secret?"

"I ran away." Only Blorfindel recognized the shame in Jerhalli's voice.

The Fitheresse's father thought that was a good idea. "You see, my dear, sometimes you just have to run away."

The armorer chimed in, "And the mail is going to let you move."

Jerhalli would not let it go, "You don't know what you're talking about!" The savagery in his voice made them all stop and face him. "I ran away. I wasn't alone. I wasn't the last one. We left them all to die! I have to carry that with me for the rest of my life. We were supposed to stop and shoot, but we just kept running. I didn't even save Blorfindel! He had to be rescued by a Tafer. You can't know." He was breaking down. "They were counting on me to shoot. <Sob> They burned the town. The bodies…" He buried his head in his hands.

"We'll, ah, take the mail shirt." Her father counted out eight gold malstren coins.

The armorer took their money and saw them out.

Blorfindel put a stool under Jerhalli. He did not notice. He pulled himself together almost as quickly as he broke down. "Blorfindel needs some armor."

The armorer wanted to say something to cheer Jerhalli, but he could not think of anything and he was afraid of setting him off again. "Of course. So you're looking for something heavier than mail?"

Blorfindel shrugged, "No, actually I was thinking more about leather – light, quick, and quiet."

The armorer shook his head but did not argue with these customers. He went to the rack. "You know, I generally ask customers to try their armor with their full kit, but I didn't expect the cittern." Blorfindel did not respond. "I might not have anything ready in your size. I keep a lot of leather armor ready, but you're larger than most. Usually the big Fitherani are looking for mail."

Blorfindel shook his head. "Too loud, and too slow."

"I thought you were sold on bands over mail."

"If I'm going to war, maybe. So far all of my battles have been about stealth."

"You just passed your archer test this year, right? How many battles have you seen?"

"I knocked out a shapetaker yesterday. I split a Tafer's skull in Kingstone. I got knocked out by a Kutel. I ran away from Foralis, too."

"You were eighty," Jerhalli insisted.

"Eighty-one. I was eighty-seven when the Kutel caught me by surprise and knocked me out."

The armorer was impressed, "Raise the trees, dell, are you sure you don't want something heavier? It sounds like you need it."

"Leather."

"I'll have to get some measurements." He started taking measurements. "How did you get away from the Kutel?"

"A slaver killed it with a crossbow." Blorfindel never knew that it was actually a different Kutel that knocked him out.

"A slaver?"

"A half-Kutel. He sold me to a traveling troupe."

"That explains the cittern."

"Actually, Milia Brightstrings is teaching me the cittern."

The armorer gave up trying to engage him in conversation. He disappeared into the back room for a few minutes and returned with a dark brown suit of hardened leather armor. "I had a Tafer order it. He said it was too tight, I bet it fits you." Blorfindel tried it on. It did fit. He put on the rest of his kit over the top. "One suit of custom leather armor, that's going to be three paddiban."

Jerhalli answered, "If we don't buy it you're never going to sell that. Two."

"If you buy armor cheap you get cheap armor, besides he's bigger than average, that means more leather."

"My office brokered your leather purchase two years ago. It doesn't cost you anywhere near that much."

"Two and a half, or you can take your stories down the street and wait two weeks for someone to make a new set."

Jerhalli counted out two silver paddiban and four copper stowsaw. "Done."

In the street outside the armorer's shop Jerhalli said, "I've got a lot of work to get to this morning. Actually," Jerhalli opened his purse, "You might as well have some coin in your purse." He laughed when he looked at Blorfindel's belt. "You might want to start by buying a purse." He handed Blorfindel seven paddiban and one gold malstren. Blorfindel had never had so much money in his life. It was more than four years pay for a member of the troupe.

Blorfindel did buy a purse in the market. He wandered around for a short while, but he was not really interested in shopping. He was more concerned about his future. *What do I do now? Biolmi has new apprentices. Jerhalli does not want me in the way, either.*

He was lost in thought and wandering aimlessly when someone called his name. It was Meresa. She had a small booth in the market selling flowers. He wandered toward it.

"Blorfindel, I never got a chance to thank you. I didn't know. I only heard this morning what that thing was going to do to me." She shuddered. "I thought he just wanted money or something. You saved my life." She started plucking flowers from her display and making a bouquet. "I'm not a wealthy Fitheresse, Blorfindel, but here. Thank you. If there is anything I can do… I don't know, what do you do when someone saves your life?"

"Uh, it's fine, really." Blorfindel did not know what to say either. "Thanks for the flowers."

"Oh, please! I mean… you're a hero. I should get you a gold talisman or something."

He had been wandering and feeling sorry for himself. Meresa's 'thank you' put him on top of the world. "No really, the flowers are perfect." His smile said that he meant it.

There was purpose in his stride and a song on his lips when he left the market. The flowers gave him a new sense of purpose. His stride brought him to Afinlia's house. There were two Fitherani working on the door when he arrived. They moved out of the way as he strutted through the doorway. "Hello!"

Jaico Silverfingers recognized Blorfindel's voice. "Good afternoon, Blorfindel," he said as he entered the foyer, "Afinlia is not at home." He laughed. "Just as well for my doors."

"I'm sorry about the door, but–"

"You should have said... The door's not important. It will be fixed today." He eyed the workers dubiously. "Or at least they tell me it will be." He took the flowers from Blorfindel, "I'll see that Afinlia gets them. Won't you stay and talk for a moment? We can have tea on the back balcony, away from this." He waived at the carpentry.

Blorfindel was better prepared for battle than for a conversation with Jaico Silverfingers. He took a deep breath. "That would be very nice, Mister Jaico."

The back balcony was very nice, as were the white wicker chairs with green velvet cushions, the matching marble-topped table, and the brightly polished silver tea service. Jaico handed the bouquet to the servant after she served the tea, "Put these in some water, please, Loasi." She took the flowers, curtseyed and left them. The pattern painted on the tea cups matched the wicker pattern on the chairs.

Jaico breathed in the tea steam and put his cup down. "We haven't had much opportunity to talk. You were in constant practice before, of course." He smiled and did not say, *Except for all the time you spent with Afinlia*. "Things were somewhat chaotic yesterday. You passed your test, congratulations."

"Thank you, Mister Jaico." Blorfindel sipped his tea. It was too hot. He tried not to let it show.

"Now that you don't have to practice your archery day and night, what will you do with all your free time?" Jaico breathed the steam again. The tea was still too hot to drink.

"I don't know." Blorfindel instantly knew that was the wrong thing to say. "I think I should get Jerhalli to teach me how to make money. That is, Jerhalli Quickshanks–"

Jaico smiled again. "I know Jerhalli. He is your cousin and quite a successful merchant. I checked up on you before you joined Afinlia for music lessons. So do you think you'd like to buy and sell?"

"I don't know." Blorfindel burned his tongue on the tea again. "I mean, that's what I should do, right?"

"You don't strike me as the type who would be happy as a merchant, Blorfindel. Incidentally, the armor suits you, if you'll pardon the expression."

"Thank you, Mister Jaico. I like it – the action, that is. Yesterday, running down the shapetaker, and even this morning when a Tafer went for his sword in Jerhalli's office."

"What happened?"

"Nothing – just a misunderstanding, but I… I don't know… I guess I'm just not used to being good at anything. When I was taking the stealth test and I beat the judges at their own game, yeah, oh yeah. And yesterday, when the shapetaker ran away from me." He managed to catch himself before he said, *And when I broke down your door on the first try.*

Jaico's tea was finally cool enough to sip. "I should thank you for that, Blorfindel. The shapetaker had me fooled. Afinlia might have been in danger." He could hardly admit to himself what grave danger he had put her in by preferring the shapetaker as a suitor. "You see, Blorfindel, I have an appreciation for fine things, and I have a fair amount of them, but above all is my daughter. Afinlia is my treasure." He stared at Blorfindel over his tea cup to be certain that sunk in. "You're a nice Fitheran, Blorfindel, but you have a long way to go. I mean, what do you have to offer Afinlia?"

"I love her."

"I don't doubt it, but love won't pay rent and Afinlia is used to a certain degree of luxury." He gestured to their surroundings. "I like you, Borfindel Brighteyes, but you have got to show me more. My daughter will not be spending a millennium in poverty just because you fell in love."

"Mister Jaico–"

"Blorfindel, I'm not saying 'no'. I'm saying 'not yet'. You passed one test this year. You need to get ready for the next one. You need to show me that you can be a good provider, not just a companion."

"Yes, Mister Jaico."

"Blorfindel, you're young. Afinlia is young, too. You may find that this is all about music and starlight. I will be very disappointed if you break my daughter's heart. I don't want her to break yours, either. Afinlia is playing. She doesn't know what she wants. Maybe it is you, maybe not."

"What do I need to do to prove that I'm worthy?"

"'Worthy' is not the right word. You should start with 'serious,' and 'committed.' Blorfindel, if you can save up two hundred malstren, I'll know that you're serious and that Afinlia means more to you than just a pretty face – that she's not just your Fitheresse of the century."

"Two hundred malstren?" *I might not make that in my lifetime!*

"Afinlia is not for sale at any price, Blorfindel. When you've saved two hundred then I'll know you can take care of her. I can't say whether she will be ready, or even interested."

Blorfindel was not listening. *Two hundred malstren! Where am I going to get two hundred malstren? They say Jerhalli is rich, but he was quibbling over three paddiban this morning. How long would it take him to raise two hundred malstren? How long would it take me to learn how to make money as a merchant? It took half a century to learn to be an archer. Can I wait another half a century to be a merchant? Will Afinlia wait? Jaico has got to be bluffing.*

Jaico was still talking, "… and, of course, it may be that another Fitheran comes to court Afinlia. She, and I, can't wait forever for you to prove yourself. If another respectable young Fitheran arrives with two hundred malstren to his name I will have to give him a chance – it's only fair, you know. Glimbel Goldbranch may have been the first, but now that Afinlia is a century and a half I expect more suitors to try their hand. Milliachi Greybark is interested, or at least his father says so, and he is from a very distinguished family. I expect that he will have little trouble raising two hundred malstren."

"So if he comes up with the gold first–"

"I'm not selling Afinlia to the highest bidder. I said that I won't let her go into poverty for love, well I won't let her go into wealth without love, either. He has the money, you have her heart – for now, anyway. I'm afraid that it is easier to win the heart of a young Fitheresse than it is to acquire wealth. I'm sorry, Blorfindel, but that puts you at a disadvantage."

"Yes, Mister Jaico."

"Listen, Blorfindel, if you can build a nice nest a bird will come. If it's not Afinlia then it will be someone else. You're an attractive, athletic, young Fitheran. When you have some gold to your name you may be surprised at how popular you become, and when the other Fitheresse start paying attention perhaps you won't be so concerned about Afinlia."

"I love her, Mister Jaico, I'm not going to give up on her just because someone else is interested in my purse."

"Good. Now all you have to do is prove it, Blorfindel. When you have the gold–"

Blorfindel was lost in thought again, *How much did it cost Linxico to set himself up with a restaurant and farms and vineyards? That has to be more than two hundred malstren. I wonder how much that magic robe is worth?* He remembered Biolmi's words from The Canopy: *'If you're willing to put your life on the line… you can make big money and do the world a favor at the same time.' The only way I am going to be able to make two hundred malstren is to take it. Korus Vet had three hundred platinum doutaks, that is twice what I need. All I need to do is catch someone like Korus Vet, and maybe keep someone else from being sold into slavery.*

"… do you understand?" Jaico looked him in the eye.

Blorfindel stood up. "I'll get the gold. I'll be back before anyone has a chance with Afinlia, you'll see. With Ilsorma as my witness, you'll see!" He stormed out. Jaico was still talking when Blorfindel jumped over one of the Fitherani working on the bottom hinge of the front door.

Blorfindel was well into the street when he realized that he did not know where he was going. His first considered stop was Milia Brightstrings' house.

"Hello, Blorfindel. I'm afraid you caught me with another student."

"That's fine. I just wanted to return your cittern." He unstrapped the instrument.

"Return it? Why? I don't need it back right now."

"I'm going away."

"Really? I guess I shouldn't be surprised. The shapetaker was looking for you, after all. You know, you should just keep it."

"I can't–"

"No, you're right." Milia took the cittern from him and disappeared into the house for a few minutes. She left the door open so he waited. She returned with a different cittern which was in much better condition. "Take this one, instead."

"But–"

She held up a tiny hand, "No. Take it. You saved my life. If it hadn't been for you that thing would be out there waiting for Chessadel's next lesson so that it could eat my brain. Take it. It is the very least I can do."

"It was–"

"No. I insist. Take it." She handed him a leather case to match the instrument.

"Thank you."

"No, thank you, and keep safe. I'll miss our little lessons," she smiled knowingly, "Afinlia will miss them, too. Have you said goodbye yet?"

"No. She isn't at home."

"You can't just leave without saying goodbye! What's she going to think?"

"I'll find her before I go."

"Of course you will. Good luck, and thanks again."

Blorfindel's next stop was the market. Earlier he had been browsing aimlessly but now he strode with purpose from vendor to vendor. He modeled his purchases after the equipment that Ammoss carried on a long trip and those useful things that Biolmi or the other Fitherani had brought on the escape from Kingstone. Soon his new backpack was heavy and his new purse was light.

Blorfindel went from the market to Biolmi's home. The archery master was teaching his new apprentices about wood grains when Blorfindel walked in. "I forgot my hunting cap."

Biolmi got up to meet him as he retrieved the cap. "They had armor that fit you? Let me see."

Blorfindel unslung his pack and stuffed his old brown hunting cap on top of his new gear. He turned slowly so that Biolmi could see the new armor.

"That's nice. I though you would have to wait for a custom job. I see you've been shopping for some other things, too. What do you need the cap for?"

"I'm leaving."

"Leaving?"

Blorfindel slung his pack back on and adjusted the straps. "I'm off to make my fortune." He did not meet Biolmi's gaze.

"You still have a lot to learn."

"I'll never learn everything that you want to teach me. I'm running out of time."

"Time for what? The test isn't sneaking up on you anymore. You have time to learn archery properly now."

"I have a new test." Blorfindel did look the archery master in the eyes now, "I have to pass Jaico's test or I will lose Afinlia."

Biolmi shook his head. "The stupid, coin-scratching seed-counter! He'll make you into his own image if you let him."

"I have to go. I have to find Afinlia."

"Oh, is that all?" Biolmi said, thinking Blorfindel's only task was to find Afinlia. "Listen, when you get done with Jaico's test, come back and get your archery in order."

"I will."

"Good, I'll be expecting you. Hey, take your cloak, it may get cold after the sun is behind the horizon."

"I bought a new one."

"Take both – that way you won't have to get your new one dirty. Save it for when you want to look good. Goodbye." Biolmi went back to the four apprentices.

"Goodbye." Blorfindel stuffed his old cloak in the top of his pack.

Blorfindel walked back toward Jaico's house. He found a spot just down the lane and waited there for Afinlia. It was less than an hour later when he saw her coming down the lane. He stepped out. She bit her lip and slowed her walk until she stopped just out of arm's reach.

He has changed, she thought. *What happened? He looks like he is going to war.* "Blorfindel, what are you doing here? If my father catches you here…" *Feadin, he isn't going to carry me off? Maybe father was right.*

"I needed to catch you to say goodbye."

"Goodbye? What do you mean? Your leaving?"

"I have to. I have to… make my fortune." Blorfindel did not really know what he was going to do, much less how to explain it.

"So that's it? You become an archer and off you go?"

"I'll be back. I'll be back as soon as I can."

"So what am I supposed to do? You'll be gone for a century having all sorts of fun all over the world, and I'll be stuck here. Father won't even pay for music lessons anymore."

"I don't know. I mean, it can't be like it was, anyway. You have new suitors. What about Glimbel Goldbranch?"

"He's just some Fitheran my father knows… ah, knew? He's dead, isn't he?"

Blorfindel tossed his head, "I think so."

"When are you leaving?"

"Now. I was waiting to say goodbye to you."

"What happened? The last time we… had a music lesson… I thought you'd be around forever."

"The last time we had a music lesson, you stood me up so that you could meet with your new suitor."

"That was father's idea!" There was a long silence. "You've changed. Then you took your test, and you broke down our door, and you ambush me on the way home, and you're leaving." She looked over his head rather than meet his eyes, "Where are you going?"

"I don't know. North. I'll go hunting Kutel."

"That's why you're wearing armor?"

"Yeah, I guess so."

"Why can't you just stay?"

"I can't." Blorfindel was not prepared for it to be this difficult. The words would not come to him. "Things have changed. Your father will give you to someone else. He said I have to make some money, a lot of money. I can't do that here, not fast enough."

"When will you be back?"

"I don't know. When I have the money."

"You're going to get yourself killed. You just passed your test this week."

"It's all I know how to do. It's all I'm good at. If I wait, you'll find someone new. Your father has him all picked out."

"I'm supposed to wait here while you have your adventures?"

"I'll be back as soon as I can."

"Just go. I have to go home now." She walked quickly passed him so that he could not see her cry.

"Goodbye." Blorfindel watched her all the way to her door. She looked very, very beautiful to him now. When she was gone he stared at the door for a couple of deep breaths. "I love you!"

He took one last deep breath, turned, and walked away.

Appendix A

Glossary

Alath – Timbrali word for blessed or sacred.

Ammoss – Tafer warrior and tracker from Dath. Foster father of Ghinlihil.

Anagoth – god of Virtue, son of Feadin.

Ardiv – brass coin current in the Shield valley and surrounding areas. Worth 4 hauger of 1/6 of a stowsaw, one ardiv will usually buy two beers at a tavern.

Arienic – god of song and gifts

Baett – Kutel god of hatred, believed to be the creator of Kutel

Biolmi Yewstaff – master Fithern archery trainer

Blorfindel Brighteyes – Fithern archer and adventurer (Blorfindel translates to "Child of Bondage")

Bur-Droo – literally "Cold Water" in the Kutel language; a Kutel city in the mountains near the Shield Valley.

Conjinese Empire – the southernmost nation known to the Shield Valley

Cral – a species of people aligned with the Kutel. They are large, averaging 9' and 850 lbs. Cral are less intelligent, on average, than Kutel. Their coloration varies widely.

Dath – Tafer vilage in the northwestern Shield Valley. Also the Timbrali word for the tree parts remaining after cutting a tree and taking the desired products.

Dell – Timbrali for "child" or "little one"; shortened to "-del" when used as a suffix.

Doutak – a small platinum coin current in the Shield Valley and surrounding areas. Worth 64 stowsaw, the dautak is not in common use. A single doutak will by a Fithern long sword. A large and well-trained warhorse might cost 20 doutak.

Dhu – god of nature, protector of all life that is unaligned with any other deity.

Feadin – goddess of righteousness.

Fitheran – species of people, or the male of the species. Fitherani (male) adults range from 4'6" to 5'5" and average around 100 lbs. The natural lifespan of the Fitherani can reach two thousand years, with 1200 being common. It is believed that the Fithern lifespan was created so that they could be gardeners of great trees..

Fitherani – plural of Fitheran or a mixed group of Fitherani (males) and Fitheressi (females).

Fitheresse – female Fitheran. They are generally smaller and lighter than males, averaging 4'10" and 85 lbs. 5'2" and 100 lbs is an exceptionally large Fitheresse.

Fitheressi – plural of Fitheresse.

Fithern – of or pertaining to Fitherani.

Fiz – Timbrali for water. Plural: Fizthe

Frenlias – Fithern god of nature, believed to be the creator of Fitherani.

Frenlias' Gift – seeds from a number of common plants which speed healing. They are known as silverseeds and bloodweed seeds by cultures separated from Fitherani.

Foralis – Small village of Fitherani; Blorfindel's (FKA Ghinlihil) birthplace.

Fummer – Hollenwae word for someone who is not stupid but does something stupid.

Ghinlihil – childhood name of Blorfindel Brighteyes.

Hauger – bronze coin current in the Shield valley and surrounding areas. Worth ¼ ardiv or 10 jertak. A hauger will buy a single simple arrow.

Hollenwae – species of people or plural of those people. Hollenwae males average 4' and 150 lbs, with females being somewhat smaller. Their lifespan can exceed 450 years, though the eldest are so sheltered by their own people that it is speculated that they might exceed 700 years in exceptional cases.

Hytrem – god of war

Ichassi – Fithern archer and sometime commander

Ilsorma – Goddess of passions, including romance and anger

Jilwanis – Renowned Fintheresse archer; mother of Ghinlihil / Blorfindel and wife of Lallium Steelhand.

Jertak – iron coin current in the Shield valley and surrounding areas. 10 Jertaks are worth 1 hauger. A single jertak might buy a piece of bread.

Kraahg – Hollenwae word for making someone angry at someone else.

Karakak – Kutel god of lightning and random destruction.

Koragen – A Hollenwae city-state east of Sekri Timbrali.

Krargle – Hollenwae word for a person who does not properly respect their own family, especially the parent-child relationship. Its use is offensive, and generally grounds for violence. In Hollenwae society it is a crime to use 'Krargle' without proof.

Kushotel – a Kutel-like creature, stronger and smarter than most Kutel.

Kutel – species or sub-species of people, or their language. Kutel average 5'6" and 150 lbs naturally, but due to culling the Kutel encountered are generally larger. The natural lifespan of a Kutel is thought to be 65 years, though their violent culture prevents virtually all Kutel from reaching their natural old age. Kutel religion insists that they were created from nothing by Baett, but their ability to interbreed with Tafers leads some to believe that they were derived from Tafers by some magical or supernatural process.

Lalliam Steelhand – Fintheran archer and warrior, father of Ghinlihil, and husband of Jilwanis. Killed by Kutel at Foralis.

Linxico Oldgrape – retired Fithern Wizard, vintner, restaurateur, and longtime friend of Biolmi Yewstaff.

Lufkora – Hollenwae word for lava.

Madrok – Hollenwae word for a fool of low moral character.

Malstren – gold coin current in the Shield Valley and surrounding areas. Worth 5 paddiban. One malstren will buy a serviceable sword or a good riding saddle. Two hundred malstren will buy 5 wagons, 10 oxen to pull them, and pay teamsters to run them for more than a year.

Manrachian Nomads – Tafers who live in clans on the plains south of Sekri Timbrali.

Order of the Circle – and group of knights based in Kingstone and pledged to Anagoth.

Paddiban – large silver coin current in the Shield valley and surrounding areas. Worth 8 stowsaw or 1/5 of a malstren. A pair of boots or a private room at an inn might cost a paddiban. Skilled artisans are paid in paddiban.

Putnu – a species of seafaring people aligned with the Kutel. They average 3'8" and 80 lbs.

Raiden – God of vengeance and hard justice.

Radorak – alternative name for Rettoric, favored by Hollenwae who consider him to the creator of their species.

Rettoric – God of the forge, forger of the world.

Sekri Timbrali – Fithern city-state south of The Shield Valley.

Shandi – A Taforam princess of The Hunt, wife of Ammoss; foster mother of Ghinlihil

Shield – language of the Shield Valley.

Shieldmaster – Chief political figure in towns of the Shield Valley. The position is appointed and traditionally hereditary. The political power of a Shieldmaster varies widely, depending on the town.

Shield Valley – Tafer nation, also known as the Valley of the Shield, centered on the Eastering River.

Shonu – capital city of the Kutel nation.

Stowsaw – copper coin current in the Shield Valley and surrounding areas. Worth 6 ardiv or 1/8 paddiban. A knife or a bottle of wine might cost a stowsaw. Most laborers are paid in stowsaw.

Tafer – species of people, or the male of the species. Tafers average 5'10" and 165 lbs, but vary widely. They also vary widely in temperament, morals, and intellect. A Tafer's natural lifespan can exceed 100 years in rare cases, though 60 is more common.

Taforam – female Tafer, averaging 5'6" and 130 lbs.

Timble – species of people. Timbles vary from 2'8" to 3'4". Weight is highly variable and generally considered a sign of status or well-being.

Tyuriaras – goddess of Iniquities – the antithesis of Feadin

Valley of the Shield – Alternative name of Shield Valley

Varren – a species of people aligned with the Kutel. They are small, rarely exceeding 3' and 50 lbs, and have dog-like features, including an exceptional sense of smell.

Varro – one of the the Varren

Wizard-King of Shonu – ruler of the Kutel

Appendix B

Currency

Name	Metal	Weight	Value	Value
Doutak	platinum	9 grams	1.6 malstren	64 stowsaw
Malstren	gold	9 grams	5 paddiban	40 stowsaw
Paddiban	silver	22 grams	8 stowsaw	8 stowsaw
Stowsaw	copper	9 grams	6 ardiv	1 stowsaw
Ardiv	brass	9 grams	4 hauger	1/6 stowsaw
Hauger	bronze	9 grams	10 jertak	1/24 stowsaw
Jertak	iron	9 grams	1/15360 doutak	1/240 stowsaw